PRAISE FOR J. CARSON BLACK

HARD RETURN

"Sweeping from suburban California to the New Mexico desert, from an assassins' marketplace in Austria to the killing grounds of Iraq, *Hard Return* is an amped-up thrill ride showcasing one of the most enigmatic and unforgettable antiheroes in fiction today. Part Jack Reacher, part Jason Bourne, Landry is a loner, a lover, a father, a killer, and the last thing his enemies will ever see."

—Michael Prescott, *New York Times* and *USA Today* bestselling author of *Final Sins* and *Around the Heart*

THE SURVIVORS CLUB

"An utterly engrossing thriller. *The Survivors Club* grips us from the very start and simply doesn't let go. The novel seamlessly achieves that rarity in crime fiction: making our palms sweat while bringing the characters and their stories straight into our hearts. Bravo!"

—Jeffery Deaver, *New York Times* bestselling author of *The Kill Room*

"J. Carson Black's *The Survivors Club* is a twisted, diabolical cat-and-mouse game that will keep you riveted."

—CJ Lyons, *New York Times* bestselling author of *Hollow Bones*

"Black serves up a breezy thriller with a killer premise: What if people who cheated death once weren't so lucky the second time around? By the time the plot snakes through twist after twist, you'll be asking yourself . . . do you feel lucky?"

—Brian Freeman, bestselling author of *Spilled Blood*

"J. Carson Black delivers desert heat with her latest cool thriller, *The Survivors Club*. Detective Tess McCrae shows us again why she's the southwest's top cop."

—Alan Jacobson, national bestselling author of *No Way Out*

THE SHOP

"*The Shop* is a hair-raising thriller from start to finish. With a complex plot and finely drawn characters, J. Carson Black draws the reader into a world where nothing is as it seems. This book is both spooky and convincing, just what a thriller should be."

—T. Jefferson Parker, *New York Times* bestselling author of *The Jaguar*

"I'm a big fan of J. Carson Black and *The Shop* is a truly original nonstop locomotive ride of a thriller. You won't even think of putting this book down."

—John Lescroart, *New York Times* bestselling author of *The Hunter*

"Fresh and imaginative, J. Carson Black's *The Shop* is a riveting read and a compelling tale of character. From FBI agents to local cops, from heroes to villains, *The Shop* is an exciting, sweeping thriller that will linger in your mind for a long time."

—Gayle Lynds, *New York Times* bestselling author of *The Book of Spies*

"Infused with an original voice and packed with compelling characters, J. Carson Black's *The Shop* is a thriller to pay attention to."

—David Morrell, *New York Times* bestselling author of *The Brotherhood of the Rose*

SPECTRE BLACK

ALSO BY J. CARSON BLACK

Cyril Landry Thrillers
Hard Return
The Shop

Laura Cardinal Series
Darkness on the Edge of Town
Dark Side of the Moon
The Devil's Hour
Cry Wolf

Standalone novels
The Survivors Club
Icon
Roadside Attraction

Writing as Margaret Falk
Dark Horse
Darkscope
The Desert Waits
Deadly Desert (Omnibus)

Writing as Annie McKnight
The Tombstone Rose
Superstitions
Short Stories
The Bluelight Special

Pony Rides

SPECTRE BLACK

A Cyril Landry Thriller

J. CARSON BLACK

THOMAS & MERCER

This is a work of fiction. Names, characters, organizations, places, events, and incidents are either products of the author's imagination or are used fictitiously.

Text copyright © 2015 J. Carson Black
All rights reserved.

No part of this book may be reproduced, or stored in a retrieval system, or transmitted in any form or by any means, electronic, mechanical, photocopying, recording, or otherwise, without express written permission of the publisher.

Published by Thomas & Mercer, Seattle

www.apub.com

Amazon, the Amazon logo, and Thomas & Mercer are trademarks of Amazon.com, Inc., or its affiliates.

ISBN-13: 9781503947436
ISBN-10: 1503947432

Cover design by Stewart Williams

Printed in the United States of America

To Pam Stack, my dear friend and rainmaker

PART 1

PART I

CHAPTER 1

Branch, New Mexico

Jolie Burke heard something.

There were plenty of noises in her house, a former miner's shack with thin walls and a corrugated tin roof. Too many to categorize, but all of them were familiar. The sound the dog made when he dipped his tongue into the aluminum water dish. The sound of the house settling—a tiny cracking sound every once in a while. The hum of the refrigerator. A car driving by at night. Voices of neighbors outside. There were so many identifiable sounds that her subconscious—her cop mind—sorted them without her knowledge: This is annoying. This is the usual thing. Cars driving by late at night—that happened, since there were teenagers living two doors down.

But this is out of the ordinary.

What awoke Jolie was another sound—a car door opening quietly.

Not the sound of the car driving up the street, or the engine turning off—

But the faint click of the car door opening, then closing. The car door coming to—just a kiss of metal and rubber suction.

Stealthy.

Her first thought was visceral: "The Inside Man"—a serial rapist who had targeted women in three states. He broke into women's houses and surprised them when they came home.

But The Inside Man was last year's news. He hadn't been active in over a year. The theory was he'd taken off for parts unknown.

She went into the bathroom where the narrow window overlooked the street. The glass was pebbled, but Jolie could see a white car parked on the street—couldn't tell much but the shape was not curvy as the late models were.

Three dark shapes approaching the front of her house. Dark. Melting into the expanse of the front yard.

Three.

She thought they might have split up, one going around the back. If that were the case, these guys were good.

She was good, too, but there were at least three of them.

Decision time.

Call 911 and stay and fight them, or slip out.

She had an escape route—out through the kitchen side door and into the garage.

Whoever these people were, they were professionals.

Her cat and dog.

The cat was probably asleep in the linen closet.

And her dog was never much of a watchdog. Despite the fact that he was a Rottweiler.

Listen to him now: not one bark.

Her purse hung on the doorknob as it always did. She grabbed it up, along with the thumb drive from the bedside table. Where was her phone? She needed to get out! Where was her phone?

Heard voices, a scuffling of feet. Back window.

Then she saw it, lying on the floor. She must have knocked it off the nightstand while she was sleeping. She shoved it into her purse. There was no time to get her laptop from her office. She kept it hidden, but the hiding place wouldn't fool a professional. She'd have to go without her service weapon, too. Earlier today a friend had come over for lunch with her three-year-old daughter. Jolie had locked her service weapon in the safe—

Jolie heard someone jimmying the window in the spare bedroom from the front. They'd found a way to disarm the alarm, and quickly. She had to go, now!

Jolie made it out the side door to the carport as quietly as she could. She could see two dark shapes—one at the window, one at the door. Weapons drawn, careful.

Where was the third?

She squinted in the vague moonlight and saw no one at the carport—her main method of escape. Why?

Her mind went to last night—the car behind her. At first she'd thought it was just another car, someone coming back from work at one of the agricultural farms, or from the small settlement south of here.

But when she'd turned, they'd turned.

When she'd reached her little pocket neighborhood, the car had turned off. One street before her street—as if they knew. . . .

Once was coincidence. Twice was—

A muffled voice. "Backyard."

Jolie duckwalked around the hood of her car. Registered the smell of gasoline but ignored it.

From now on, it would get noisy.

She prepared. Did she really want to do this? Maybe it would be wiser to slip over the neighbor's wall into their backyard, and then out to the alley. But what if there were more than these three?

She didn't want to involve her neighbor.

She got into position, hand ready to yank open the door, and hit the alarm button to unlock the car. The shrill alarm was deafening. She dove inside, just as the two shapes in the front yard yelled and hurtled toward her. The car started immediately—she was worried the lever wouldn't hit reverse the first time—but it did. Jammed it in reverse. Hit the gas and rocketed backward, nearly hitting one of the two men in black coming at her.

Instinct and training kicked in—think evasive driving maneuver—

The car swapped ends in the street and the next thing Jolie knew she was hurtling down toward the corner.

Within a minute a car was on her tail. Screaming around corners, headlights juddering in her rearview. She came to the Y in the road—make a decision! One way led to a lonely road with plenty of curves that slowed you to a crawl up the hillside to expensive homes—a maze of one-lane blacktop dead ends. The other shot through the last of Branch and out to the highway.

The lonely highway.

Neither choice was optimal.

But one was easier—turning right. Right on the road out of Branch.

The moment she turned she realized it might be a mistake. Why didn't she swap ends again and head for the middle of town?

Afterburners on. Nothing ahead of her. Jolie peered in the rearview—no car behind her. No car speeding, no headlights. How could that be? They had to be running dark. She squinted at the mirror, almost willing a dark shape to come hurtling toward her from behind.

Out in the lonely expanse of New Mexico desert now.

This time she did see headlights, way back.

But coming.

Coming fast.

She goosed the accelerator, prepared for the car to respond.

But the car engine wasn't as smooth.

Something was wrong.

She pushed on the accelerator again, hard, but after a half-hearted surge, the car slowed.

The engine was knocking. Out of gas?

But she'd filled the car yesterday. She looked at the gas gauge. The needle was on empty.

Smelled gas at the same time—how could she have missed that?

But I filled it yesterday, her mind insisted. Did they siphon her gas?

"Shut up," she muttered. "And suck it up."

Now what?

She had to ditch the car. Had to find a place where she could hide it.

There was an old ranch house on the right. Middle of the night, nothing stirring. The road led to the ranch house and two outbuildings. She drove onto the washboard dirt road, nursing the car and glad there was a slight decline in the path, her eyes cutting to the rearview mirror, looking for headlights, and then she was there. No lights on in the house. No cars.

The place was abandoned.

Jolie doused her lights, drove behind the barn.

Just in time. The car shuddered, stinking of gas, and died. She opened the barn door and saw piles of junk—but enough room in the aisle for her to push the car in.

It was not easy, but she managed. The last little bit, there was a slight decline. The car rolled to a stop.

She pulled the doors closed and barred the gate.

Pulled out her phone.

No bars.

"Shit!" she muttered. She looked around. Jolie knew this area well. There was a lot of land, but very few houses. Hardly any around here. As she recalled, the closest building was abandoned—the Circle K.

It had been closed a couple of months ago.

But Jolie remembered the pay phone on the wall outside. She hoped the pay phone still worked. It was a shot. No way would she stand by the road and hang her thumb out—whoever the people were who came to her house would still be looking for her.

She estimated that the Circle K was five or six miles away. She'd been a long-distance runner in high school. She'd also had to run to pass the fitness requirement as a sheriff's recruit in Florida, but that was over fifteen years ago. Unlike many of her hard-ass, gung-ho friends in the Branch Sheriff's Office, she was in good shape. Good shape, not great shape. That hadn't mattered—until now. She would go cross-country, in the desert.

Hell, they gave death row inmates one phone call.

She'd make sure hers would count.

- — -

There wasn't much cover but there was some—creosote bushes, mostly. Jolie kept track of the road but stayed about ten lanes off it, on the far side of the barbed-wire fence that seemed to go on forever. She'd stuck to a jog-trot as long as the moon was bright.

No one had driven by on the two-lane rural road. Not surprising—it was probably around two in the morning.

Way up ahead she finally saw it. A square building paralleling the road. She squinted. Black against the dark gray of the surrounding terrain. The pole sticking up into the night sky.

The Circle K.

She tried her phone again. Still no bars.

Jolie always thought she was good, but not lucky. Now she hoped she would be both good *and* lucky. She altered her path, moving diagonally in the direction of the store.

At the barbed-wire fence thirty feet back from the road, she removed her shirt, doubled it up and placed it over the lower strand of wire. Held it down, bent it in half and stepped through. Donned her shirt again on the other side.

SPECTRE BLACK

The moon had slipped behind a cloud. Everything got a whole hell of a lot darker. Jolie slowed to a cautious shuffle—there were gopher holes out here and she didn't want to break a leg—but kept moving in the direction of the Circle K.

The road was empty at this time of night. Flat around here, just some low hills far away to the south.

Jolie tried not to feel disheartened.

She told herself she would be careful. If she heard an engine she would hide in the tall grass growing in the ditch alongside the road. It wasn't much cover, but some.

It was one of those old Circle Ks built in the seventies. It sat there like a building block against the navy blue of the night sky and a billion stars. The front plate-glass windows and door had been boarded over with plywood.

But, as she remembered, there was the pay phone on the side wall. Crazy.

It felt too much like a nightmare where you thought you had help but you didn't. Where your last hope was an old pay phone at an abandoned convenience store in the middle of nowhere and you expected to hear a dial tone but of course there wasn't one. That would fit in with the way things had been going of late. In what dream could this phone possibly work?

Not gonna happen.

It's there. Try it.

She darted across the patch of ground, aware of how exposed she was. Pressed against the wall, picked up the receiver. "This is crazy," she muttered, just as she heard the dial tone.

She punched in the number of the only person in the world she knew she could trust. The one number she had committed to memory.

The phone rang. The message came on.

"Talk."

Jolie heard the rumble of an engine, way off in the distance, finished her message and headed for the brush by the side of the road. She squinted in the direction of the sound, but saw nothing.

But a car was coming. No headlights; it was running dark. Way out there on the road. A big engine—

A muscle car.

The engine idling along, the car moving slowly. The sound of the deep-throated engine reverberating off the pavement.

But she couldn't *see* anything.

Every instinct told Jolie the driver was looking for *her*. That might not be logical, but instinct trumped logic every time—especially in this kind of situation. So if she was going to hide, it had to be now. She stayed behind the Circle K, climbed back through the fence and into the dark and fallow field.

She lay flat on the ground and squinted at the road. The car came closer, the shuddering engine loud—

But *still* she couldn't see it.

She needed to make sense of this—now. Someone was looking for her.

She was surprised, but not as surprised as she would have thought. Jolie disciplined herself to clamp down on the adrenaline, use her head. She knew the car. She knew the owner.

The car was now right in front of her. Virtually invisible. But then she saw *something*—a diffused red glow, possibly the interior of the vehicle, barely there. She couldn't see the car but she could see negative space: what resembled a cutout of the inside of the vehicle, dim but there. Just enough light to illuminate some of the driver inside.

As the car came abreast of the Circle K she could see the ghost of the door strut, the shape of the window, one or two shapes reflected off the dash inside.

But nothing else.

Jolie was ninety percent sure the car belonged to the kid, but there were plenty of black muscle cars in this town. She could be wrong. She needed to expand her horizons, think of who else might have a car like that. She couldn't assume anything at this point.

Think! Who did she know who owned a muscle car? Plenty, at the sheriff's office. It seemed every other guy she knew had bought into the muscle car dream: late model Mustangs, Chargers, Challengers, Camaros. Many of them black, silver, or charcoal gray. Mean machines.

And the sheriff's department was full of practical jokers. Their favorite victims were the women cops in the department, which was probably the way it was everywhere.

Maybe that was it, one of the guys playing a practical joke on her, but she didn't think so.

Whoever had come to her house meant business.

The car slid past like a shark cruising through murky water. No light delineated its shape except for the inner cherry glow, so faint she sometimes didn't see it at all and the whole thing just . . . disappeared except for the noise. She could track it better with her ears than her eyes. Past the Circle K, the car picked up speed and hit the afterburners, the red glow turning into a thin trail as the car accelerated.

Then it was gone, rumbling off into the distance.

Now you see it, now you don't.

The moon had broken through the clouds; it was bright enough to see where she was going now. Jolie broke for the fallow field behind her, hoping for an undulation in the ground, a fold that would hide her—

And found it. A quarter mile away, after a hard run, she landed stomach-down in a small ditch.

Cold out here.

Minutes dragged by.

It seemed like hours.

Just as her heart rate returned to normal, she heard the noise of the engine again.

The muscle car cruised back the way it had come. Almost as if the thing were an entity unto itself, patiently stalking her. The loud engine reverberated. She knew from that sound that if push came to shove, it would scream like a catamount. She peered over the hump of earth and grass and looked.

The ghost car turned in to the Circle K.

At least she thought it did—

Keep your head down!

Jolie realized she'd squeezed her eyes shut. It took every trick she knew to open them. She was *that* scared.

The driver cut the engine. Jolie heard the creak of a car door opening, then the stealthy click of the door latching shut. The sound of shoes on gravel. Sound carried out in the boonies.

Voices. She couldn't understand what they were saying.

She recognized one of them, though—

The man shouted, "Jolie! I know you're out here. Why don't you come out and we'll talk?"

Don't move.

"Jolie? I just want to talk to you. Don't play games."

She heard someone else talking on a phone, but couldn't hear what was being said. Then: "Where the hell did she go?"

Another voice said, "She could be in the next county by now."

Jolie recognized this voice, too. For a moment she was stunned, but then she realized she'd been expecting it all along.

"If she knows what's good for her, she's already gone."

The car door opened and clicked shut again. The engine gunned. The car pulled out onto the highway. Jolie couldn't help but look at it—

What she could see. Just the dark that was darker than the night, and in the center of it a faint infrared glow.

Then the lights came on and the car arrowed down the highway, the taillights eventually swallowed by the dark.

CHAPTER 2

San Clemente, California

"Tennis balls."

"Cool, huh?"

Cyril Landry held the lime-green tennis ball, aware that he was not hefting it with confidence.

Which was unlike him.

"Don't worry," the cricket-like man in the gaudy Hawaiian shirt said. "It won't go off on its own. Has to be activated by the racket."

"Not any kind of racket," Landry said. "Is that what you're telling me?"

The man in the Hawaiian shirt nodded and his gray ponytail nodded right along with him. "That's correct. You're right as rain. Otherwise . . ."

He left it open to conjecture.

Landry had gone out for a day of paddleboarding, but as the sun dropped low over the water, he'd stowed the board and paddle into his Subaru and wandered into downtown San Clemente for a bite to eat.

Even at this early hour the restaurants were crowded, so Landry ducked into this cubbyhole of an antique shop, with an eye on the Beachcomber Bar and Grille across the street, hoping a table would open up.

A friend had told him about the old hippie. Landry wasn't in the market for anything right now, but curiosity had finally gotten the better of him. His friend had said, "You won't believe this guy. He was in Nam. Some elite squad, what I heard. He sells knick-knacks and the occasional Hellfire missile."

His friend had been joking about the Hellfire missile. At least Landry thought he was.

But once Cricket Man, aka Terrence Lark, knew he was for real, he'd shown him some nice stuff.

Amazing stuff.

"If you're interested, let me know," Lark said, before tucking the tennis ball reverently back into the box with its mates.

- — -

After his solo dinner, Landry walked by the shops and restaurants down by the water. The whitewashed stucco buildings dated from the 1920s. Almost all of them had red tile roofs. The Spanish colonial-style look had been a requirement when the resort town was built and incorporated in 1928. At the time the town was called "San Clemente by the Sea."

San Clemente appealed to Landry. He liked that it felt like a small town tucked inside a large sprawling chain of cities and freeways—quickly accessible to airports and ways in and out of LA.

He always looked up the celebrities and famous people in the towns he decided to live in, and San Clemente was no different. San Clemente didn't have a lot of notable natives. Richard Nixon's Western White House was here. But otherwise, the pickings were scarce: Lon Chaney, Lon Chaney, Jr., Cara Fawn—a porn star—and Carl Karcher, the founder of Carl's Jr. Such a beautiful place—idyllic. You'd think San Clemente could have done better than that.

On Friday night, the street was a hive of locals and tourists.

SPECTRE BLACK

Every shop was open at night. Throngs of people bubbled along the sidewalks like packing peanuts on a conveyer belt, only these packing peanuts were dressed in T-shirts, shorts, flip-flops, and swim trunks. There were surfers, baby boomers, beach bums, working stiffs, Maserati owners, chefs, charter boat captains, and the younger families who came from the bland neighborhoods across the San Diego Freeway where houses were measured more in square feet than originality. Landry did not like the fact that there were more of these houses every day, perched on the buff and gray hills like Monopoly hotels. But who was he to judge? The millennials made good money. Landry saw them coming into town for dinner and shopping with their spacious SUVs and collapsible strollers and very cute offspring.

Landry blended in, just another beach bum/surfer type. Every picture tells a story and he made his own. His longish brown hair had gold streaks in it, which he had applied himself. A goatee concealed the lower half of his face. Even the car he drove, the 2000 Subaru Outback, fit the mold. He rented a seventies-era bungalow on Avenida De La Estrella, a short walk up the hill from the main drag and the pier and the ocean.

San Clemente was easygoing and forgiving. He had plenty of time for his new pastime-bordering-on-passion: paddleboarding.

Del Mar was a short drive up the freeway. He could watch his brother's racehorses run, although he missed being on the backside in the mornings. But he couldn't drive in through the horsemen's gate. He did not have a license. To apply for one, he would have to be fingerprinted.

Worse, he would be recognized right away.

Landry walked up the steps to his bungalow. He scanned the pocket yard, looking at every potential hiding place, his roof and the roof next door, his door and the door next door. Finally, he ducked under the banana tree and, key ready, eyeballed the small pebble he'd set on the middle of the doorstep. It was still in place. Only then did he unlock the door. He pushed the door open and stood to the side. SOP—Standard Operating Procedure.

Inside the bungalow, Landry's gaze made a visual sweep of the room—the configuration of the furnishings. Everything looked the same. He eyeballed the kitchen alcove. Nothing had been touched.

He took the hallway to his bedroom, opened the walk-in closet and reached into the jacket pocket of his navy suit for his other cell phone. Walking back into the living room, he punched in the number for the answering service and entered the security code.

As he waited, he stood inside the doorway looking out at the patch of ocean off to the north. The air, redolent of the ocean, blew past him, fluttering the banana tree leaves. The sky had turned the color of a red plum. It would be a nice night to sit out on the terrace with a beer.

The message played.

"It's Jolie. I'm at an old Circle K outside Branch, New Mexico. Mile Marker 138. I need you to come. Hurry."

He made a note of the time, date, and number, so the phone company could track the location, then punched it in. The phone rang but there was no answer.

CHAPTER 3

Bill Cannaly, a former Special Forces helo pilot and one of the good guys, connected Landry with a pilot friend of his in LA who agreed to fly him in to the Las Cruces International Airport. The first thing he'd said when Landry contacted him was, "You have a pink sheet?'"

After 9/11, passengers carrying a firearm on every plane in the United States, private or commercial, required a permission sheet also known as a "pink sheet."

A few months ago, when he'd had a little free time, Landry had devoted a day to producing a stack of twenty pink sheets. They had to look official, so he'd taken his time to do it right. He'd manufactured pink sheets for every occasion: military, paramilitary (mostly police), private security—you name it. It was intricate but mind-numbing work. By the end of the day he had twenty pink sheets, and all of them would pass muster as legitimate.

The big problem was the hologram that appeared on every sheet. It wasn't easy making a fake look like the real thing.

The gold-leaf holograms were difficult to reproduce. Landry had fudged a little and used a combination of zinc and some pieces of gold leaf cut from one-hundred-dollar bills.

For this flight, Landry chose the dummy company he had christened Secret Circle Security. He went through the security area, producing his H&K MP5, and a .32 Automatic Colt Pistol so small it could fit inside the span of his hand.

Tom, the pilot, was a good guy—solid. He'd been in Iraq around the same time Landry had. All the way to Las Cruces he recounted harrowing stories of near misses and fellow pilots now dead.

Landry said nothing of his own exploits.

They arrived in Las Cruces just past eight o'clock in the morning. It was already a scorcher.

Using the alias Chris Keeley, Landry rented a white Nissan Versa. No one would look twice at a modest compact rental like the Versa. There wasn't much of a selection. He had a choice between a red and a white one, and chose the white. Red attracted attention. White was not only a generic color, but it deflected heat. In the summer, New Mexico was hot.

Landry took a few photographs of the car with his phone. It was expected these days—no one in his right mind would rent a car without at least a cursory look. Landry wanted to be seen as a typical customer.

"How you doing?" the rental car employee said, a hint of desperation in his tone. Four minutes under the hot sun and the guy was already wilting.

"Almost through." Landry wanted to be unmemorably memorable, like any other anal-retentive car renter who resented the idea of being charged an exorbitant fee for a pea-gravel dent.

- — -

Landry drove west on Interstate 10. He passed the turnoff to Tejar, where Jolie Burke had worked previously as a sheriff's deputy. She'd changed counties, although you wouldn't know it from the terrain. This part of New Mexico looked like any other part of the Chihuahuan Desert. Miles and miles of greasewood, pale mountains like cardboard cutouts in the distance, and parched-looking grassland. Branch, New Mexico, was located on a state road northeast of Deming.

Landry used to stop for lunch in Deming when he drove cross-country. Used to.

Then he'd read about the cops there, a story about a man suspected of carrying drugs secreted in his person. He was subjected to two forced colonoscopies and various other invasive indignities. The police found no drugs and were slapped with a lawsuit for 1.6 million dollars. The man prevailed—eventually. Years later.

Landry had always thought of New Mexico as a laid-back state, not as tightly wound as neighboring Arizona. But he'd been reading about bad cops in Albuquerque, the state capital.

Maybe the cops in New Mexico had watched one too many episodes of *Breaking Bad*.

He took the exit for Branch. The road looked just like most of the roads he'd driven through in this part of New Mexico.

He used a burner phone to call the pay-phone number Jolie had given him. He didn't expect an answer. He had tried her six times before. She had never called him back. Maybe she'd run out of change making the first long-distance call. Maybe she didn't have her purse with her or a credit card. But he'd keep trying the number on the off chance she was in the vicinity and could answer.

This time, though, someone picked up on the first ring.

Landry squinted at the blue mountains in the distance. There was a mirage of gray water just underneath them, appearing and disappearing like quicksilver. He kept his eyes on the road and listened to the silence. Imagined he could hear breathing. Like the watery mirage in the distance, the silence stretched out.

He listened but said nothing.

The phone disconnected.

He removed the burner phone's battery and threw it out the

window. Landry drove through a short mountain pass and was met with more grassland and fallow fields, the road a black ribbon to the next range of low mountains. The sunlight picked out a glint or two of metal at their base.

Cars.

Police?

Landry knew the traffic laws in New Mexico. Unpaved dirt roads were forty-five miles per hour. Two-lane paved roads in New Mexico were fifty-five miles an hour. This was a two-lane paved road, so he kept to a steady fifty-eight mph. No one would pull him over for that, and if he stuck with the speed limit in this flat country he might actually draw attention.

The mirage in the center of the road resolved itself into three vehicles.

Three Chevy Suburbans, approximately two miles ahead. All of them dark in color, grouped near the road's junction with a ranch road that wandered off to the right.

The checkpoint looked official, but you never knew. He glanced at the H&K MP5 and the .32 Automatic Colt Pistol he'd brought on the plane. It lay on the seat beside him in plain sight. This was ranch country. The laws were lax, and the police wouldn't look twice.

If they *were* police.

More likely, if it was a checkpoint, he would encounter Border Patrol. This area wasn't that far from the Mexican border. The grouping of vehicles ahead didn't look like Border Patrol, though.

Orange traffic cones spread out across the road—one for each lane. But there were no temporary speed limit signs intended to bring the driver's speed down to a crawl. Landry squinted against the glimmer of the road in the sunlight. Yes, two cones. One planted in the center of the right lane and one in the left. For all intents and purposes blocking the road.

Something wrong here.

Manhunt? Police action? But the Suburbans didn't look right. One of them dated back to the nineties.

Militias. He remembered reading an article about a group in Nevada. He knew that there were people just like them in a number of the western states, New Mexico in particular.

There were two kinds of militias. One, a military force raised by the civilian population to supplement a regular army during an emergency.

And two, a military force engaged in rebel or terrorist activities, often in direct opposition to a regular army.

In Nevada people dressed up like their idea of soldiers, stopped people at "checkpoints" and asked them for ID. They were not police officers. They were not sheriff's deputies. They were not U.S. marshals. They were not state police.

Many of them were cop wannabes.

Fakes.

His mother would have said they had a "case of arrested development."

Of course, even fakes could be dangerous. In fact, fakes were probably more dangerous, simply because they had to prove they weren't fakes.

Landry noticed one of the figures—all in black—leaning against one of the Suburbans. He was the picture of inattention.

Landry knew he could handle them. He knew he could handle their friends. He would have no problem kicking their asses into next week for impersonating a police officer or worse, a member of the armed services. The question was, did he want to?

He was dressed to fit this car: the tourist T-shirt, the flip-flops, the shorts, the sunglasses. The average-guy haircut. The Timex. The fast food wrapper balled up on the dash and the Big Gulp in the console cup holder.

A box of tennis balls on the seat.

He removed the balled-up fast food wrapper—it was from a Dairy Queen brazier in Las Cruces—uncrumpled it and laid it over the Colt—

And slowed down like a good boy.

A big guy in combat boots, a ball cap with an official-looking insignia too hard to read, a black bulletproof vest, and Army fatigues you could buy online, stepped toward him and raised his hand. He bristled with weapons—a sidearm on his hip, a rifle slung across his back. Big kid playing dress-up. Another stood nearby, a Bushmaster cradled in his arms.

Landry obliged by stopping. He buzzed down his window and looked up at the guy. His gape was excellent—sterling. He knew he looked like a cowed tourist.

The dress-up guy tipped the bill of his cap and said, "Can I see some ID, sir?"

"May," Landry said.

"What?"

"*May* I see some ID. You can, physically, but you're asking."

The man stared at him.

Landry gave him a vague smile—his professorial face—and tried to look clueless. He knew the guy was no cop. Not even an undercover cop. Cops were not allowed to stop people and demand their IDs. Not in any state in the union, with the exception of Arizona.

For a moment Landry considered taking one of the guns from the fake cop and pistol-whipping him across his beefy dumb face, but decided against it. Maybe the guy was from Arizona, and didn't know any better.

So, innocent as a lamb, he dug out his wallet and handed the man his license.

"Is there trouble, officer?"

The guy held his license and looked at it hard. "Where are you going, Mr., uh, Keeley?"

"Is there something wrong? I'm going to Branch to see my sister."

He looked at the license one more time. Reluctant to let it go. But when you pretend to be a cop, you have to act like one. "May I look inside your trunk, sir?"

Landry pulled the latch and the trunk popped open.

The guy stood there for a few minutes behind the car. Landry watched him in the rearview. He raised the trunk lid for a quick look and pushed it shut again—

Which was a good thing for him.

The duffle in the trunk was Landry's "run bag"—a bag packed for him to grab up at a moment's notice. He kept it in his closet, packed with the basics. The run bag contained shampoo, bath soap, pain meds, an extra phone battery, a suit and a dress shirt laid out and folded neatly, dress shoes and socks, work boots, jeans, a baseball cap, and an emergency medical kit. It also carried twist-tie plastic cuffs and loaded magazines.

One reason he rarely flew commercial.

Landry heard the crackle of the walkie-talkie. The man was talking into it, wandering this way and that behind the car. For entertainment, Landry studied the two people leaning against the bumper of one of the Suburbans, a short, squat woman and a stringbean man, both dressed in paramilitary outfits and black Kevlar bulletproof vests. The bulletproof vests were decorated with Velcroed epaulets—a nice touch—and the camo pants contained plenty of pockets for their lip balm and breath mints. Someone had a mom who liked to sew. Landry thought it must be hot as hell in those vests, but if you want to play cops and robbers, it's the price you pay. Landry also got a closer look at the three Suburbans. They had a lot of miles on them, especially the one that was mid-nineties vintage. The others were in the right decade but were dusty and dented.

The first man came back around to the driver's side window. "You may go, sir," he said, just as a walkie-talkie crackled on the hip of the fake policewoman.

Landry sat there, his hands on the steering wheel, ten and two.

You have no fucking idea how lucky you are.

The guy had expected Landry to drive off. He was discombobulated. He wiped at the sweat on his cheek and said, "That a tennis racket in your trunk? Guess you're a tennis player, huh?"

"Just an amateur," Landry said. "But it's fun."

The guy fumbled for words. Finally he said, "Good job."

Whatever that meant.

Landry took his foot off the brake and eased it onto the accelerator. He pulled away, almost running over the man's feet. The fake cop jumped back, and Landry smiled as he watched the little band dwindle away in the rearview mirror.

He'd seen better playacting at a Punch-and-Judy show.

CHAPTER 4

After a few hills, the road straightened out through a wide, flat valley. It was an agricultural area: beans, chiles, and cotton, the road a black arrow straight to hazy blue mountains in the distance.

The milepost number grew higher. When it passed 120, Landry actively started scanning for a Circle K. He was only eighteen miles away from Milepost 138.

He drove past several farms, everything from a few acres and a farmhouse to massive agricultural concerns. There were three big farms and two small ones. The big farms looked new and well kept; acres and acres of farmland hemmed in by twelve-foot-high chain-link fences with concertina wire on top. The wire was new and shiny. He noted complexes inside complexes and rectangles inside larger rectangles. The buildings looked new and state of the art, made to loosely resemble the gracious haciendas of California and Mexico. All of them appeared to have the same architect. The only differentiations in the buildings were the individual layouts and the colors of the buildings. One farm had beige walls and rusty-brown metal roofs. Another had white outbuildings and slate-gray roofs. Another had beige buildings with red roofs. A white sign flashed by: "Jordan H. Green Experimental Agricultural Station: Your Tax Dollars at Work." Another sign, also white, but with blue letters instead of black: "Heron Lake Agricultural Farm." Landry looked for a lake but didn't see one. He did see irrigation ditches, though.

The third big farm was called "The Valleyview Experimental Agricultural Station." Like its companion farms, the Valleyview Experimental Agricultural Station was neatly laid out with computer motherboard precision. There were two gigantic manufactured steel buildings and several smaller ones, all fitting together in a pleasing manner, divided by paved roads lined by poplar trees. A small airfield and hangar were situated at one end of the grid of bean fields.

He slowed a tick—no one else on the road—as he drove past the mega farm, instinctively enjoying the layout, the neat interlocking parts. Precision was something that appealed to his eye. He had always been drawn to circles and squares and triangles. Geometry had been his favorite subject in school.

He watched the farm dwindle in his rearview. The land became fallow farmland again and the odd patch of desert. As he left the valley and the farms behind, the road climbed a little.

Up on the left he saw a child's building block of a structure—the Circle K. An old one, the kind he used to hang out at during his youth. The pole rose above it but the sign was gone, except for a rusty square frame.

Landry didn't alter his speed, but drove past it, cop style. First, get the lay of the land. Then, go back. At approximately two hundred yards beyond the Circle K, Milepost 138 flashed by.

He scanned the road, looking for anything or anyone, but saw nothing. He turned around and drove back, pulling off the road into the pitted asphalt parking lot. Aimed for the tamarisk tree at the edge of the lot near the rear of the building, and parked behind it. This way he was hidden from the road on one side and blocked by the bulk of the abandoned building on the other.

SPECTRE BLACK

He saw the pay phone on the side of the Circle K. Turned on his 4G and punched in the number Jolie had left with his answering service. The phone rang.

Landry had mixed feelings about tamarisk trees. They were salt cedars, imported from the Mediterranean. They clogged up rivers and streams in the west, killing the natural flora and fauna, and they sopped up a lot of water. On the other hand, their shade wasn't just good, it was spectacular—the deepest, darkest, coolest shade you could find anywhere. At this time of day, going on eleven in the morning, the area under the tamarisk tree was as black as ink.

Landry went out on the road and looked from every angle. The car was, for all intents and purposes, invisible.

Just in case someone pulled in (unlikely, as the Circle K was obviously abandoned) Landry opened the trunk and pulled out the spare tire and the jack. He left the trunk open and set the spare tire against the car and the jack near it. It would look like he was just getting ready to work the tire.

He leaned against the car, staring out at the road and the shimmering blue mountains to the east, and once again punched in the number of the pay phone.

This time he let the pay phone ring again and again and again while he scanned the desert for movement.

She did not come.

- — -

But someone did. Or rather they drove by, in a hurry: two Tobosa County Sheriff's cars, light bars blinking. They whisked past, going at least eighty miles an hour, in the direction Landry had come from. They disappeared over a hill and the sound diminished.

Landry wondered where they were going in such a hurry, but

decided it was none of his business. He continued to wait for Jolie Burke, staring out at the desert, and tried calling again.

The same result. Nothing.

Another city or county car—this one a plain wrap—blew through, followed by a tall white panel van. After that, nothing. Landry continued to try the phone at the Circle K periodically, as noon turned to afternoon. One hour turned to two hours turned to three hours. The sun moved and he moved with it, staying in the shade of the tamarisk tree.

For hours at a time, the road remained empty. There was very little traffic either way. Maybe one or two cars, zipping by.

No sign of Jolie.

He checked his answering service: nothing.

Maybe she was waiting until it was dark. But Landry couldn't stay out here much longer. Even though there was little traffic on the road, the disabled car would become conspicuous at some point. That point hadn't been reached yet, but it would soon.

He counted only fourteen cars in a three-hour stretch, all whizzing past.

Late in the afternoon, a rancher drove into the lot and parked near the tree. He leaned across the seat and yelled through the open window, "Need help?"

"I got this," Landry said. "Thanks."

"You sure?" The rancher turned off the engine and got out of his truck. He wore a straw cowboy hat, a snap-button plaid shirt, and boot-cut Wranglers. Wranglers and Roper boots. The man's face was seamed and brown, like a gingersnap cookie. He reached out and shook Landry's hand. "Name's Jerry Boam."

"Boam? Like the giant bottle of wine or the first king of Israel?"

The rancher laughed. "Both, I reckon. My parents, God rest 'em, had a sense of humor. Funny thing is, they was both teetotalers."

"I've heard everything, now."

"Nope. There's plenty more where that came from. My sister's name is Margarita."

Landry covered his eyes against the glare. "I'm new here, came to see a friend of mine. Her name's Jolie Burke. Do you know her?" He thought for a moment. "She live in Branch?"

"Yup. She's with the local sheriff's."

"Sounds familiar. Local girl? You sure you don't want a lift?"

"No thanks, I'm good." Landry grinned. "It's time I brushed up on my tire-changing skills."

"Seek and ye shall find, that's what the Lord says." The rancher reached into his breast pocket and pressed a pamphlet into Landry's hand. "We're all travelers in search of answers. I think you'll find some comfort here."

Landry looked down at the religious tract in his hand. Boam hopped into the truck cab, started up the engine and cocked his elbow on the door. "You see those sheriff's cars?"

"Sure did."

"You know what they were going to?"

Landry shook his head. "No idea."

"Guess I'll hear about it on the news. Or on the Internets. You take care now and drink plenty of water. It gets hot out here."

Landry held up his water bottle with a grin. "What are the motels like in Branch?"

"Oh, fair to middlin'. The Satellite INN is nice, though. Wife's cousin works there. They got cable TV, even serve breakfast. Nothing fancy, just some coffee, rolls, butter patties. Swimming pool, too. I remember when the place was built in 1963. Most modern thing I ever saw. Oh, if you do like wine, which I do *not*, there's a winery right here in Branch. Think it's over by the Walmart."

"Thanks."

Boam nodded to the leaflet. "Be sure to read that now, there's nothing like God's Word to set you straight on the path." He saluted, put the truck in gear, and drove away.

Dusk came. A few official-looking cars and the tall white van went by—this time in the opposite direction. And this time, they were in no hurry.

Curious, Landry checked his Samsung 4G. No bars. He'd called the pay phone intermittently, but getting a signal on his cell phone was catch-as-catch-can out here. He waited some more. The sun began to show through the tamarisk screen. The white Nissan sat there with the wheel propped against the back fender, telling its story. Someone had a flat tire, and that same someone had gone to get help. Landry left the car where it was and walked out into the desert.

There wasn't any high ground to watch the Circle K from, so Landry burrowed down in a desert wash an eighth of a mile away. He lay in a prone position at the lip of the arroyo's bank and watched the Circle K through his nightscope. Every once in a while he called the pay phone.

It stood to reason that Jolie would wait until after dark to make her move.

But she didn't.

Night stretched into morning. Landry shifted positions a few times for comfort. Toward dawn, the cold seeped through his clothes from the ground. Deserts were dry places; hot during the day but cold at night.

No one approached the disabled Nissan Versa.

Not on foot, not by car. Whatever the cops and other officials had been racing to was over with.

The road remained empty.

Long before dawn, Landry knew that Jolie would not be coming. She hadn't taken advantage of her window of opportunity, and now that window had closed.

She might be looking to find him in some other way, and so he would stick around Branch and let himself be seen. Hopefully she *would* see him.

But for now, Jolie Burke was in the wind.

- — -

He ate an early breakfast at Dina's Diner next door to The Satellite INN in Branch, tipping the waitress enough to make her happy but not enough to make him stand out. Before that, he'd ducked into the bathroom of the neighboring Texaco for a quick strip wash and a change of shirts.

Landry had adopted his "average dad" look: sports sandals and plaid cargo shorts covered by a big T-shirt featuring a sun wearing sunglasses.

Despite multiple deployments in Iraq and Afghanistan, Landry had managed to avoid tattoos—except for one, a snarling mountain lion on his upper arm. The tattoo was easily hidden by a short-sleeved tee.

Landry had a fellow Navy SEAL to thank for his lack of tattoos. Jim Doolen (now deceased) was his superior officer and a good friend. Jim had spotted Landry's abilities early on. He'd taken Landry aside and suggested he think twice about getting more tattoos. After his service, Landry might have few options for work, and he should keep every option still available to him, open. Tattoos were memorable, and would likely disqualify him from some jobs—especially if those jobs were covert.

Tattoos didn't matter to Landry much either way, so he took Doolen's advice.

In the military, there was always pressure to conform, but Landry had been immune to outside pressure. What other people thought about him or said about him didn't matter much. He knew that at some point he would leave the military, and he also understood that his skill set was limited—elite though those skills might be.

He was also blessed with a forgettable face: good-looking enough, but without the edginess of handsome. He wouldn't scare anyone, but he wouldn't engender any romantic fantasies, either. Landry's face could blend in. His best looks were "affable and open," and "I'm in my own world—don't bother me."

He looked like someone's dad. He looked like that for a reason. He had a daughter.

Here, in a small town where he looked like a tourist whose wife and kid no doubt were sleeping in at The Satellite INN while he had a quiet breakfast to himself, Landry opened the newspaper he'd picked up at the vending machine inside the door of the restaurant, half an ear on the babble surrounding him. He learned two things immediately. One, there was good fishing in the mountains north of here.

And two, one of the militia members at the checkpoint had been shot to death yesterday morning.

The article in the paper was mostly photos. The *Las Cruces Sun-News* had decided to go artistic. Four photos. One large—above the fold—and three smaller shots.

Plenty of ink.

Landry found himself looking at the crime scene—the three Suburbans as he remembered them, a detective in the foreground looking down at a marker, a plastic pyramid with a number on it, like you might see at a car wash. In the background the squat lady in the Kevlar vest from yesterday appeared to be wandering aimlessly. Of course it was a static picture, but that was the feeling Landry got.

Another photo featured one of the traffic cones that had blocked the road. An artistic shot: the aftermath of a shooting, the cone lying on its side. The photog must have thought it conveyed a higher truth. The cone represented the victim.

Beyond the cone was just the very edge of what looked like a combat boot toe sticking straight up, the rest mercifully covered by a tarp.

He wondered which man had been killed. Was it the one in the ball cap who had asked to see his ID, or was it the man who had been standing with the squat woman? Landry thought it didn't much matter—he certainly didn't know any of them—but he was curious.

The accompanying article was long on photos and short on information. At approximately eleven in the morning a man in a white subcompact car had tried to run down the person manning the checkpoint. The victim was not identified—"Name withheld pending notification of the family"—but the article did say he had been shot twice: once in the chest and once in the face. After taking several shots at the fleeing car, the two surviving members of the checkpoint patrol had tried to resuscitate their friend. But Landry guessed he'd died instantly.

Luckier than most.

He looked out the window at the parking lot, which was jammed with cars. He counted four white subcompacts, including his own rental. Good protective coloration as far as it went, but he wondered if he was now a suspect. He had driven up to that checkpoint in the midmorning. Somewhere between ten thirty and eleven a.m.—eleven fifteen at the latest.

Fortunately, there were witnesses. The squat woman and her string-bean friend. Neither one of them looked very bright but they might remember the man who shot their pal.

Except that Landry knew witnesses were notoriously unreliable. When he'd driven up, they had been leaning against one of the Suburbans, arms folded, chatting. They might have spared him a glance, but maybe they didn't. Maybe they didn't really see him at all. What they would have seen was their buddy leaning down talking through the driver's window of a white subcompact car. They might have been able to see the driver through the windshield but the sunlight was bright and harsh. And they'd probably operated under the tacit agreement, *You take this one, and I'll take the next.*

He had the distinct impression that the squat woman and the beanpole boy had been enjoying their day playing soldier.

Landry was amazed that either one of them had been able to offer any description at all, other than the word "white" and subcompact. Pretty good, although he suspected that someone else had come up with the term "subcompact." They probably said something like "small car." None of the three would qualify as bright bulbs. They had made up their own little checkpoint with their own little made-up police force, mainly because no one told them they couldn't. The federal and local governments wouldn't want to get into a firefight with them, or even arrest them, since it would be bad publicity or, worse, a showdown that could result in injuries, deaths, and lawsuits. He'd seen it before: a hands-off policy that was really a wish-it-would-go-away policy. In his opinion, this policy led to a lot of swaggering assholes stopping people and checking their IDs. And eventually that would lead to tragedy . . .

Which it had.

Landry himself had complied because he had better things to do than teach them a lesson.

Apparently, someone else wasn't so easygoing.

He checked into The Satellite INN and asked for a second-floor room facing the street, which also happened to be Branch's main drag.

His room was like any other motel room at this price point: it contained a swaybacked queen-size bed covered by a rust-and-brown

SPECTRE BLACK

floral bedspread, a TV in brackets in the corner, and a waist-high counter fronting a mirror so he could see the wall art above the bed in its reflection. The art in question was a mustard-colored print of a button-eyed female puppet—vaguely Hopi. Thick swabs of paint and the lack of a nose or mouth told him it was a DeGrazia print.

Landry walked out onto the second-story walkway and leaned on the rail, looking down at the kidney-shaped pool. Families had taken it over, their voices rising along with a splashing beach ball.

Like the other old motels on the street, The Satellite INN came from the Space Age. In New Mexico, motels with space-race themes sprang up like mushrooms in the late fifties and early sixties, partially to reflect the optimism of the era but also betraying the sharp edge of fear underneath. Developers wanted to make all of it fun—and accessible. Thus the atom symbols and movies about space aliens, who always seemed to invade places where few people would feel threatened because they didn't live there.

Deserts like this one.

Landry walked to the end of the building. From here he could see the parking lot the motel and the diner shared. Two of the other white cars had gone—so much for protective coloration from police looking for a white subcompact.

He had a few options. He could ditch the car or hide it—or he could leave it where it was.

How many white subcompact cars were there in this town? He'd noticed several just on his drive into town—at least nine or ten, maybe more. And that didn't take into account the outlying houses in their minisuburbs. Small but sporty utilitarian cars were making a comeback. It stood to reason that people who wanted new cars in a town of this size and tax base would go small—something affordable but modern. *Doable.* In San Clemente and LA, Landry was used to seeing BMWs, Mercedes Benzes, and the odd Maserati. No one would drive a Maserati out here. They'd be more likely to drive a Dodge Ram.

And if they couldn't afford a Dodge Ram, they'd buy a Nissan Versa, or something like it.

He heard a "whump!" and the beach ball sailed up and over the railing. Landry picked it up and punched it back down. One of the grownups yelled "Thanks!"

He calculated the odds of being pulled over because he was driving a small white compact.

He looked down at the car, parked facing him, the silver sunshade propped up in the window. A car in a parking lot was less likely to attract the eye of a law enforcement officer than a moving vehicle. Even if he was pulled over—which would have to be under extraordinary circumstances—what then? He had a rock-solid alias. He'd used a legitimate credit card at the Budget in Las Cruces. He looked like your average citizen, just making a run to the store to buy refreshments for the wife and kids.

Would there be a store-to-store, house-to-house search?

No. The law enforcement agencies would assume that whoever got into the gunfight with the militia would keep on going, right through Branch and on to whatever place they could find to lie low. They might ditch the car and steal another. They might keep driving until they could get lost in a good-sized city, like El Paso.

What Landry couldn't figure out was how he'd missed the other car. It must have shown up right after he went through the checkpoint. He didn't remember seeing any car behind him in the rearview mirror. Some cars had flashed by the Circle K, and only a couple had been white. But nothing about them stood out.

Maybe the shooters turned off somewhere and took a different route.

The important thing was to get back out to the Circle K and wait for Jolie.

But first, he went for a walk.

CHAPTER 5

Three blocks down on the main drag Landry found a used car lot, one of those places where they try to rope you in with easy-money payments for the rest of your life.

At the front of the lot was a 1997 blue Aerostar panel van that had been driven up onto a platform facing the street. Painted on the window was a white cloud with red lining, and inside the cloud in bold blue letters it said "$1999!!!!!"

Landry inquired within.

He had changed his look again. He'd shaved his facial hair, for one thing. At the Walgreens two doors down from The Satellite INN, he'd bought a couple of plain T-shirts and cheap aviator shades. Back in his room, he'd stretched the tees out so the material looked tired, and added cotton balls to the back of his mouth to make his face look wider. He'd also wadded up a shirt and stuck it in the waistline of his old jeans to give himself a small belly. Old work boots completed the picture. As Landry walked out through the parking lot to the street, he'd dropped a piece of paper. As he'd bent down to pick it up, he also scooped up a little dirt and black from the asphalt, which he used to grime up the shirt a bit.

A salesman crossed the lot toward him. They could have been twins, except the guy wore a short-sleeved button-down shirt and slacks of some cheap shiny material. He looked wilted from the heat, and vaguely desperate. "How do you like her?" he said, patting the fender of the van as if it were a horse.

"Can you come down on the price?" Landry asked.

"Oh, I can't do that, friend, I'm sorry. It's a ridiculous price as it is."

"Can't haggle a little?"

"I'm afraid not. You want to test drive it? This baby is solid, and if you're in a job where you need to carry equipment, this is a real workhorse."

Landry reached into his pocket and pulled out a wad of cash. Flashed the roll. "I have fifteen hundred. All I'm gonna spend."

The guy grinned. A good trick to look amused with sweat trickling down your face. "It's nineteen-ninety-nine! A great bargain."

"I can pay you cash right now. Fifteen hundred."

The salesman drew in a breath. "Got yourself a deal, mister."

After the paperwork was done, Landry said, "Is there a Walmart nearby?"

"Oh, yeah, we've got a brand-new one. Right up Powder Road, at the intersection with Garcia. Four blocks and over the new overpass."

The Walmart was the anchor store, but to Landry's delight, there was also a Sportsman's Warehouse. He bought two of the least expensive hunt cameras he could find, and a blue work shirt.

He needed to change the look of the van, give himself a reason for being here. He bought a can of black poster paint and stenciled "Diaz Landscaping Service" in small block letters on both sides. The takeaway: a landscaper no one would want, slapdash and amateurish.

Just beyond the Walmart the land stretched out, mostly open space except for a few ranch houses sprinkled here and there. And several acres of staked vines. Yet another crop in New Mexico: wine.

Back at the abandoned Circle K he parked again under the tamarisk tree and waited. He had a box of donuts and a to-go cup of coffee from a Dunkin' Donuts. He put the box on the seat and kept the door open, sitting in the driver's seat, just a Diaz Landscaping employee taking a break in the shade before driving on to the next job.

Few cars went by. No one spared him a glance. The shade from the tamarisk tree was dark as ink.

Periodically, he rang the phone at the Circle K.

Nothing happened.

There was very little traffic. He stayed there for three hours. By that time he knew Jolie Burke was not coming.

It was hot here in full summer. The desert could sneak up on you. Landry had seen that many, many times in Iraq and in Afghanistan. One minute you were fine, and then suddenly, you were overwhelmed. Sunstroke happened to hikers all the time. Not just hikers, either, but strollers. People out for a walk on a nice morning. He'd read about a hiker who had recently succumbed in a tame desert park in Tucson, Arizona. The woman in question was in her twenties and an avid hiker, and this was just a couple-hour hike on a designated path in a relatively tame county park in June. She did everything right. It was early in the morning. She'd had friends with her. She had water. She had trail mix. She had a phone. Probably had all the up-to-date hiker attire and equipment as well. But for whatever reason, she went into cardiac arrest and they could not revive her.

If Jolie was out in this desert, she had been here for at least sixty hours. Some of that was night, but a lot of it was day.

He scanned his surroundings. The land was mostly beige in color, depending on the time of day. There was a striation of pale green where mesquite trees followed the trickle of white sand that called itself a watercourse. All of them dry at this time of year. Dips and washes and small promontories of rock, primarily igneous and metamorphic. But to the naked eye it was a uniform tan, all the way to the washed-out blue mountains.

The sound of a ringing phone would go a long way out here. But it had not drawn her in.

Jolie Burke was gone. His guess? Someone had her, and was preventing her from leaving. He'd heard the desperation in her voice, the edge of fear. Jolie Burke was good at masking her emotions. She was good at keeping her own counsel. And yet he remembered hearing it in her voice. As if she were hanging by one fingertip on a high-tension wire.

She might have escaped whoever it was who had been holding her, but maybe they had found her. She could be anywhere by now. She could be in Branch, or she could have been taken out of state. Or—he glanced in the direction of Mexico—out of the country.

Or she could be dead.

It turned on a dime: just like that. One minute he was waiting. Scanning the horizon, hoping for her to come. And the next he knew she was never coming.

It was time for Plan B.

Whatever Plan B was.

CHAPTER 6

Jolie Burke lived in a rented house on Turner Avenue, an old part of town. Turner Avenue was a generic name for a street where the houses were jostled together cheek by jowl, many of them with small but cluttered yards. Toys, old cars on blocks, dogs of unusual ancestry, and old walnut trees pushing up the sidewalk. Most of the houses were plain-wrap Victorian, which meant they had wood siding and porches with spindly posts. The spindly posts outside Jolie's place were painted dark green. Landry noted the home protection sign planted in the grass. He also noticed that her yard was neat and the plants and tree were healthy.

There was an empty lot on one corner and a convenience store on the other.

Landry made one pass by. Hardly anyone was out on the street. None of the dogs were barkers. They either sat morosely in the shade or trotted up to the fence to get a look at the man driving by. It was a weekday and many of the driveways were empty—people at work. Only one middle-aged woman, dressed like a hippie from the sixties, black hair down to her waist, was spraying her flowerbed with water. She was careful not to look in his direction as he drove past in his Diaz Landscaping Service van. He could have been on the moon for all she cared.

There was an alley behind the row of houses, choked with weeds, smelling of garbage and the sharp, medicinal stench of alcohol. Landry had counted the houses—Jolie lived four down from this end of the street. He cruised through the alley between the two rows of backyards facing the alley, parking as close to the back wall of Jolie's yard as he could get.

Nothing going on in the hot sunlight. Everyone either at work, or at school, or indoors under the air conditioners. Landry noted several swampbox coolers, could hear them rattling on the roofs.

You could have staged a theater production here, and no one would notice.

Landry parked up close to the wall behind Jolie's place. In his blue work shirt, jeans, work boots and cap, he looked like a guy sent to clean up the backyard. He even had a rake and a plastic garbage can.

This wall had been added to—it was much higher than the other walls on the alley. He tried the gate but it was locked.

As he approached, he heard a bark. A suspicious sound, low and guttural.

Of course she had a dog. She was a cop. Cops by nature were paranoid. Cops by nature were all about mitigation. Mitigation and control. Control your immediate space, keep things from getting out of hand. Smother trouble in its sleep. If at all possible, run to meet trouble and hit it before it could hit you. That was the reason her wall was higher—the new blocks creating a sort of waterline. Gray on the bottom, and coral on top. He had no doubt her house would be hard to get into. There was already a regular obstacle course. High wall, big dog, alarm service sign.

He could jimmy the back door if he could get past the dog. But Landry doubted if Jolie would leave it just at that. Cops—at least cops like Jolie—tended to be anal when it came to personal protection.

Landry looked around.

Nothing going on. Just the heat, the sun bearing down on his head.

He climbed up onto the wall.

The dog was a Rottweiler. He was lying down in the shade of the house, by the sliding glass door out to the yard.

The yard wasn't dry and parched and half-dirt, as some Landry had seen as he drove past chain-link fences and old pickets. In the shade on the terrace was a paradise of potted plants and flowers, colorful blooms—pinks, whites, deep-rose-colored petunias, small cacti in pots, a veritable rain forest of ferns and exotic bushes and small fruit trees.

Smelling of water.

The terrace dark from a recent spraying.

Her neighbor? A friend?

A boyfriend?

Or was she holed up there, hiding?

The Rottie woofed once from his spot on the cool terrace.

Hard to know if he was friend or enemy.

There was water in his bowl.

There was food in another bowl. Big bowls for a big dog. A full bag of Pedigree Large Breed dog food was propped up against the redbrick house.

Someone was taking care of the dog—and the plant. Maybe it was Jolie, hiding inside the house or staying elsewhere and coming by to look after him, or maybe it was a neighbor, or maybe it was someone she worked with at Branch Sheriff's Office.

If he knew one thing, it was that nothing would likely happen here except at night, under the cover of darkness. If he stayed around here much longer, landscaping van or not, he would draw attention.

He was ninety-percent positive that if Jolie moved in and out of the house, or if her agent moved in and out of the house, they would do so by night. If she had someone to care for the dog, that person would likely come either early in the evening or early in the morning. Usually people who took care of pets had to work around their own schedules, unless pet-sitting was all they did.

No car in the driveway—at least not now. So Landry was leaning toward the theory that whoever took care of the Rottweiler and the plants wasn't staying there.

He drove two blocks to the Subway shop he'd noticed on the way in to the neighborhood, and bought two sandwiches. One for himself, and one for the Rottie.

It didn't take him long to install the two hunt cameras—one focused on the back door and one at the front. First, Landry tossed meat from the sandwich to the Rottweiler. The dog ate it and lumbered over for more, tail wagging. Landry thought: *now or never.* He hopped down from the wall into the yard and was nearly licked to death. He found a lawn trimmer in the storage shed, put it in the van and drove back around to the front. There, he ran it around the little patch of lawn.

He had an audience of none. The carports and driveways were still empty and no one was about, not even the hippie woman with the long black hair. The sound of the lawn trimmer, he knew, would be an expected sound and no one would question him being here. He stopped partway through, found a suitable place for the camera, made sure it lined up with the door, and installed it—two minutes tops. He did the same in the backyard.

He wanted to know who was taking care of the dog. Jolie, or someone else? He wanted to know if her place was being monitored, or whether or not the house needed monitoring at all. If they had her—whoever "they" were—they would not bother monitoring her house. Unless they thought someone was coming.

Unless they knew about Landry himself.

It occurred to him that whoever had taken Jolie might be the same person feeding the dog—just to maintain the status quo.

SPECTRE BLACK

Landry raked the small yard, making plenty of noise. The Rottweiler decided to join in, wriggling his hind end and dashing around the small yard before wriggling again.

A real killer.

After raking for ten minutes, Landry took a break and looked for the home alarm sensor leading to the central control box. He found the magnet where he expected to find it: attached to the doorsill. A home alarm system like this one passed a minimal amount of electrical current to the magnet. The current arced across a very short distance between the sensor and the magnet, sending it back and forth—a cycle. If that cycle wasn't repeated constantly, the alarm would go off. Say a window was opened, or a door—that would break the cycle.

Landry donned latex gloves from one pocket of his jeans before reaching into the pocket of the other, past a roll of electrical tape and a couple of bobby pins until his fingers closed around a sheet of tin foil. He fed the tin foil into the narrow crack between the doorjamb and the door—it was a nice tight fit. As long as the foil pressed against the sensor, he could open the window or door with impunity. The foil acted as a de facto magnet, aping the alarm's cycle.

Next came the deadbolt.

Wisely, Jolie had made her home security redundant. She had deadbolt locks as well. But any lock could be picked. Landry removed one of the bobby pins and bent it into a right angle. He removed the second bobby pin and straightened it out flat, all the way. He started with the straight pin, working it back and forth inside the lock, then added the pin with the right angle. He worked the two of them until the latch clicked.

Inside, Landry walked down the hallway, reconnoitering, and made sure he knew the house. Next, he returned to the open door on the left. This was Jolie's home office. Inside, he smelled stale air. The house was cool, though—Landry had seen and heard the working swampbox cooler on the roof. It sounded like a bucket of rocks.

A black-and-white cat was curled up on the desk chair.

The desk was clear, except for a jar of pens and pencils. He'd hoped for a laptop but found none. Under a standing lamp a printer sat on a stand you'd buy at OfficeMax, paper stacked on the shelf beneath. He opened the desk drawers, but he saw nothing important in them. He went to the filing cabinet with its four drawers, and used the bobby pin to open each of them.

The filing cabinets were half empty. The cabinet held old files from old cases, some even from Florida.

Who used filing cabinets anymore? These days a person could file everything they wanted on a USB disk.

He searched everywhere for the computer and for a USB disk, but found nothing. Wondered if she'd taken her laptop or if someone else had come along and taken it.

There was nothing else. No iPad, no tablet of any kind. Just a potted plant. He poked his finger in the pot and the soil was crumbling and dry. The pet sitter apparently wasn't a plant sitter. He went to the kitchen and took down a glass from the cabinet, filled it with water, came back to the office and dumped the water on the plant.

A little bit of the sun came through the slats in the blinds, and the cat stretched and then curled up again, covering its face with one paw. It ignored him completely.

Landry liked cats. They minded their own business.

The missing laptop (if there *was* a missing laptop) meant a few things. She could have taken it with her, she could have cleared out fast and hidden it, or the person who fed the dog and cat could have been charged with keeping it.

Or whoever had abducted her in the first place also had her laptop.

The cat came into the hallway and cried at him, turned around and went into the kitchen and stood by the refrigerator. It looked at him briefly, then focused its attention on the refrigerator. It didn't

SPECTRE BLACK

cry and it didn't beg. Just stood there expecting him to open the refrigerator and give it something to eat.

Another reason he liked cats.

There was no pretense with them: they were what they were and they wanted what they wanted. They didn't have to get all polite about it.

Still gloved up, he opened the refrigerator. He saw no cans of cat food. He looked in the cupboard next to the refrigerator and found some cat treats. He didn't know how much to feed it. The whole bag? Or just a couple? He settled on a handful, and shook the treats on the Saltillo tile floor. The cat ate each one delicately and looked at Landry for more. As if it hadn't eaten anything at all and was starving.

"I met a con man like you once," Landry said.

The cat gave him a look, then turned his back and cleaned himself.

Landry didn't want to spend too much time here. He searched the house thoroughly but quickly, found nothing associated with Jolie's job as a sheriff's deputy, except for a couple of uniforms in her closet.

If Jolie had been abducted—and when she'd called him, she had escaped from somewhere—then when did she contact the person who fed the dog and cat? Did she call her after her escape?

She'd called the right person. The water bowls were full. Both the cat and the dog looked fine to him.

Back in the yard, he stowed the lawn trimmer back in the shed. He said to the Rottweiler, "Some watchdog *you* are."

Next, he went to the donut shop two blocks down from the motel. The donut shop was called Duncan's Donuts, which not only treaded on a well-known copyright, but also went well with Dina's Diner. He briefly wondered if they had all gotten together in a town meeting and decided what to name their businesses to present a unifying, alliterative theme. Maybe there was also a Rosa's Restaurant, or a Ginny's Gin Mill.

Landry knew that the FBI would send an agent to investigate

45

a missing cop, no matter what the jurisdiction. They would do this within three days. If he hadn't wasted time waiting by the Circle K, fruitlessly calling the pay phone number, he might have been able to intercept the agent, find out what he knew, and become his replacement. But Landry had no idea how long Jolie had been missing. He was way too late to intercept the FBI agent now.

But he could still strike up an acquaintance with the right cop. He could still pump him for information, if he did it skillfully.

And so he chose the donut shop.

Landry had dressed like an off-duty cop, which basically meant jeans (the more faded the better), sneakers, and an open-necked polo shirt. The polo shirt was banded at the bottom, a cop trick used to conceal a gun or knife secured to his belt. The shirt puffed out a little above the band, so there was no telltale outline. The banded polo shirt, along with the fact that the jeans had plenty of legroom to fit over boots (or a leg holster) did double duty, making him easily identifiable as law enforcement or former law enforcement. He could be anything, from a retired cop to an off-duty cop to an undercover cop. His hair was short but not too short.

There were uniformed cops here—three of them at a four top. The table, like his own, was on a single stand and tottered a little under their elbows, just like his did. Landry put a matchbook under the table, to add to the matchbook already there. He had the newspaper open and coffee at his elbow, and he could watch them.

And then he realized he was being watched himself.

A good-looking woman stared at him from her table, her gaze open and interested, before returning to her iPad.

Landry liked that she didn't attempt to hide her interest. That set her apart right there.

He looked at her, willing her to look back up, but she didn't take the bait. She appeared to be concentrating on whatever she was reading.

SPECTRE BLACK

Dark hair with blond highlights swept up and back with one of those stick things women put in to keep their hair from falling down. She was nice-looking. Slender, with a strong face that he had seen on some Brazilian models, bold but narrow, high cheekbones, a flare at the end of her long, thin nose, dark lipstick. She wore a deep cerise blouse, collar out, under a dark navy suit. Expensive leather shoes, lots of support. Hose. In this heat.

A professional. The question was, a professional *what?*

He stood up and walked over to refill his cup at the coffee-and-tea station near the window. Took his time, looking out at the parking lot—

And saw what he expected to see. One row back, sun glinting off the windshield.

Landry felt a motion behind him, a misplacement of air. The slightest rustle. An expensive sound. Out of the corner of his eye he saw a sliver of her suit jacket and a hand with short nails polished smooth. He caught her scent—subtle but enticing.

She filled her coffee cup and reached past him for the half-and-half jug. No perfume, just the clean scent of soap.

He looked back at the car under the hot glare of the New Mexico sun. It was black, a plain-wrap Crown Vic. He couldn't see the back plates, but he knew what they would look like. They would be white.

The lady was an FBI agent.

He felt the air whisk against him and she was gone.

He did not look around, but kept his eyes on the plate-glass window. The interior of the donut shop was reflected in faint outlines. He saw her pull out her chair and sit down. She did not look back at him.

As he walked back to his table, Landry kept track of her out of the corner of his eye. Looking for eye response but getting none. She seemed absorbed in her iPad.

He set his cup on the edge of his table. Three-quarters of the ceramic mug teetered in thin air before falling to the floor with a crash.

He hunkered down, head low, scanning the room. Looking for a quick eye response, and seeing it everywhere: "flash focus." Everyone's eyes turned immediately to the sound of the ceramic breaking. Except for the woman. Instead of looking at him, she was assessing everyone else's reaction. He liked that, too.

Finally, she turned her head slightly in his direction. Their eyes met. He threw her a rueful smile as he helped the busboy pick up shards of ceramic.

The busboy apologized and Landry told him he didn't need to, it was his fault, no problem. All the time, watching the woman out of the corner of his eye. The boy bustled back with a replacement mug, and Landry walked back to the coffee station.

Once again, his eye went to the window, the ghostly reflection of people behind him. But she was fast. Already beside him, reaching for the half-and-half. "Your handle should be closer to your belt," she said. She poured the cream into her cup and walked away.

Landry fought the urge to look down at his shirt, looking for a telltale shape, but ultimately, he did. As God intended, the knit material puffed out over the band of his polo shirt, completely concealing the H&K snugged underneath. She'd seen nothing. He assumed she'd made him because he had come dressed for the show. That was all.

Maybe he could get her to tell him what she knew about Jolie's disappearance, if she knew anything at all.

Landry stared into the plate-glass window. She had her phone out, her head tipped forward, engrossed in whatever she was doing. Then she looked up at him, and their eyes met through the window's reflection.

SPECTRE BLACK

It was faint, a ghostly image, but Landry saw that her face was impassive. Not just impassive. She held him with a cool stare that his body responded to.

She dismissed him and looked back down at her phone.

Landry remained where he was, staring into the window. She did not look up again. She ignored him. He stood there, shaking a packet of sugar, eyes holding her reflection. Then he put the coffee mug down next to the coffee machine, turned around, and walked in her direction. She sat at a table where people had to funnel past her to get to the door. As he passed her, he felt her gaze on his back.

He'd walked here. Duncan's Donuts was only five doors and one four-lane bridge down from The Satellite INN.

He stood just outside the shop, taking in the air, looking at her car, but not looking. Clearly, the FBI agent had targeted him for some reason. Maybe she suspected he had something to do with Jolie's disappearance. Or maybe she thought he was the guy who shot the militia guy at the checkpoint. There were plenty of maybes. It was her turn to make a move.

And he'd give her that chance.

He stood just to the side of the door, pulling a cigarette from the pack he always carried. He didn't smoke, but it was a good piece of stage business—a reason for him to pause.

The door's bell jangled behind him.

"How long will it take me to find out what you're really up to?" she said. Her voice was low but musical, with an underlying sarcasm. He liked it. She stood next to him, eyes forward, taking in the view.

Landry pushed the cigarette behind his ear. He did not look at her. "Do we know each other?"

"I know you," she said, staring at the parking lot. "I've run into your kind before, plenty of times. You think you're fooling people, but you don't fool me. You can dress like a cop but that doesn't mean you are one."

"I'm not such a bad guy. I've been known to grow on people."

"That kind of thing takes time, and I'm a busy person."

Landry removed the cigarette from his ear and flicked it into the parking lot. "Then I guess we have nothing to talk about."

He crossed the lot and followed the road back toward the motel.

He'd spent some time studying the horse whisperers. The famous one, Monty Roberts, once got a deer to follow him over miles and miles of open country. It took patience, but the main thing the man did was *never* pursue the deer. He made it so that the deer wanted to pursue him. The animal never felt threatened. And Landry had learned that to walk away would very often lead his intended target to him.

It did this time, too. She fell into step beside him. Landry smiled.

She repeated the line she'd used before. "How long will it take for me to find out what you're up to?"

"What I'm up to?"

She continued to keep her eyes forward. He walked fast, but she had no trouble keeping up. Expensive shoes with sensible heels: practical. They took the sidewalk on the four-lane bridge spanning the riverbed. It was well past eight and there were few cars on the bridge at this time of the morning. The clean soap scent of her followed the breeze—sometimes strong, sometimes faint, sometimes non-existent.

"So what do you think?" Landry asked, walking faster.

"What do I think about what?" She had to take a fast stutter step every now and then to keep up with him. He was tall and had long legs—no one said life was fair. "You're a cop."

Landry said nothing, but increased the pace. She took faster stutter steps.

"Who are you with? Sheriff's or PD?"

SPECTRE BLACK

He said nothing.

"Or an outside agency?" She stopped, wiped at a bead of sweat on her cheek. Beautiful. Even the sweat bead was beautiful before she mashed it with her beautiful finger. He noticed her nails. Deep purple, engraved with turquoise *fleurs-de-lis*.

Landry stopped as well. She was tall, but he was taller. She tipped her face up to him and he felt the thrill again, only this time it wasn't in his stomach, but in his groin. A thrill down deep in the muddy bottom silt of him.

"I'm retired," he said.

She came closer, mashed up close against him, lifted a manicured hand and touched him.

Landry felt the thrill. It was like a short, sweet carnival ride. He felt a lot of things. But the one that screamed at the top of its lungs was the wire. It thrummed like a guitar string all the way up his body.

"Where'd you say your motel was?" she said.

- — -

It was great and it was awful.

Thrilling and stupefying.

She hit every note.

There was one moment he thought he'd been devoured and what little remained had been left by the side of the road for the buzzards.

At first it was brilliant. Stimulating. Beyond stimulating. Then it passed the point of pleasure to wanting it to be enough to waiting for it to be over. His own pride was his worst enemy. She kept at him. He lost count of the hours, which could only be marked by the moving bar of sunshine across the bed.

They were too loud. *She* was too loud. Like she had something to prove. In the fifth inning, he was starting to dislike her. At the bottom of the ninth, he hated her.

He was lucky to have made it to the seventh-inning stretch. By that time he was running purely on pride.

He couldn't stand the stink, even if it was arousing. The sweetness of her fresh-soap skin cloyed. It gave a clean soap smell a bad name.

And it was no fun to feel like a pile driver, looking into the eyes of not just a stranger, but an alien.

Her eyes changed from time to time. There was lust, yes. Unquenchable lust. But also contempt. Cold contempt. He had misjudged her. She'd presented someone else to him, cool and composed, attractive and . . . normal. But now, her eyes were like fixed turquoise stones in her head, her face a mask of incredible but virulent beauty.

His body hurt. It didn't want to go again, but again and again she picked at him. Nasty words, contempt, belittlement—switched out with the most ridiculous of compliments, heaps of praise. A wheelbarrowful of praise like heaped roses, once beautiful, now fading, damp, smelling of the dirt and decay. The smell of the grave.

A supernatural experience.

She wanted to go again, and again. It challenged his manhood, it challenged who and what he was, because he knew she was willing him to fail.

When she'd shucked her clothes, they could not wait to get at each other: a windfall. A gift. And then there were the repeat performances, three strikes and he was out. After that there was the contempt. Icy.

He'd once ridden a horse who would not submit, and to his great shame he rode that horse and rode him and rode him and rode him until it stopped, head down, sweat dripping from its hide, and gave up. Just gave up and gave out.

Now he felt like that horse.

And her screaming. It felt playacted, but he knew she was enjoying herself. Had to be. But there had been knocks on the door. There had been voices outside on the walkway. There had been banging on the wall. And muttered comments he could hear: "This is a family motel."

Landry didn't believe in shame—he'd dumped that Catholic idea long ago when he had to go and kill people in a foreign country.

But he felt it now.

He felt hollowed out, cored.

Finally, she fell into a deep sleep. Hours later, she still slept. The sleep of the fulfilled, the slightest smile on her lips.

Landry couldn't sleep, though.

He wanted to get away from her. So he took a long, hot shower followed by a long, cold shower, and pulled on his clothes. He looked through her purse and found her service weapon and FBI creds. Her full name was Carla Angela Vitelli.

Then he went for a walk.

A long one.

- — -

When he returned, she was gone. There was just the smell of sex. And underneath, the smell of rage.

He'd gotten nothing out of her on Jolie's disappearance or where she was in the investigation. And he'd left a lot on the field.

He walked back to the donut place. The FBI car was gone.

He didn't go back inside. Half of him thought she might be waiting there, some sort of weird sexual ambush.

What did she want from him? He couldn't figure it out. She had told him nothing. Was she working the case, the missing persons case of Jolie Burke? How did he show up on her radar? How had she made him? Did she connect him with Jolie Burke in some way, or was he just cannon fodder? He'd kept in good shape, and maybe he gave off some kind of vibe. It had happened before. But not with an FBI agent.

She had targeted him for some *reason*.

He should have paid attention. He should have caught on much, much sooner.

When their eyes first met, mirrored in the plate-glass window, he'd felt something in his jaw—like a tiny wire being pulled. That was his warning apparatus. It had saved his life many times in Iraq and Afghanistan. It was like a sixth sense, only more visceral than that. Just a tug inside his jaw, mirrored by a not-unpleasant stirring in his gut.

Danger.

But he'd ignored it completely. While he'd been targeting her, she'd been targeting *him*.

Whatever her game was, the FBI woman was dangerous.

He stood outside the donut place, looking back across the bridge over the dry riverbed at the motel sign, neon-bright against the sunset. He should go back to the motel room and get some sleep.

The sun's orange eye squinted under a pile of black clouds. The road was dark but tinted gold. He ran out of sidewalk and walked on dirt.

The day had been windless, hot and dry, but now it was heavy with the promise of rain. As he waited for a car to turn onto a cross street in front of him, he heard the crunch of shoes on dirt and felt a displacement of air behind him. He turned around. But there was nothing—no one. He smelled aftershave.

He turned in a circle. It was getting darker by the minute. The sun's eye was all but closed now. Above Landry was the embankment where cars came down the exit ramp from the bridge. Their tires hummed, amplified by the sound bouncing off the low guardrails. One after another they came, stopping before turning right in front of him.

The sodium arc lights on the bridge came on, casting an orange glow.

SPECTRE BLACK

The cars might have accounted for the displaced air. If someone's car window was open he might possibly have smelled aftershave.

He squinted in the direction of the receding footsteps, expecting to see a figure in the gloom, but there was nothing. Just the desert and a string of stores on his side of the road.

The wind was scented with the coming rain. He listened hard—and listened to the footsteps. They were barely there: a rhythmic crunch of shoes on dirt.

He stared hard, but the walker was nowhere to be seen.

But he saw something.

The air seemed to waver. There was a rhythm to it. A walking rhythm.

But no walking man. The landscape was intact, the road markers, the buildings, the signs. He could see them.

Way off in the distance the shape that was not a shape seemed to catch the light, and crinkled like a funhouse mirror.

Did he really see that?

The sound of footsteps had long since receded, drowned out by the traffic.

Whatever it was he thought he saw, it had dwindled to nothing.

A dust devil, maybe.

But it didn't act like any dust devil he'd ever seen.

- — -

The next morning Landry cruised by the police department parking lots and the sheriff's office parking lots, looking for an FBI car. But there was nothing remotely like it in any of the lots, visitor lots, or any of the other surface parking. The PD and the Sheriff's Office were both small enough entities that they didn't have parking garages.

How did she find him? Or did she just sense that he wasn't legit?

He went over what she'd asked him. *Are you with the Sheriff's Office or are you with PD?*

Why had she homed in on him? He didn't fool himself that she just wanted to have sex. There had to be something she had wanted from him, and he was sure it had to do with Jolie.

The woman had a strange way of interrogating him.

He shrugged it off—for now, anyway. Some things had to just sit, off to the side, until his subconscious found the answer, or new information came to him. Perhaps she was just a sex maniac looking for a retired cop; maybe that was her thing. As far as he could recall, she'd never mentioned Jolie Burke. Never mentioned a missing cop at all.

Time to check on Jolie's place. This time he took the white car and left the landscaping van in the motel parking lot. Someone in Jolie's neighborhood might have seen it. A landscaper would be there once, but probably not the following day.

Only fifty feet up from The Satellite INN was another traffic light. Every time he reached the intersection, the light turned red, and today was no different. So he waited and took in the ambience: an old lady sitting in the covered bus stop, two teenagers leaning against the poles holding the roof up, ignoring the old lady and each other. A female jogger in a tracksuit stretching a hamstring, affording the stopped traffic a generous look at her trim backside.

Landry wasn't worried about driving the white car. There had been nothing more on the shooting at the checkpoint, except the article rehashing the story and reiterating that there were no suspects. There had been mention of a white subcompact, but so far he hadn't seen or heard of a make or model.

He thought it was strange that there wasn't anything new. It had the feeling of old news—already not worth reporting about. Branch was not a small town, but it wasn't quite a medium-sized town either. Small enough, he would have thought, to consider the shooting a big story.

Maybe the police were holding back some vital piece of information. Or else they weren't, and were just a Mickey Mouse police department with nothing to recommend them but their uniforms. He'd seen that in many towns.

He parked in front of Jolie's place. Carrying a newspaper, he went up the walk to the house and rang the bell with his elbow. It bonged through the house while he looked around. No one anywhere. Unless someone was looking out, unseen, from the houses next door or across the street. In the shade of the porch, he was able to look at the camera and run it back. He saw the house sitter. A dark-haired woman, early forties, wearing jeans, a knit shirt, tennis shoes—and a sheriff's shield on her belt.

She walked up to the house, disarmed the alarm, unlocked the door, and went inside. He watched as she let herself back out, approximately fifteen minutes later. He wished he could see the kind of car she drove—if she had driven a car at all. Maybe she lived nearby and walked from her place. He looked at the time: five seventeen in the afternoon. Probably she came straight from work to feed the dog.

Landry knew her pattern now, which would be helpful.

He'd already decided what to do with the cat and the dog.

For now, he let the hunt cam run. Late afternoon turned to dusk and then to dark, the porch security light automatically coming on above. He was about to stop and reset the cam, when someone else appeared on the screen. "Well, well," he said.

His sex partner, the FBI agent, appeared.

She looked straight into the camera, a self-satisfied smirk on her face. Then she crossed her eyes.

He drove by the donut shop. This time there was no FBI car in the lot. He parked the Nissan in the lot and walked the couple of blocks back to the cop shop.

He hurt in places he didn't know he had. It was enough to make him swear off sex—almost. He sat near a group of rowdy cops, who drank coffee and tucked into their breakfasts like longshoremen. Some, he sensed, had come off shift, and some were about to go on.

From their badges, he knew they were with the sheriff's office.

He pretended to read the paper and drank his coffee and waited for Jolie Burke's name to be mentioned. "You know what I'm saying. They're all about equality, but she left Jeff Beebe high and dry. He's doing double duty—her caseload on top of his. I heard she didn't even call in."

"I know Jolie—she's not like that," the younger cop said. "Maybe something else is going on, like something . . . personal."

"Like what?"

"I dunno."

"What are you saying?"

"I'm just saying she would've called in."

"I'm sure she's just enjoying her *va*cay."

"Unless something happened to her."

"A little early to think that, wouldn't you say?"

"It's not like her to not call in," the younger man said.

There was a moment of quiet. Landry couldn't tell if they liked Jolie very well or not. It felt more as if they were all contemplating their own possible disappearance.

"Not to worry, kid," the same cop said. "Jan's taking care of her pets while she's gone."

Then the older guy said, "You heard about the robbery in Tejar."

No one said anything.

Finally the gruff older guy said, "I wouldn't put too much stock in what the media says."

"Yeah—assholes."

There was quiet. Then another guy said, "But *Jesus*—if it was true. It was like a Clint Eastwood movie."

"Yeah, so they *say*," the deep-voiced guy said. "Probably, they made it look bigger than it was." Added, "You ask me, someone like that, who shoots up a city street? Trouble. She probably asked for trouble and got it. Hate to say it, because she seemed OK, but . . . that kind of shit comes back to bite you in the ass."

Landry listened, a half smile on his face. He'd been there. Not for the bank's ATM smash-and-grab, not for the subsequent shooting (Jolie had used her long gun), but later, for the cleanup.

They'd done a good job, cleaning up. One of the robbers had a brother, and that brother came looking for the famous cop who killed his sibling.

If he and Jolie Burke were lucky, no one would ever know what happened to that fourth member and ringleader—the one who stayed in the comfort of his own home while the others drove a car into the wall by the bank's ATM and came running out with the money.

The ringleader had been cremated. The only problem for the cremators: there was no name to go with the person they cremated; all they had was ash.

Landry and Jolie. They had worked together. Like a well-oiled machine.

"Hey, how's your daughter doing?"

"Good. She and John named the baby after me."

They talked about that for a while.

Then one of them said, "You seen the FBI agent?"

"What FBI agent?"

"What's she doing here?"

The older guy glanced at the younger guy. "Maybe she's looking for Burke. Maybe that's her assignment."

Another voice said, "Yeah. She's hot."

"Where'd you see her?"

"Here."

"Here?"

"Yeah, you must've been asleep at the switch."

Another cop said, "She was right at that table over there. Yesterday."

"The woman with the long hair? The one with the great ass?"

"You got it, brother."

The cop who was quiet—there was always a quiet one—spoke up. He said, "I think she's a cousin or something."

"A cousin? What're you talking about? Whose cousin?"

"Jace Denboer. She's his cousin."

"That little shit? The one with the Camaro? Took the leg off that homeless guy and didn't even get a traffic violation?"

Someone else said, "No, she's his sister."

"Half sister," someone else said. "She's his half sister."

"So the Denboer kid has a half sister who's an FBI agent. Cozy."

"He doesn't need a cousin who's an FBI agent, you ask me," another cop, the skinny one, said. "Nobody gonna give *him* any trouble."

"Got that right."

"Untouchable," the oldest cop said. "And don't you forget it."

Landry drove back to the motel. The FBI agent, Carla Vitelli, was related to some rich kid who was a reckless driver and took a homeless man's leg off. Jace Denboer.

Every town had one. A royal family. The tradition had probably been handed down from the dawn of time, down through the ages—the Dark Ages, the Enlightenment, the Industrial Age. The wealthiest families and most royal of the royal, the cattle barons and railroad barons and captains of industry all the way down to small-town mayors. Every municipality, every small town, had a family. It had become a meme: "To the manor born." Apparently, in this small city, the Denboers were the royal family.

Which explained a lot. It explained why Vitelli had felt entitled. It explained why she'd run roughshod over him—

Literally.

There was at least one family like that in every town.

Vitelli had felt extremely entitled. In fact, Landry was still recovering from her right to entitlement.

He approached The Satellite INN from behind, across an empty lot, a scrub patch of desert. The white subcompact rental car was in back, one of ten to twenty other cars there, give or take. His van was out front.

A sheriff's cruiser had pulled up catty-corner to the rental Nissan, as if planning to stop an escape in its tracks. Landry could hear the crackle of the unit's radio.

He looked up at the open door to his motel room on the second floor. A hive of activity. Deputies in tan uniforms, big-hipped from their duty belts, coming out with white trash bags in their gloved hands.

Landry felt the tickle of hair on his neck just before he heard a loud engine gun down the side street and screech into the dirt lot.

"Police! Don't move! Hands on your head!"

Landry obeyed.

CHAPTER 7

"Can you tell me what you're charging me with?" he asked the deputy who had cuffed him and was marching him toward a sheriff's car.

"You have the right to remain silent, and if I were you I'd do just that."

"I'll take it from here," a gruff voice said. Landry turned his head to look at him. The man was older, beefy, with a gray mustache like a whisk broom.

Landry had already been to the Tobosa County Sheriff's website, and he knew who the man was. He was the Tobosa Sheriff's Office's undersheriff, Walt Davis.

The undersheriff grabbed Landry's shoulder and spun him toward his own plain-wrap Crown Vic.

———

Landry was delivered to the Tobosa County Jail in the back of the undersheriff's car, already handcuffed and chained. They must think he was dangerous, or perhaps it had been reported that he was dangerous, and they were taking no chances.

Containment.

There was a separate entrance for arrestees, and in this smallish cinder block building that entrance was in the back, as it usually was. Davis marched him up a loading ramp and into a gray hallway with gray linoleum and gray-painted walls. The only brightness was the row of fluorescent light panels at intervals along the ceiling, which seemed to chase the shadows into what few corners there were. The artificial light made it brighter than day, like those warehouse shopping marts, only worse in every respect. He could smell disinfectant that did little to mask the odor of piss and vomit.

He knew his first stop would be Intake. It would be a long, drawn-out process, designed to humiliate and cow him.

The first precept for cops was control. Clamp down on the perpetrator so he can't make a move. Intimidate him into not even thinking about resistance. Always, the goal was to cut off rebellion at the source. Police were trained to run to meet trouble, to stop it before it could get any traction at all. Police work was based on the concepts of prevention and containment. Never let the tossed match turn into a brushfire.

Landry understood this and even admired it, but he had been on the wrong end of this policy before, and he didn't like it.

He didn't like it now.

The undersheriff called to one of the guards. "Don't bother with the other stuff, just give him the once-over and get him in lockup. I've got twenty-four hours."

There was one other man to be processed before him, so he waited. As he waited, his mind ran through the possibilities. The number-one possibility: his car, a white subcompact car, had been seen going through the checkpoint shortly before one of the militia members was shot to death.

Landry knew that the guy who stopped him at the checkpoint did not write down his driver's license number or even jot down the license plate of the car. The other two people at the checkpoint had been engrossed in conversation. Landry was sure the big guy who stopped him had not looked inside the duffle.

Pretty sure.

And if he had, what were the odds of him talking about it? He'd remarked on the box of tennis balls on the seat and the racket in the trunk—that was all. But maybe Landry's memory was faulty and the man had unzipped the bag and looked inside.

No, his memory wasn't faulty. The guy did not look inside the duffle. One, he didn't have time to, and two, Landry would have heard the duffle zipper open.

Even if he had looked through the duffle, he had been killed shortly after Landry went through. He might have remarked to the other two about something he saw in the duffle, but again, Landry was sure he didn't open it.

Another car, another white subcompact, could have come by within the hour, and that car could have contained the shooter. The two other militia members struck Landry as not too bright. He doubted they had seen that kind of carnage before. A man being blasted by a shotgun—a man they knew. A man they spent time with.

They would have been in shock.

So were the police interested in his car? After all, it was a white subcompact.

But no one knew Landry in this town. No one could have looked at the white Nissan Versa and known he had rented it. He had used a different identity to check in to the motel.

The only person he had spent any time with in this town was Agent Carla Vitelli. Perhaps she suspected him and somehow found a way to link him to the car?

It was hard to think in here. There were a number of mentally ill people around him. All of them claiming to be innocent. Some of them screaming, some of them crying, one of them vomiting, some of them just sitting there staring into space. A few talked casually to one another, as if they were in bleachers at a ball game. Landry sat quietly and nobody talked to him. To his right was a homeless man who hugged himself and sang under his breath. To his left was a big hulk of a man, Hispanic, with the concentrated visage of a sumo wrestler. Except he wasn't naked, fortunately for everyone there. He wore a tank top and those long, sloppy shorts that only looked good on basketball players, and blinding white top-of-the-line running shoes.

The homeless man smelled. The hulk smelled good. But both smells were overwhelming. Between the two of them Landry could survive only by breathing through his mouth.

Chains rattled. Someone snored. He could smell cigarette smoke clinging to a lot of unwashed bodies. Time dragged by. A fly lit on the homeless guy and he freaked, and someone dragged him away. The Hispanic guy did not seem to notice. He just sat there, elbows on his knees, fists cuffed together, staring straight ahead.

There were madhouse cries every once in a while, and shuffling feet, and chains.

Finally Landry was walked over to the intake desk. There was plenty of shame to go around, and a police jail was the perfect place to showcase it. The man at the desk looked at his ID and driver's license: "Chris Keeley." He went through the contents of his wallet and confiscated money. He paid particular attention to Chris Keeley's one credit card. Landry wondered if this small-city police force in New Mexico pulled the scam that many others did. If they would trump up a charge and confiscate his assets.

Good luck with that. Chris Keeley had the credit card but nothing in a bank account except enough to keep the savings account open. One hundred dollars, in a bank that nobody had ever heard of.

The man processing him had a placid expression. He must have seen every possible permutation of man, and gave off the impression that nothing fazed him. He had an indoor pallor that went with the artificial light.

Next up, Landry thought: *fingerprints*. Only the man didn't take fingerprints. He didn't take a mug shot, either.

Good thing.

Or maybe a bad thing. If there was no record of him, they could do anything.

I've got twenty-four hours.

The undersheriff had treated him as a special case.

This arrest was off the books.

As far as they were concerned, he must appear to be who he said he was. Chris Keeley, no wants, no warrants. A high school teacher from Albuquerque, New Mexico. His wallet showed pictures of his wife and kids. He had a driver's license, a Triple A card, and one credit card.

He was not questioned.

Landry asked the officer leading him to lockup what the charges were.

"Vagrancy."

"I'm staying at The Satellite INN motel."

"That's nice."

"If I'm staying at a motel, that's not vagrancy."

"You'll have your day in court."

No use arguing with him. They sent him through the showers and gave him a yellow jumpsuit and a pair of flip-flops that were two sizes too small and slippery when wet.

He was locked in what looked like a cage you put dogs in, only twenty times bigger. It appeared to be temporary, like a cage set on the floor, until they made up his suite. His box was on one side of the room and there were four other cages opposite his. There were only three other inmates, so they had the place to themselves.

One of the inmates wailed like a banshee. It was constant. Landry was mildly successful at blocking out the sound.

There was no theater seating, so he found a place that wasn't taken and sat down, knees up, feet flat on the concrete floor, back against the wall. He was forty-eight years old now, pushing fifty, and his years as a SEAL had compromised parts of his body in many ways—wear and tear. Despite a daily routine of flexibility training, he knew that in normal circumstances, his body would act up.

Fortunately, that didn't apply to emergency situations, and did not impinge too much on his particular skill set. The learned memory was still there. He could still kill a man in a few seconds if he needed to.

Time to cool his heels and wait to see what would happen.

- — -

A half hour in, a jailer came for him. He was marched down another gray hallway and buzzed through two solid steel doors, deeper into the building, and deposited into a cell of his own. This cell had a bunk, a toilet, and a sink. Landry doubted that the faucets were Moen.

The door slid open and closed electronically. All the cells surrounded a common area.

The common area had chairs and a couple of tables. A little like those breakfast nooks at the Comfort Inn, except these were gray, metal, beaten up, and cheaper. Landry could see that the chairs and tables were bolted to the floor. A guard stood on duty. Two inmates sat at one table, watching a soap opera on TV.

He was surprised there were still soap operas on TV. He guessed there weren't many channels on the TV in the common area. Landry lay down on the bunk and stared at the ceiling, trying to figure out what the game was. He was aware that he had been moved in the wrong direction, deeper into the jail. He'd require a bed, a sink, and a toilet. Which meant they would be keeping him for a while.

No one came to talk to him. No one came with forms to fill out; no cops came to question him. They were a conspicuously incurious lot. It was just him and the squirrel cage and the sound of the soap opera on TV. He thought of other things while he waited. He had waited for longer periods in worse places than this—in the desert heat, over 120 degrees—many times. If anyone was made for waiting, Landry was.

The day passed, but as he suspected, no one came to release him. The little block of sunshine from the narrow window high above moved along the floor. There was one guy across the way who cackled like a crow. One guy who had a screaming fit was moved somewhere else. There was a smell, too. Old clothes, old socks, body odor. Aftershave.

He thought about aftershave, and how he'd smelled it on his walk back through the darkening day, but saw no one. Had he been imagining things?

Night came and went. The TV droned on. By then he'd reconnoitered, but found nothing remotely interesting. There were only a few channels on the TV, and they were mostly the kind of crap you get with basic cable: infomercials and talk shows. Plenty of magazines. Dog-eared copies of *Popular Mechanics*, a *Time magazine* from two years ago, and a Holy Bible.

Landry could sleep anywhere, so he lay down on the bunk, closed his eyes, and drifted off.

The next day, the sun poked through the window again.

The electronic gate shuttled sideways and a guard brought him a tray with some inedible food on it. It looked like a sausage patty and egg, but just barely. He didn't know if it was the fluorescent lights overhead or the meat, but it had a greenish tinge.

But there was coffee.

He was grateful for the coffee.

The guard was a big guy, possibly a high school football star a few years before. He had that corn-fed Nation's Breadbasket look—a crew cut and wide blue eyes. He could have been a farm boy from the 1950s.

As Landry accepted the tray, the guy leaned in to him. Broad face, plenty of muscle in his arms and chest. He whispered, "I don't know what your game is, but stay away from her. Got that?"

"Stay away from whom?"

"You know who. My fiancée."

"You know *whom*."

"What?"

"You know whom. Not who. Who's your fiancée, so I'll know to stay away from her?"

"You know *whom* it is, but I'll spell it out for you. Carla."

Landry ignored the kid's mangled grammar, and decided to play dumb. "Carla who?"

The kid's face turned murderous. "Carla, the *lady* you've been harassing."

"I haven't harassed anyone, that I know of."

"Think again."

"Are we going to play twenty questions?"

"You know *whom*," the kid said again. "Carla Vitelli. She's with the FBI, so you'd *better* leave her alone."

Landry looked at the kid. Maybe he was connected in this town. Maybe his father was a big deal. Or his mother was a big deal—Landry didn't want to be sexist about it. "The FBI agent? She's your fiancée?"

"That's right. So don't go sniffing around, okay?"

"Okay." Landry wondered how much the boy knew. He must be in his early twenties, although he looked eighteen. Did he know about the marathon at The Satellite INN?

No. If he did, he might have got to Landry in his sleep—and

Landry might never have awakened to find out about it. The kid looked like he had a short fuse, and Landry suspected he had the potential to kill. He knew that much about him.

Corn-fed tried to stare a hole in him. His eyes were the color of faded blue denim. He could have been just a kid, but he would be the kind who would cross the line without very much thought at all.

Landry wondered why he hadn't been assaulted. Perhaps the kid was just a jailer, and had no power, despite being affianced to an FBI agent.

Or maybe the kid was waiting for a better chance.

- — -

But it wasn't the kid who moved him to the deeper recesses of the county jail. This guard was male, plump, and feminine, built like one of those punch clowns, the kind you'd hit in the face and they would come bobbing back at you. All his weight was below his waist. This time Landry's hands were cuffed, the manacles threaded through a waist chain that went well with the leg chains. They shuffled him through many corridors that grew successively darker, until he reached dungeon status—this must be where they kept the hard cases.

There were several cells lining the walls, but only one was occupied.

"Why am I here?" Landry asked the punch-clown guard.

Unsurprisingly, the guard's voice was on the high side. "You'll see," he said.

He sounded nervous. He looked nervous, too, glancing around often and then averting his eyes from the cells on either side.

"Is this some kind of punishment?" Landry asked.

The guard hit the button and the door to the occupied cell slid open partway. Inside was one big guy. He must have been six-four, six-five.

SPECTRE BLACK

The guard brandished his stick. "You stay back now, Earl!"

Landry took Earl in at one glance. Shaved head, tats all over, including a rather fetching banner across his forehead that spelled SATIN. Landry almost made a remark, something to the effect that he should ask the tattoo artist for his money back, but he didn't want to start off on the wrong foot. His new cellmate grinned. He had meth teeth; the bottom row looked like a half-eaten cob of corn. The Incredible Tattooed Man. He had the full sleeves and art climbing up his neck like a thick vine. Landry was betting full-body suit, and wondered if he'd get the opportunity to see for himself. (Not that he wanted to.) Earl had jailhouse muscles, which in Landry's opinion were about as useless as no muscles at all.

Besides, it wasn't about muscles. It was about leverage.

Landry was betting, though, the guy had something else to back it up—something sharp. In addition, he probably had a pretty slim grip on reality.

"Why am I here?" Landry asked again.

"This is just temporary," the guard said. "Overcrowding."

Landry remembered most of the cells around him in the last pod had been empty.

Landry's new cellmate started toward them. It made him think of wolves coming after the weakest lamb. The guard brandished his club and yelled, "Stay back, Earl! You know what happened last time."

Earl seemed to sink back, like an animal putting weight on its haunches, ready to spring. He made a noise somewhere deep down in his throat. All of it was way over the top, and Landry wondered if perhaps this was some kind of a joke.

The guard removed the extraneous hardware. Landry stood quietly while he did so. He ignored Earl.

Earl continued to make the sound in his throat. Half growl, half whine.

The guard backed out hastily, hit the switch, and the gate rattled shut. "Play nice," he said, before walking away, leaving the two of them alone.

Landry went to the bunk that had been made up and sat down, facing Earl. "Hello, Earl. I'm Cyril. This is how it's going to be. I'll leave you alone if you leave me alone. How's that?"

Earl just stared at him with his shiny, bat-shit-crazy eyes. He literally *was* a mouth-breather.

"Let me rephrase this, Earl. We can do this the hard way or the easy way. Let's make it the easy way, okay? I leave you alone, and you leave me alone."

Landry gave him a look that would be as strong as a handshake. A look that said, "We have a deal."

Then he lay back on the bunk and waited.

- — -

Earl behaved himself for the most part. He lay on his bunk and hummed tunelessly—Landry thought he recognized some of the songs, most of them from the seventies. The time when disco was king.

But Landry also knew that at some point Earl would stop humming disco and come for him.

It was a kind of stalemate. Landry lay on the bunk, arms cradling the back of his head on the flat and spongy pillow they'd provided. The pillow and the sheets smelled bad. Maybe it was mold; maybe it was something deeper, like desperation. Earl didn't help. He was the kind of guy who sweated a lot. The stink clung to him, and more than once Landry had to turn away and breathe through his mouth. It was a metallic stink, a vaccination stink. With just a hint of brimstone.

The hours went by. All of it seemed pointless. Landry didn't know why he was being held, but he assumed it was because somebody wanted him held.

He also assumed somebody wanted him dead. If that was true, Earl was the guy for it. Earl was perfect for it.

Landry listened. All of him was on guard. It was like being back in Afghanistan—every sense heightened. He knew it was coming. He knew this was a setup, and as strong as he was, he needed to be ready. Earl might be a meth head, but he'd probably been offered a nice reward to maim or kill Landry. That would make him extremely goal-oriented.

Landry got all this just from the way Earl looked at him. As if Landry was a big Thanksgiving turkey on a platter with all the fixings.

Like now. Earl caught his eye and grinned, as if he knew what Landry was thinking.

Time went by. Nothing happened.

The tension grew. It had weight. Landry thought perhaps he should just get it over with and kick Earl's ass. There were a number of ways he could do it. A chokehold. He could kill him instantly, but he thought that would only put him in more hot water.

Still, in war, you always took the advantage. And you went all the way if there was any doubt—

He heard Earl stir. Pretending to be asleep, Landry let one eye open a slit. Earl was sitting up. It had been swift and quiet. He heard the soft rustle of the meth head's jumpsuit rasp across the made-up cot. Heard the light stamp of his feet onto the floor: one, two.

Landry closed his eyes.

When Earl came for him, Landry was ready. He lay still on the bunk, but opened his right hand, stretching it as hard and straight as he could make it, fingers and thumb far apart. Landry slid off the bunk, and did his best to look confused and frightened. Let the guy advance until he was half a foot away. That was the moment Landry had been waiting for. He struck fast at the man's trachea, snapped his hand out so quickly Earl didn't know what happened. Landry made sure not to hit him too hard; he wasn't about to kill the guy. Earl raised both hands to his throat, and that was when Landry followed up with the second blow. Hands cupped, he stepped into the guy and smacked both ears at once. Again, he didn't put much force behind it, but clapping the man's ears did the trick.

It was over in seconds. Earl stumbled like a drunk stepping into a pothole and went down, his shiv hitting the floor with a clatter. Out cold.

His eardrums broken.

Landry walked over, raised him to a sitting position against the wall of the cell, and made sure his breathing passageway was clear. It was the least he could do.

"Buck up," he said. "You'll be okay."

Doubtful the guy could hear him.

CHAPTER 8

Landry lay in his bunk, waiting patiently for the racket to recede. There had been quite a commotion: jailers yelling, Earl coming to and trying to stand up. His inner ears all shot to hell. He'd fallen down twice now. His panic started low in his throat before revving up into a loud but eerie siren. Landry didn't dwell on Earl's punctured eardrums.

After Earl was carted away, Landry sat on his bunk and thought things through.

Earl had a shiv. He had been bent on killing him. In fact, he seemed almost desperate to get the job done. Still, Landry thought it was a flat performance. Earl might have done an adequate job, if he were dealing with someone who didn't know how to fight back, but he had been hopelessly overmatched.

Someone wanted him dead, or at the very least, out of commission. And the easiest way to get to someone was inside a jail. It was an enclosed space. There was nowhere to run. And all you needed were for the guards to look the other way. You couldn't beat the talent pool inside. There were all sorts of crooks in jail, many of them homicidal. Mental illness was the order of the day. There were people who would kill for a pack of cigarettes. There were people who were happy to maim and kill just for the hell of it, like Earl.

But Earl had been . . . rusty, and so it had not worked. That didn't mean they wouldn't try again. Landry had been locked in a place where he couldn't escape.

So who would want him dead, or at least discouraged? He went through the list. At the top was whoever had taken Jolie. Next would be someone he'd rubbed the wrong way.

He knew the perfect candidate: the FBI agent, Carla Vitelli. She and her fiancé, the corn-fed boy who had been dumb enough—or prescient enough—to threaten him.

He blamed himself for a blatant lack of chivalry. He'd left the motel room while she slept—he'd been rude. He regretted that. There was a certain etiquette in sleeping with someone you didn't know, and he should have stuck around.

In his defense, he could not stand to spend one more minute in that room with her. She was obsessive. She reminded him of a horse soldier who ran his horse over broken ground for miles and miles, whipping him all the way. It was almost as if she wanted to kill him as much as she wanted to fuck him. Maybe she wanted to kill him *more* than she wanted to fuck him.

He figured she'd picked him up because she thought he'd lead her to Jolie.

Remember the hunt cam stunt.

Why did she do that? To let him know she was looking for Jolie Burke, or let him know she knew where Jolie was?

Or maybe she was just a lunatic.

Generally speaking, most people who rose through the ranks to be FBI agents weren't lunatics. But Carla Vitelli certainly brought the average down.

Earlier today, the punch-clown prison guard had come to check on them. Landry could tell from the man's expression that he'd been expecting something other than what he'd seen. What he'd seen was Earl lying on the floor, bloody and unconscious. Landry

SPECTRE BLACK

got the feeling the punch-clown prison guard had planned to call for paramedics. It was just that he'd called the paramedics for the wrong person.

The shock on the guard's face, though: priceless.

After the paramedics came and removed Earl from the cell, after the punch-clown prison guard asked if Landry knew what had happened (Landry said he had no idea; he'd slept right through it), he was left alone. He thought at the time that the prison guard was afraid of him, that he would get reinforcements, but none came. And so he lay on the bunk, doing math problems in his head. He let his mind wander to see if there was some place he had not looked for Jolie.

He knew that soon he would have another prison mate.

So he waited, and saved his strength.

He would be ready when they tried again.

- — -

But it turned out, they didn't.

Three hours later another guard showed up, consulted his clipboard, and said, "Chris Keeley?"

Landry hopped down from his bunk and walked to the cage door. "Do I have a lawyer yet? I asked for one yesterday."

"You don't need a lawyer," the guard said. He opened up the door and stood back. Landry walked out. His legs felt a little shaky, and he didn't know why.

Maybe it was the aftereffects of sleeping with Carla Vitelli.

The guard handed him over to a sheriff's deputy, who took him out a loading dock ramp into the blinding sunlight and ordered him to get into the back of a sheriff's unit. He pushed Landry's head downward as he climbed in. SOP.

"Where are we going?" Landry asked when they were rolling.

"You'll see."

They didn't go far. The sheriff's office was across the large parking lot from the jail.

"You going to try anything?" the guard said.

"No."

"When we get inside, I'll see if I can get the handcuffs off you."

Inside, the air conditioning smacked him in the face. The sheriff's office was a showplace, different from your average city building—especially in a city this small. For one thing, it was five stories tall. In the foyer, one wall was all glass and looked out on a fountain. It had a modern industrial look that you see in glossy magazines, lots of browns and tans in the palette, walls of mottled granite, metal tarnished an artful coppery-gold. They took the elevator up to the fifth floor, which was all one big suite: the sheriff's office. Landry had been in governors' offices a few times in his life, but this office put anything he'd seen to shame. Including one wall dedicated to an aquarium.

Sheriff Ronald Waldrup sat at a massive desk in front of a polished black granite wall with the "Tobosa County, New Mexico" seal emblazoned upon it. Waldrup's desk was flanked by a New Mexico state flag on one side and a United States flag on the other. On the desk was a small microphone, the kind that city council members used in their chambers.

The whole effect seemed counterproductive—the stage set dwarfed the man.

The sheriff studied Landry. Landry thought of a little kid sitting at his father's desk. That was, if the kid was wizened and resembled a stoop-shouldered monkey.

"So, are you the one-man crime wave people say you are? Mr. er . . ." He looked down through his reading glasses. "Keeley?"

"I haven't committed any crime."

SPECTRE BLACK

Waldrup assessed Landry. He pulled off his large glasses and rubbed them with a cloth. "We have reason to suspect you in the disappearance of one of our detectives."

"Who would that be?"

"Detective Burke. Jolie Burke."

"Can't say the name rings a bell."

"Is that so?" The sheriff leaned to the side and consulted with the deputy in a low whisper. Ending with, "Is she here?"

"Yes sir, she's waiting in the anteroom."

"Show her in."

Landry knew who it would be.

Carla Vitelli entered. She wore a dark blue suit that flattered every curve. Her hair was pulled back into an economical bun. She held a folder at her side. She stopped beside the desk and set it down before the sheriff, then stood beside the desk with her hands folded in front of her, eyes on Landry.

Sheriff Waldrup dipped his head toward the tiny microphone, which Landry suspected doubled as a recording device.

"Go ahead, Agent Vitelli."

She cleared her throat and gave them a summary of Cyril Landry's crime. He had set up a hunt cam on Jolie Burke's property after she had gone missing.

"And what does this signify?" The sheriff spoke into his microphone. "What is your conclusion?"

"My conclusion is that he was stalking Detective Burke."

"No, I wasn't," Landry said.

"Probable cause," said Sheriff Waldrup. "If you indeed set up a camera to watch Detective Burke, it appears evident that you *were* stalking her." He leaned forward a little more. "How did you come to cross paths with Detective Burke?"

"I met her at a conference," Landry said.

"What kind of conference?"

"Comic books."

"Comic books?"

"Yes."

Vitelli stared daggers at him. "He's lying," she said.

"You don't have enough evidence to charge me, so why don't we just go our separate ways?"

"You seem to be a transient."

"No, I'm just passing through."

"You set up those cameras."

"I'm sure somebody did. But it wasn't me."

"He's lying," Agent Vitelli said.

"I have been told I have an unmemorable face. I get mistaken for other people all the time."

Sheriff Waldrup covered the microphone with his hand and said something to Vitelli, who knitted her brow and looked stony. Landry guessed he was asking her if she had seen Landry setting up the hunt cam.

Waldrup nodded to the deputy. "He can go. Process him out."

The deputy nodded.

"I hope you'll at least validate my parking," Landry said.

Vitelli glared at him, but said nothing.

"It's a shame," Landry said to Carla as he was walked to the door. "We could have been something."

The guard took him back to the intake desk at the jail. Only it must have been the output desk, still inside the inner shell of the jail.

A man sat at the desk. He looked fastidious—the only person in the place who looked that way. His hair was combed neatly to the side. He had a neatly trimmed beard. He was youngish, and wore stylish clothes—at least for a jail—and wire-rimmed glasses.

SPECTRE BLACK

"Mr. Keeley?" he said, looking up from an open folder on his desk. "Chris, correct?"

"That's my name."

"You probably know this by now, but we have decided not to extend your stay."

"Good, because there was too much chlorine in the spa."

The man laughed. It was a tiny laugh, mirthless. "Very funny."

"Can you tell me again why I was held?"

The man twiddled a pen in his fingers. "It says here . . . vagrancy. But it turns out that someone made a mistake—not one of ours, of course. I'm terribly sorry for your inconvenience."

"So I'm free to go."

"Yes."

"How's Earl?"

"Earl?"

"The guy I bunked with."

"He had a bad reaction, I heard. Had to go to the hospital. . . . Why?"

"No reason. So I'm free to go?"

"Absolutely." He pushed Landry's folded clothes and shoes across the desk toward him. "There is a restroom down the hall." He gestured in the direction with his chin.

"So this was a mistake."

"Yes. A mistake. I'm terribly, terribly sorry."

Landry thought that the person who was truly sorry was Carla Vitelli.

CHAPTER 9

By the time Landry got back to the motel, it was going on three in the afternoon.

Someone had targeted him for death. As if whoever had jailed him went under the theory that Landry posed some kind of threat and should be eliminated, and that person had acted on that theory.

But it hadn't panned out, so they let him go. Whoever wanted him dead had to have his hooks deep into the sheriff's office, or at least the county jail.

He cut diagonally across the empty lot toward his room. It might be wise to move to another motel; leave the white car there and take the blue van. He needed to clean up first.

As he took the steps up to the second story, he glanced back at the white rental Nissan, still parked in the same place, nose to nose with a car in the next row. It was in the same place he'd left it. He approached the room from the back and from the right. The shades were drawn. He'd left the TV on to fool people into thinking he was still inside.

The room was clear, as he'd expected.

They—the sheriff's department—knew where he was. They had searched his room, but he knew they had found nothing—everything but a change of clothes and a few traveler's basics had been left in a storage unit two blocks over.

SPECTRE BLACK

Probable cause these days, in certain towns, in certain counties, in certain states, in certain regions, could be stretched beyond recognition. Stretched, wrung out, hung on the line, ironed, folded, spindled, and hung up in a closet. If they'd been playing by the rule of law, they would have had no probable cause to arrest him. And they certainly had no basis to let him go, after he dispatched Earl.

Police in this town were a law unto themselves.

He wondered how Jolie had fit into this brave new world in Tobosa County.

The police had become paramilitary. Police and sheriff's departments across the country were getting more and more hardware that they didn't know what to do with. They had everything they needed to fight a ground war. Army surplus was king. SWAT gear, tactical vests, armor-plated vehicles called MRAPs (Mine-Resistant Ambush Protected vehicles), tear gas, M-14s, grenade launchers.

Considering the fact that municipalities liked to get their money's worth, he was lucky to be alive at all.

He checked the door for anything unusual. Saw nothing that would raise the alarm. Peered in through the tiny gap in the drapes. Unlocked the door, stood at the side, and kicked it open.

Nothing.

He made a quick search of the room. No one hiding in the shower stall, no one in the closet. No bogeyman under the bed. He checked for bugs, too—was quite thorough about it. Stood on the bed and unscrewed the light fixture. Nothing he could see stood out.

It was good to luxuriate under a hot shower.

It was going on five p.m. when he changed into the blue work shirt, jeans, and work boots, drove the blue van to Jolie's neighborhood, and parked it out front.

He waited for Jolie's fellow detective to come by. It didn't take long. The woman drove up in a late-model car, on the inexpensive side but immaculate. She parked in the driveway and followed the stepping-stones to the front door, unlocked the iron door and the inner door, and went inside.

He looked around. No one was out and about. Going on dusk. The blinds to the house were closed.

Then he walked to the door and rang the bell.

She opened the front door but left the iron door locked. Peered out at him, her face betraying nothing.

"Is Jolie here?" he asked. "She said to come by and we'd settle up." He motioned to his truck with the landscaping logo on the side.

The detective was no pushover. "You'll have to come back later. Jolie's out at the moment."

Landry let his disappointment show. "Do you know when she'll be back? I have a job in Deming tomorrow that's gonna take several days, and to be honest . . ." He slouched a little, swiveled to glance at his van. "I usually get paid up front—she's really good about that—and I kind of need the money."

She wasn't buying it. "Tell you what," she said. "If you give me your number, I can have her call you."

"That would be great." He reached into his pocket, pulled out a burner phone, and texted her the number. No more tearing off slips of paper to scrawl on, or asking her to go pull off a sheet from the pad by the phone. No muss, no fuss. She looked down at her own phone, then slipped it into the pocket of her jeans—

And started to close the door. Landry said, "If you talk to her, tell her Cyril came by."

"Who?"

"Cyril. She'll know."

"Cyril. Like the saint? Saint Cyril?"

"That's the one."

He waited on the street parallel to Jolie's. Fifteen minutes passed, then twenty. A few minutes after that he saw the headlights of the detective's car pulling onto the road. He stayed at least two

SPECTRE BLACK

lights behind—there were three traffic lights before she turned into a newer neighborhood. The streets were quiet, with tall palm trees and pueblo-style condominiums, most of them pale yellow. Brown poles stuck out of the top of the stucco near the roofline like the pegs on Frankenstein's forehead. Typical New Mexico fare. Landry stayed way back and out of sight with the van, training binocs on her. She pulled into a condominium's driveway, the automatic garage door opened, and she drove inside. The garage door rattled back down.

He parked around the corner and walked past. It was getting dark. He wished he'd been closer and at an angle where he could see if there was another car parked inside.

Jolie had chosen the right person to look after her place while she was gone. But she didn't know the danger. Landry did.

He punched in a number he knew by heart. His neighbor, Louise, the sixty-seven-year-old transplant from Washington, DC, where she'd worked in the State Department.

She answered immediately.

"How's Barkley?" he asked. "Is he still with us?"

"He died two days ago."

"I'm sorry," Landry said. The wolfhound was old and sick, and even though it had been coming for a long time, he knew Louise was heartbroken.

But it did clear the path for him. "Will you do me a favor?"

- — -

Landry made the arrangements. It would entail another break-in at Jolie's, but he knew she'd thank him later.

If she was still alive.

He firmed it up with Tom, the pilot who'd flown him out here. Gave him instructions where to go and when would be the best time.

"I've done extractions before," Tom said.

"Just do it soon. I have a bad feeling."

He sat alone in a booth in Dina's Diner with his own image beside him in the mirror. Wondering if Jolie was still in communication with her fellow detective and pet-sitter. Maybe she'd left for parts unknown. If Jolie was alive, if the detective passed on his message, she would text him—unless she thought it was a trap.

If Jolie was on the run, she'd confided in this woman. Or at least, trusted her fellow detective to take care of her animals.

Landry felt good about that—but he knew that the enemy was much more dangerous than Jolie's pal could imagine.

He felt it—felt it in his jaw. An electric feeling: *By the pricking of my thumbs, something wicked this way comes.*

- — -

Back at the motel, he turned on the television.

The evening news came on—local, not national. Canned music blared like trumpets at a medieval fair. It was the same canned music he'd heard on several local news shows throughout the west. He thought they must all go to the same canned-news-music provider.

Behind the boyish-looking anchor and the female anchor in the blue suit, words flashed large on the screen: "Midtown Shooting."

Ted Landigran, the boyish anchor, adopted a grave expression. "We now bring you live to the scene of a shooting in midtown where three people are dead. We have a reporter on the scene. Gary, tell me what you know."

They went live to Gary, who looked a lot like Ted Landigran, except his hair was brown and Landigran's was blond. He gripped the microphone hard, his voice strained. Still, he did a decent job.

There had been shots fired and a man screaming.

A jogger who lived in the neighborhood heard shots around three thirty in the afternoon and called the police.

SPECTRE BLACK

The door to what looked like a duplex was open and in the garish light of the camera Landry saw what might or might not be a small section of a blue-jeaned leg. According to the news report, there were two bodies in the front room, and one in the back bedroom.

Back to Ted Landigran. He looked deadly serious. His handsome face had been transformed into a full frown, his eyes large and sad. When he spoke, he didn't have the bantering tone he'd used for the Street Fair story. His voice was now measured and sad.

Footage ran of a police officer unspooling crime scene tape from a wheel, walking carefully around the edge of the house. The duplex was probably built in the seventies—fired-brick adobe painted over with white. The camera panned to a car in the driveway, then to a couple of people inside the doorway, barely visible, wearing what looked to be hazmat suits. One big guy stood there, his latex-gloved arms hanging out from his side, ignoring the camera.

Ted Landigran did not give the names of the three people in the duplex. But Landry could guess who they were.

He would know soon enough if he was right.

A knot of people stood nearby. One of them was being interviewed by the reporter. They'd all heard shots fired. They'd all heard a car drive away at a high rate of speed.

Ten minutes later, the victims were identified. Landry didn't recognize the names: Gary Short, James Berk, and Amy Diehl. But he recognized the photos that flashed on the screen not long after.

Two of them—one of the men and the woman—had manned the checkpoint the day Landry had driven through, right before the third member of the group was shot to death.

More information came in. One witness described the car, a late-model white subcompact. The car had sideswiped a pole with the right front fender.

Landry got up, turned the TV off and the light out and stood back five feet from the window. He could see his rental car from here, the white Nissan Versa.

It was still nose-in to the other car. But now he could see that there was a difference to the shape of the hood. Now that he looked. The hood looked bent up just a little on the right side.

Something had changed. He didn't know what, but he trusted his instincts. The dull electric feeling in his jaw was back.

He grabbed the few things he'd left out in the room, once again glad he'd taken the time to leave the run bag and its contents in the storage facility. He left the TV on, and the bathroom light, and pocketed the key. He'd throw it in the nearest Dumpster he could find. He wiped down everything with a towel from the bathroom just to be on the safe side. Made sure no one saw him before walking around the end of the top floor and down the steps past the pool. It was full dark now, but there were plenty of lights. He kept to the shadows and started walking.

Sure enough, two city police cars swooped by—no sirens but they had their flashers going and the light bars on. They slowed and turned into The Satellite INN parking lot, and gunned around the back.

He found a place where he could watch the activity. It wasn't perfect, just a sorry-looking tree at the edge of the back lot. He lay in the dirt and watched. One thing bothered him. Would the police know he had another vehicle?

As time went by, he realized they didn't. All their attention was on the Nissan Versa. In their excitement to bird-dog the vehicle used in the shooting at the checkpoint, as well as the shooting of the two other militia members, they had ignored every other car in the parking lot. They inspected the car. The tow truck showed. Officers went up the stairs to his room. Four cops on the walkway, weapons leveled, creeping alongside the wall. The two cops in front closed to either side of the door. One cop going high, one cop going low. Another cop stepped forward and banged hard on the door and stepped quickly back out of range. "Police!" he shouted. Of course there was no answer. Landry wondered if they would get the battering ram, but decided that would be overkill. One of them would just get the manager. And as he predicted, a cop took off down the steps and around the motel toward the office, and came back with the key moments later.

Back to one cop high, one cop low. A crowd was beginning to gather in the dirt lot—people from the neighborhood and some of the guests.

Landry noticed the SWAT team sniper, if things got out of hand. All they needed now was the big fat MRAP to come lumbering in.

Another knot of law enforcement watched as the white Nissan was winched onto the bed of the tow truck.

He glanced back at the open doorway of his former motel room. SWAT in black. Cops taking the rear. All of the cops were with the sheriff's department. It seemed to Landry that a whole lot of nothing was happening, although everyone was quick about it.

They would see the car rental agreement for Chris Keeley, but that would be as far as it went.

Cops stood around the white car. Peering in the windows. Talking about it to one another.

They knew what they had: this was the white car used in the shooting at the checkpoint. You could almost see the wheels turning in their heads. If this was the car driven by the shooter of the militia members who'd witnessed the shooting at the checkpoint, then it stood to reason that it might also belong to the checkpoint shooter, who had killed the other two to cover up his crime.

Everything nice and neat.

Easy peasy.

There couldn't be two white subcompact cars coming through the checkpoint around the same time. Too much of a coincidence. This had to be the car, and Chris Keeley had to be the shooter. And so they would look for Chris Keeley, even if they didn't know who he was or why he had gone on a crime spree.

Their theory: Chris Keeley had come back to eliminate the witnesses.

Landry thought about his own alibi—his stay in jail—and realized he didn't have one—not for this afternoon. The two militia members in the house were killed after he was released.

The news said the shots had been fired at three thirty. And he had been out of jail since three p.m., give or take five minutes.

He had a white car fitting the description. He had been seen around town. He had slept with the FBI agent. He had been arrested and detained for no plausible reason. Then he had been put into an empty cell pod with a psychopath.

For a guy who flew under the radar, Landry realized he'd made plenty of enemies already.

Starting and ending with Agent Vitelli.

— · —

By two in the morning, the cops were done. Everyone cleared out except for one unlucky cop stuck with guard duty. He stood on the walkway outside the room, slapping his nightstick against his palm and watching the moths play ring-around-the-rosie near the light by the door.

They must have thought Landry was long gone. If he was smart, he would be.

But Jolie was still missing. She'd called him for help and he wouldn't abandon her now.

He still had the van. Everything he'd brought with him other than the clothes he'd changed out of had been moved to the storage bay.

The white car had done its job. Now it was time for the blue van to shine. First, though, he would wait to see how this played out. He wouldn't go to the van for a while.

And so he walked.

He found another motel, this one on a side street off the main drag on the other side of town, one of those old motor courts that was even older than The Satellite INN. This one had survived the forties and fifties. There was a sleepy quality to the place. He liked it. The rail-thin man at the desk had a Middle Eastern accent. He also had very white teeth and an engaging smile. He gave Landry the key to the unit at the back of the courtyard.

An oval expanse of lawn sat in the center of the lot, units on either side and two additional units at the end, which formed a "U." Croquet hoops were set up inside the grassy oval.

Inside his room it was dark and smelled old. The bed was made with a white chenille bedspread, a yarn saguaro cactus in the center. Quaint. Landry had a feeling that this was a place where people minded their own business. There might be a sex trade going on here, or other nefarious dealings, or it might just be the kind of place where the well heeled would never go.

Landry sat on the lumpy bed. He speculated about Carla Vitelli's motive for targeting him. Maybe she wanted to sleep with him, but maybe she didn't. Maybe she just wanted to check him out. A sex marathon was a funny way to check someone out, but stranger things had happened to him. She'd seemed insatiable at the time, but Landry wasn't so invested in his sexual prowess that he couldn't discard that theory. Maybe she'd faked her passion.

But could she fake her anger?

Maybe.

What did Agent Vitelli want from him? He thought back to the donut shop. He knew she was FBI and he'd gone out of his way to interact with her.

He had hoped she would tell him something about her investigation, but instead there had been the sex marathon.

Followed by her mugging for the hunt cam.

Landry didn't know what to make of this. She was smart enough to figure out he was looking for Jolie. She was smart enough to find the hunt cam, and she was rash enough to show him that she'd found it. But after all that, there had been nothing.

Except for his arrest. Except for the fact he had been put into that cell pod with Earl—*alone* with Earl.

Which was it, though? Did she want Earl to kill him or at least beat him up badly, or did she want to set him up for the shooting deaths of three people?

Landry got up and washed his face. The idea that she'd kill two people to link him to the checkpoint shooting, just to get back at him, was outlandish. Crazy.

But the Nissan was a generic type of subcompact, similar to many other subcompacts from the same year. Landry had thought it out the day he'd driven into town. He'd decided the chances of anyone noticing one white subcompact in a parking lot full of similar cars would be minimal—statistically.

He'd been wrong about that.

He looked at himself in the mirror. The eyes in the mirror met him dead-on.

His Nissan Versa had been in pristine condition yesterday.

So when did it sustain front-end damage?

CHAPTER 10

The crunch of car tires on gravel outside awakened him. He glanced at his watch: just past ten a.m. The sun would be up, but the cheap motel room was still dark.

He peered out between the drapes. A police car drove through, without stopping.

Last night Landry had parked the blue van in front of an empty motel room on the west side of the motel's U-shaped drive-around. The police car drove right past it and followed the gravel lane back out the other leg of the U, waited for traffic to clear, and drove back out onto the street.

They were looking for him. They were looking for Chris Keeley, to be exact. The guy who had almost killed a fellow county jail inmate.

The guy who had been set up to take the fall for the deaths of the two militia members.

Landry stepped into the shower and was disappointed that the water was tepid and stayed that way. He was pretty sure he had the whole picture now. Someone shot the one guy at the checkpoint. That same someone boosted Landry's rental car and shot the other two militia members—the man and woman who had witnessed the shooting. He must have worried that they would talk to the police.

After the second shooting, he'd returned Landry's car to the motel parking lot and called in the tip.

There was only one person he'd spent any time with here in Branch: the FBI agent. Only one person who knew about him—

Their time together had ended badly. He'd thought he had seen the last of her, but then she'd shown up on the hunt cam at Jolie's place and taunted him.

Had she been watching him before they met?

He remembered her saying: "How long will it take for me to find out what you're up to?"

Not long after that, he was arrested.

And not long after *that*, he was moved deeper into the jail to share a cell pod with a psychopath bent on killing him.

Did someone *want* to kill him?

Did *she* want to kill him?

He'd managed to turn the tables, putting Earl in the hospital.

Instead of further punishment, he was released. He was arrested for no reason, moved deeper into the county jail for no reason, and released for no reason he could see.

His rental car had been damaged and used in a drive-by shooting. If he hadn't been on his game, he would be back in jail right now. He would be charged with first-degree murder.

It had to be Carla Vitelli.

He wondered if she'd really been assigned to Jolie's case. He had assumed she was the FBI agent sent to investigate Jolie's disappearance, but maybe she wasn't.

If Earl had beaten him to a pulp, he would be in the hospital now. In the hospital, or dead.

Vitelli couldn't have it both ways. She couldn't have him beaten up to teach him a lesson, but then try to pin the militia members' shooting on him.

That made no sense. If he was injured badly, or killed, he would not be around to take the fall for the militia members' deaths.

SPECTRE BLACK

She pulled strings in this corrupt little city to get him thrown into jail with Earl to teach him a lesson or out and out kill him.

When they couldn't kill him, they decided to release him and frame him for the deaths of the militia members. This accomplished two things: get rid of Landry, and kill the witnesses.

He dried off from his shower and pulled on the shorts he'd worn a couple of days ago.

Something was wadded up in the right pocket.

Landry pulled out the crumpled leaflet, "Choose Jesus!"

He chucked the religious tract into the wastepaper basket—three points—and sat on the bed facing the mirror, listening to the faint breath of traffic out on the street. Thinking about the FBI agent, wherever she might be. Thinking about her fiancé. Thinking about Earl.

Jerry Boam. The name intruded. Landry knew himself well enough to know there was a reason why it did.

Landry pictured the Circle K and the tree and the shade that concealed his Nissan Versa.

How had Boam known he was there?

He saw in his mind's eye the police cars speeding past, heading to the site of the shooting, and later, driving much slower on the way back. They had driven straight past the Circle K. Landry thought this was because they'd expect the shooter to put as much distance between himself and the scene as possible.

Probably twenty cars had driven past. Landry had decided to stay put there for two reasons: one, he was waiting for Jolie, and two, his car could not be seen. He'd even walked out onto the road and looked for it from both directions, and had satisfied himself on that point.

But one car *did* pull into the parking lot—the truck belonging to the old rancher, Jerry Boam.

Why?

Landry couldn't think of a reason. Boam's truck was fine—no flat tire, no problem with the engine. The convenience store was abandoned. There was nothing to stop for.

Something else bothered him.

The name "Jerry Boam," sounded made-up—a play on words. *Jeroboam* was another word for a double magnum of wine.

Landry wondered if Boam had come up with the name on the spur of the moment, or if he'd thought it up ahead of time. He looked down at the thin, glossy paper, a minimagazine like *Awake*, the tract Jehovah's Witnesses left stuck into the screen door when the inhabitant inevitably didn't answer.

If anyone would have the persistence to find someone, it would be the Jehovah's Witnesses. If Landry was to be found, it stood to reason the one person most likely to find him would be a Jehovah's Witness. Or the next best thing: a religious person. Landry wasn't sure what sect Jerry Boam belonged to, but the man had sure enough figured out there was someone parked behind that tree.

Landry flicked through the four paper-thin pages, mostly illustrations and one Bible story. The story was a familiar one: Jesus turning water into wine.

When he was a boy, he'd attended an informal Bible school at Santa Anita, mainly because his mother wanted to keep him out of trouble and there was no church nearby that had a catechism class he could attend. The school, started by the racetrack chaplain, was an informal gathering. He attended with the other children who grew up on the backstretch—the children of grooms, exercise riders, trainers, the people who worked the grandstand and the gates—a community built around the racetrack.

Landry knew his Bible stories well enough.

He read the passage in the magazine.

"*When the wine was gone, Jesus's mother said to him, 'They have no more wine.' Nearby stood six stone water jars . . .*"

"'*Fill the jars with water,' He said, and so they filled them to the brim.*"

"*And Jesus turned the water into wine.*"

Landry could hear Jerry Boam's voice, soft and measured, like voices were in the west. "*You be sure to read it, now, there's nothing like God's Word to set you straight on the path.*"

Boam spoke to him, but Landry recalled that he had actually been looking *beyond* him, squinting against the sunlight, peering into the desert.

Landry had seen that look before. Not in the pale blue eyes of an old rancher, but in the eyes of his buddies in Iraq and Afghanistan. There were always horizons to scan, and eyes to scan them. Fighters were constantly looking for trouble, constantly taking in data—a sweep of desert here, a palm grove there. Looking for something out of the ordinary: a movement where there should *be* no movement. A shadow where there should *be* no shadow.

Landry had waited by the Circle K for a day and a half, but Jolie'd never appeared. The only person who *did* appear was the old rancher, who had shown up on the first day.

Be sure to read that now, there's nothing like God's Word to set you straight on the path.

Landry could hear his voice. Yes, it was a voice of the west, but it also sounded like the voice of a man who was trying to be quiet. Trying to keep his voice down. Landry pictured Boam. The way he looked around, the way he looked into the desert, the way he kept his voice down. Conversational, yes, but quiet.

Maybe he was worried that someone was listening in. Maybe he was worried about a parabolic mic.

It was time to change vehicles again. Although Landry had ditched the landscaper sign, the van had spent some time in The Satellite INN parking lot, long enough for someone to remember it. Better safe than sorry; he couldn't take the chance that someone might link the van to him. He drove out of Branch to the next town, Lunaria, New Mexico, which was smaller and poorer but still had car dealers. He decided on another car no one would look at twice, a 2004 crimson Suzuki Forenza with a three-thousand-dollar price tag. He traded the blue van—sans the Landscaping legend on the sides—and made three hundred bucks on the deal.

Landry was still dressed like a guy on vacation: the long shorts, a T-shirt, running shoes, sunglasses. He'd dyed his hair reddish-blond. He'd also grown some stubble, which he shaped into a goatee-in-training. Landry did the "Dad on vacation" very well.

He was a dad who was just scraping by, driving an eleven-year-old Suzuki Forenza. Everything about him said white bread—your average Joe.

He'd paid cash for the Forenza, told the car salesman he'd got the cash from his credit union. He showed one of his false IDs, a driver's license for Barry Westerlin. He'd retired Chris Keeley, buried him in a little patch of desert out on a lonesome dirt road between the two towns, toasting him with a bottle of Fat Tire beer.

After that he drove back the way he had come and looked for the winery on the outskirts of Branch. He'd driven past it on the way out of town. The Wildcat Red Winery was a one-story territorial-style building facing the road. Burnt-adobe brick, arches in the front. Probably built in the 1970s. Beyond it sprawled acres of staked vines on the yellow-brown land.

There were no cars out front. Landry wondered if a winery in these parts could succeed. He parked the Forenza, got out, and walked inside. A bell rang as the glass door opened.

The place simulated a wine cellar. Dark and dank-smelling,

SPECTRE BLACK

plenty of wine barrels with display glasses and bottles on top, walls of cubbyholes for wines to lie flat, and a counter in the back. There was also a cooler for white wines, beer, and sandwiches.

Landry looked around, picked out a nice pinot noir, and walked to the counter. No one else was in the store, so he had the full attention of the guy manning the cash register.

"Nice choice," the man said, peering at Landry over rectangular half-glasses: far-sighted. He was tall and lanky. Anglo, but his skin was dark as caramel—probably from spending time outdoors. About fifty. He wore a graying ponytail caught up by a leather thong, a work shirt, and jeans. He could have mirrored Landry's landscaping clothes.

"That's a nice red. Would you like to try one of ours?" the man asked, wrapping the bottle in butcher paper.

"That would be nice."

The man poured a sample into a wineglass from the rack behind him.

Landry swished it around in his mouth and looked up at the ceiling, as if weighing a great problem. Then he looked into the man's eyes and said, *"Tres jolie."*

He pushed Jerry Boam's religious tract across the desk in the man's direction to gauge his reaction.

The man didn't react at all. He seemed contemplative.

Landry said, "I'm looking for something a little bit more full-bodied. Slightly impudent, with a penchant for hand-to-hand combat."

The man still did not react, but continued to stare at him over his half-glasses. No shock, no disgust, no fear or nervousness, no delight. Finally, he said, "Can I ask you a question?"

"You *can* ask me a question, sure. It's a free country." Landry knew he sounded schoolmarmish—he just couldn't stand poor grammar.

But the man smiled, clearly pleased. "Yes, you're right on that count. *May* I ask a question. Who's your favorite saint?"

"Saint?"

"Saint. You know, like Saint Nick. Saint Paul. Saint Peter, Saint—"

Landry smiled. "I'll take 'Cyril' for five hundred, Alex."

- — -

The ponytailed storekeeper's name was Rand McNally. (He said his parents had a weird sense of humor.) He invited Landry to ride in his 1979 Ford truck, complete with an old camper shell. They drove out of Branch and passed through the smaller town, Lunaria, where Landry had bought the Suzuki Forenza. McNally drove to the outskirts of Lunaria to a neighborhood of cheap tract houses. "She's here?"

"Hold your horses."

He stopped just past the driveway. All the houses looked the same. Two floor plans, depending on how many bedrooms. Nineteen seventies construction, fired-adobe walls, long and one story. McNally backed the truck into the covered carport and up to an aluminum fishing boat. It looked to be about ten to twelve feet long, with a small-horsepower tiller-steered outboard engine titled up in back. Landry's father had owned a boat just like this one. He called it a "car topper." Landry noticed there were fishing rods, too, already rigged up, along with two tackle boxes—one large, and one small.

McNally expertly backed the trailer hitch to the hitch ball and completed the connection, before climbing back into the truck.

"Let's go," he said.

They drove out of town and picked up the highway again. Landry didn't know the roads around here, but he knew direction. They were heading east, toward Las Cruces. "Where are we going?" he asked.

"Want to keep it a surprise."

"I don't like surprises."

"You'll like this one."

"There's a big lake north of here," Landry said.

"Sure is."

They drove in silence for a while.

Landry said, "What do you know about this?"

"This? Not much. Jolie's a friend, she asked me to help her, so I did."

"You don't know who she's in trouble with?"

"She didn't tell me. She's good people, so when she asked for help getting lost, I helped get her lost."

"You're used to doing stuff like this?"

"I used to be with an underground group."

"What kind of underground group?"

"Environmental."

"Oh. Like burned-down ski resorts? Stuff like that? Ecoterrorism?"

"More like chaining ourselves to trees, but yeah, thirty years ago, that's what I did."

"You want to tell me where we're going?"

"You'll find out soon enough."

"You think somebody bugged your truck?"

He shrugged. "Stranger things have happened."

"I could check it for you."

"Okay." He swerved over to the side of the road. Landry had him get out, looked in the places he thought there might be a microphone, but more important, he checked for a transponder.

Nothing. "Anyone notice what you're doing? Anyone on to you?"

"Honestly? I don't think so."

"Good enough."

At Las Cruces they took I-25 north to the turnoff for Elephant Butte Lake. Rand followed the blacktop down Marina del Sur, where the boats were. There were a lot of them, cheek by jowl in their slips.

Shade canopies kept the sun off the docks. There were plenty of docks, slips, and boats. Contrast that with the solid blue of the lake. It was a long lake, hemmed in by biscuit-colored ground—scrub desert, mostly. There was a formation Landry took to be Elephant Butte, wading in the water like a hippo. He could see the white striations along the bottom of the rock and along the shore—the water level was down. Everything in the west was in a state of drought, so it didn't surprise him.

Landry shaded his eyes against the glitter of sunlight on water. "So she's here," he said.

"Yup." Rand backed the trailer down the ramp to the water. "Figured she'd just be one in the crowd."

Landry shaded his eyes. "There are houseboats here?"

"Plenty of them. Lots of cruisers, too. There's a camp store, too, all the comforts of home." He nodded to the boat. "Get in."

They headed out into the lake, followed the shoreline on the other side.

Landry spotted the cabin cruiser in a small cove, just around an outcropping of rock. The rock hid the cove from both directions. He grabbed the binoculars.

And there she was.

CHAPTER 11

Jolie Burke looked the same except for her hair, which had been cut short and colored black.

She had them in the binocs. Anchor already pulled up and the boat drifting a little. She was positioned at the console, ready to take off if she needed to.

McNally produced a flag—a denuded branch from a creosote bush, a blue pair of Jockey shorts tied to the top.

Landry mentioned to McNally that his grasp of high tech was mind-boggling.

Jolie dropped the binocs to her chest and shaded her eyes. Then waved.

He missed her long, golden-brown hair, usually pulled into a ponytail or bun, but otherwise, she was the same Jolie. She wore shorts, boat shoes, and a square-necked embroidered peasant top, the kind you got from Mexico.

The white-and-black Bayliner cabin cruiser had a swept-back aerodynamic design. It looked new. It was about thirty-five feet from stem to stern. The Bayliner would make a good drug-running boat. He wondered who owned it. They came to and tied up.

The boat's name was written in dark red cursive near the bow: Texas Red.

Landry said to Rand, "This your boat?"

"Belongs to a friend of mine."

"Texas Red. Great name." He added, "Won a Breeders' Cup race."

The boat rocked gently as they stepped onto the gunwale. Jolie wasn't a hugger and neither was he, but they hugged, anyway. He could feel her slender body mold against him, more slender than she used to be.

She stood back, holding his hands, and gave him a solemn look, then broke into a smile like a sunrise.

He felt his own heart respond.

She gave him a quick tour. The cockpit up top was spacious. You could call it stylish. Down below Jolie walked them through the boat—the galley with its small dining area, two berth beds, the head, even a wide-screen TV.

"It's about half and half, getting reception out here," she said.

At first glance, she looked like a party girl, but Landry knew it was just the look she'd adopted to stay under the radar. Anyone who took a second look would see the quiet strength underneath the painted exterior.

They sat down at the dinette. Rand remained standing. He seemed to be debating whether to leave them to talk alone, or to stay. "I'll be outside if you need me."

Jolie nodded to him.

Landry realized it had been a year since he'd seen her. They'd been lovers then. As much as two independent people could *be* lovers.

"What happened?" he asked.

"Three people broke into my house," Jolie said. "One of them was my boss."

"The sheriff?"

She recounted events. From the members of her own department—including Sheriff Waldrup himself—breaking into her house, to her escape, to ditching her car in the barn. She told him about the

SPECTRE BLACK

moment she realized that Jace Denboer and the sheriff's office were on the same team.

"Looking back, I know I was capable of handling this on my own, but I thought of you. I thought I could use the backup."

"You did all right on your own," Landry said.

"Yes, but we're far from done."

It left the two of them together, elbows on the table. "You know what sheriff's offices and police departments are doing all over the country, don't you?" Jolie said. "They're seizing assets."

Landry nodded. It was a common practice.

"I have no problem with seizing assets from drug dealers, but somewhere along the line, here in Branch, the sheriff's office decided to go after innocent people. Or at least people who should be presumed innocent."

"The new deputy, Dan Atwood, seized the wrong car from the wrong guy."

There were plenty of horror stories, many of them in New Mexico. Police departments that used any excuse to claim a "civil asset forfeiture."

Originally, the purpose had been to bring down the untouchable drug dealers and members of organized crime. But now that many counties were strapped financially, more and more jurisdictions divvied up spoils of war—mostly cars. It didn't matter if you were a drug dealer or a shoplifter, if they could take your high-ticket item legally, they did. Some departments kept the swag for higher-ups, targeting desired items.

Say, if you wanted a Corvette.

Just go ahead and place your order. Good luck to the person who got ticketed in a traffic stop and lost his car. Once it was gone, it was gone.

"So who did he take the car from?"

"Jace Denboer. Jace Denboer's 2015 Camaro."

Jace Denboer. Landry remembered the cops talking at the donut shop. The kid's father owned the town and the county. Taking the kid's Camaro was a major infraction.

"I can see why the kid—the deputy—got confused," Jolie said. "He sees them doing this, day in and day out, targeting people with nice cars, nice homes. These are wealthy, influential people. I've never been in on those 'after-school' meetings—where Branch's finest divvy up the spoils—but I know what goes on. You wouldn't think there was much money in this town, but there are plenty of people who live on the outskirts, plenty of people with money. Some are retired executives, enjoying their place in the sun."

"They have lawyers, don't they?"

"Yes, but there's also intimidation. Threats."

"Threats?"

"And blackmail. The sheriff's department chooses their victims carefully. What with all the bureaucracy, promises, time stretching out over months or even years, a lot of people just give up. Hard to believe, but they do."

"Okay . . . so what happened after Atwood took the car?"

"It was worked out. Within the hour. They turned the tow truck around in the *street*, they worked so quick to get the car back to Jace. But a week later Dan Atwood was gone."

"Is he still gone?"

"No."

"Where is he?" Although Landry was sure he knew.

"A worker found a body in a bean field—what was left of a body. They had the teeth, though. There was DNA."

"You think it was because he seized Jace Denboer's car for five minutes?"

"It's the theory."

"The Denboers killed him?"

"I didn't get that far. It could be anyone. There are some guys . . .

he could have gotten crosswise of them. And you can be sure nobody else in the sheriff's department wants to prove it. Half the force is corrupt, and the other half is running scared."

"Why are you on the run?"

"Because I was the one assigned to investigate Danny's death." She opened a drawer and produced a lightweight laptop. "Rand gave me this to use. The files are already on here."

She showed him the murder book for Dan Atwood. A description of the crime scene, sketches of the body, aerial view, a list of physical evidence, grisly photographs.

Atwood's body had decomposed considerably. Atwood was shot execution style—a .22 slug, placed right at the junction box. That didn't mean he'd been shot by an expert. Anybody with a television set would know that a .22 to the head at close range did the most damage. Every cop show in the history of the world had gone over that ground at one time or another.

Jolie's theory was that the hole had already been dug and he had been kneeling at the time, shot in the back of the head, and fell forward into the shallow grave.

So she'd looked for enemies. Atwood wasn't popular. For one thing, he was a rookie. A freshman, basically, in a high school full of jocks. Jolie recalled some awkward moments, some practical jokes, the usual hazing. The "kick me" sign on his back.

He'd been partnered with three different deputies, and none of them could stand him. Policing was a dangerous job. A cop needed good backup. That bond was very important.

No one wanted to partner with him.

Still, when he'd had the opportunity, he'd made the big move. He'd taken Jace Denboer's Camaro.

And then he was gone. He didn't officially quit, but it was assumed he'd taken the coward's way out.

Jolie said, "But why would he leave all his possessions? Why wouldn't he try to get back some of the money he'd paid on rent? I was making headway, and then, just like that, I was reassigned. The sheriff gave the case to Jacobs, probably the worst detective we have, does the very minimum. A few of us have a saying: 'If you want to bury something, give it to Jacobs.'"

"So what do you think about this kid? What was going on with him?"

"I think Dan Atwood found out something he shouldn't have."

"What would that be?"

"I have no idea."

They went through the murder book.

Atwood had disappeared in late spring. May 8th to be exact, when he didn't show up for his shift. They'd tried his cell and his home phone: nothing. Sent a deputy to cruise by his house. Two days later, it turned out that he had formally quit— by letter. It was a short, typed letter of resignation, pleading an emergency at home. In Sitka, Alaska.

His reason for quitting: his brother had cancer. He left an address for the sheriff's office to send him his last paycheck.

Then his body was found in October by a farm worker.

Jolie's theory was some kind of animal had dug him up. The burial site was only a few yards in from the roadside fence. Not in a row of beans, but in the patch of dirt and tall grass by the fence. The confrontation between Dan and his killer might have happened on the road. Maybe someone had pulled over; maybe there was some kind of altercation. Of course this was all conjecture. There was little evidence left, since it had been months between the time Atwood disappeared and the time he was found.

"If it was a bean field, wouldn't someone find him pretty fast?"

"The field was fallow."

Landry remembered the drive to Branch, the big agricultural farms that stretched for miles alongside the road. Three of them in a

SPECTRE BLACK

row, and two smaller ones, mom and pop concerns, on the opposite side. "Which farm?"

"Valleyview Experimental Agricultural Station."

Landry said, "The one nearest to town. There was a lane with poplar trees. And an airstrip. And bean fields."

"You have a good memory. That's the place."

"Who found him?"

"One of the farm workers checking irrigation ditches. He smelled it, thought an animal had died out there, and went looking for it."

She described the scene. Something had been out there digging— "An animal of some sort. Maybe a dog, or a coyote. Or a bobcat."

According to the interview with the worker, he'd smelled decay, and then he saw something brown, the dark soil clinging to it—a bone. Disarticulated, probably dug up by a predator. They'd pulled the arm out. The body was degraded, part of it mummified. And clinging to the corpse was a tan shirt—the color deputies wore. And a badge, smeared with dried mud but still reflecting the sun.

Landry pictured the farm. Rows and rows of dried, reddish-brown beanstalks—at that time of year they would look a lot like shredded wheat cereal. A corpse would fit right in. Muddy brown from the dirt, hard to see. Hard to see, but easy to smell. Still, who went out that far into a fallow field?

"May," he said.

"Yes, May." Jolie turned the laptop toward him.

Landry looked at the corpse again. There was the bean field. Just as he had imagined it. The row of tall poplars way in the background. Sheriff's deputies and detectives standing around.

More photos. Atwood *in situ* in the grave. Atwood placed on a tarp to be moved. Atwood zipped into a body bag.

Photos of the grave from every angle. An aerial view of the farm as well.

Evidence markers had been placed here and there. One next to a rusty nail. A fast-food wrapper that had been wadded up and blanched white from the wet, coated with mud. But inside one fold it was bright yellow.

Landry said, "I saw someone sitting outside near the Walmart the other day. At a taco place. The wrapper was yellow."

"The Chimi Brothers has wrappers like that," Jolie said. "Atwood disappeared in May and wasn't found until October—that's five and a half months. I interviewed the servers at Chimi Brothers. I asked them if they recognized Dan Atwood and if they'd ever served him. It was a stretch, but I asked them if they had ever served him in *May*. I even asked them if Atwood might have been with somebody."

"Let me guess," Landry said. "You got nothing."

"No one remembered serving him, or even seeing him. It was too long ago. Whatever encounter they'd had with him—if they did at all—wouldn't have been memorable. And for all I know there's another three or four Mexican chain restaurants with yellow wax paper."

"There *are* another three or four Mexican chain restaurants."

She shook her head. "There you go, correcting people's grammar again. It's like you have Tourette's syndrome."

"It's habit."

"It's a bad habit." She grinned, to let him down gently. "There's other stuff you need to know."

"Like what?"

"I went out on a date with Jace Denboer."

"What was it like?"

"Unpleasant. Awkward. *Weird*."

"Did he ask you out again?"

"No."

"Why'd you go in the first place?"

"Why do you think? To check him out."

"And what did you find out?"

Jolie told him.

CHAPTER 12

Everything about their "date" went wrong. Jace showed up at her door with flowers. She asked him in and put the expensive red roses in a vase. Roses always reminded Jolie of funerals—although usually they were white. These had a moldy smell, as if they'd been kept in the back cooler at the Safeway for too long.

She asked him to sit down and he sat on her couch. He wasn't much for small talk, so Jolie found herself having to fill the gap. Imagine a rich kid like him not being able to hold up his side of the conversation, but that was how it was. He wasn't shy; he wasn't awkward. Maybe the word for him was "distracted."

As they walked out to the car, he rested his arm around her shoulder. It lay there like a dead animal. Jolie knew then that this was a bad idea. *Worse* than a bad idea. It would be a long evening, and she was already making plans to find a way to duck out after the main course.

And that was when she saw the car for the first time—up close. How hideous it was. In the late afternoon sunshine, she could see the uneven paint job, almost like a lava flow only sanded down. Whoever had painted it made mistake after mistake, slapping on more coats of paint to cover it up, and finally they just sprayed another two or three coats on, really rough—almost like powder.

"It looked like a chunk of charcoal."

This was his pride and joy? Jolie would have unloaded it ages ago.

They went to an upscale restaurant. The Cliffs was up in the foothills where the tony places were. California Fan Palms, their trunks ringed with white fairy lights, led to a circle around a fountain. The restaurant consisted of three brown stucco cubes scattered among beautiful gardens and tall palms, and they all looked down on the small city through walls of glass. So nice, but to her the glass fronts made her think of ice. It made her feel cold.

Maybe it wasn't the place so much as the person she was with.

Of course there was valet parking. Jolie noticed that the valet was courteous and treated Jace's car like a freshly laid egg, despite its condition. He must have seen it many times.

But Jolie couldn't help but notice the stark contrast between the expensive restaurant and Jace's chariot.

She described the car again to Landry. Almost as if she had to get it *right*.

It was so *ugly*. Something you'd see at a chop shop. The way the paint was slapped on it, so dull that it seemed to swallow the light. Jolie thought it was some kind of primer, although she'd always thought of primer as gray. An eyesore.

This was the precious car Dan Atwood seized?

Hard to wrap her mind around.

The date—and it really had all the awkwardness that the word *date* implied—lurched on from there. There was very little in the way of conversation. It was strange. The waiter, the maître d', the table settings, the sparkling glasses, the linen, the view, the low voices and clink of silverware—it should have been a magical evening. The exquisite lighting, and the *food*, which was excellent. Perhaps the best meal she'd ever tasted.

But the company . . . Jolie said she was probably not the best conversationalist in the world, but compared to Jace Denboer, she was brilliant. She tried a half-dozen times to get him to talk about *something*, before realizing that she was trying too hard and probably came off like a performing monkey.

"To say it was small talk would be insulting to all the small-talkers out there," Jolie told Landry. "He had virtually nothing to say. He just stared at me and kept asking me about myself. He just phrased it in different ways.

"Honestly. I don't even know why he asked me out. Except for talking about the car, and asking me inane questions, like where was I from, was I a good shot, did I like cars, who were my friends. Like he was testing me, somehow.

"He just kept staring at me, as if he expected me to produce a litter of kittens. It was like he didn't want to be there at all—I got the impression this was something he had to do. Like an arranged marriage. He excused himself partway through dinner and went off to the bathroom and God only knows what he did in there. If he was jerking off, I'm pretty sure he wasn't thinking of me. It was a total waste of time, on his part as well as mine. I'm surprised we lasted an hour. It was like he had to be there. He definitely didn't want to get me in bed"—she shuddered at the thought—"and I don't think he made eye contact with me the whole evening. The only thing he did to impress me was to let me ride in his car. And that strange stunt with the shirt."

"His shirt?"

"I'll get to that."

At one point during dinner, Jace grimaced and said, "What's that smell?"

Jolie didn't smell anything except the food. But Jace became increasingly agitated. He called the waiter over and questioned him at length. That's when it came out: he believed there were cardamom seeds in the salad.

The waiter told him there weren't. Jace became even *more* agitated. Jolie didn't smell anything out of the ordinary. He questioned the waiter at length about it. The waiter even brought the chef out to explain the ingredients, but Jace didn't believe either one of them.

"The cardamom seeds were the most important thing he talked about all night," Jolie said. "Between the flat affect and the paranoia, I'm wondering if there's something medically wrong with him. He's in his midtwenties—twenty-four, to be exact—and that's about the age when schizophrenia begins to take hold in young men. The weirdest thing was that damn car."

"But it gets even weirder than that."

She told him.

Their dinner didn't take long. After Jace's minitantrum, he tersely ordered the check and they left. He drove her straight home, without saying a word. Still agitated.

Angry.

Seething. Jolie could feel it. She could almost smell it. Like an animal backed into a den.

The last of the sunset lost its color. They reached her street. The one thing the neighborhood had was good streetlights. Probably put in years ago when the tract houses were built.

He insisted on walking her to her door. It felt like one of those old movies from the fifties or sixties—she was surprised he didn't ask to see her dad.

Jolie thanked him for the evening. Again, like the 1950s. Maybe *Father Knows Best*. He stood there, looking at her, his face pale in the dusk. She couldn't read him.

"The flat affect. There's something really wrong with him. He said, 'Just a minute.'"

He walked back to the car. He turned his back on her and ducked through the open window of the Camaro, as if he were looking for something. Reaching in, fiddling with something.

Jolie carried a gun in a specially made compartment in her purse, built for concealed carry. She unzipped the bag and curled her hand around the stock, finger on the trigger. She didn't want to turn her back on him to go into the house. Jace and his butt-ugly car were approximately twenty feet away. As a cop, Jolie knew the "twenty-one-foot rule." If a man threatening you was within twenty-one feet, you had to shoot immediately to stop him from getting to you. He could get to you in an instant, across twenty-one feet.

Heart thumping. Mouth dry.

But determined. She'd been trained always to shoot to kill.

His back was still to her as he leaned into the car. He was stretched forward; she could see the waist of his jeans pull down just a little. Jolie wondered if he was reaching into the glove compartment, even now grabbing his own weapon. Was that his plan? To shoot her? *Why?*

Why would he take her out to dinner and then shoot her at her door?

The sky was turning darker by the minute. Jace and his shadowy Camaro were getting harder to see, even with the streetlight reflecting down on them. He remained bent, his upper body inside the car. Rummaging. Rummaging around for something. Jolie's hand tightened on her Sig. Then, still bowed over, he reached down to his waist, rucked his shirt up and pulled it over his head. His bare back to her.

"He took off his *shirt*."

Jolie could see the faint outline of what must be his head, his arms. He'd ducked in again. Now he was wrestling with something, pulling it over his head.

He was *changing* shirts.

- — -

Landry said, "He changed shirts."

"Yes and no."

"He didn't change shirts?"

"It wasn't really a shirt . . . it was more like a poncho. But I couldn't see it very well. Whatever he changed into, the . . . the *garment, it* was . . . it made him . . .transparent. I could see the interior of the car right *through* him."

Somewhere out on the water, a motorboat whined by. There was another noise, too, louder than you'd expect: a fly buzzing at the inside window. But Jolie heard nothing, saw nothing on the boat—everything she saw was interior. She was back at her house with Jace and the Camaro.

She said: "It wasn't the best view in the world, but I could see the interior of the car.

"I could see it right *through* him. The steering wheel, the passenger window, the street scene beyond.

"That red light on the dash, too. The infrared light. And the windshield—I could see the control panel; it was faint but I could see it. Right through him, but no interior lights."

"No interior lights?"

"None."

Landry waited. She wasn't done.

"The poncho was fairly big. Hip length. I could see his legs, his feet, but I couldn't see his waist. It was . . . disturbing. Freaky. Like something from a horror movie. I could see his jean legs, his shoes, halfway up to his waist. Above that, nothing."

"Nothing?"

"Nothing, except . . ." She looked him in the eye. "I could see his head, from the neck up.

"*Just floating there.*"

CHAPTER 13

Landry said to Jolie, "How well do you know Jerry Boam and Rand McNally?"

"Very well."

"Are you sure?"

"I am."

"Why?"

"Because both Rand McNally and Jerry Boam lost loved ones to homicides."

"Both of them? In Branch? They were your cases?"

"Just Jerry. He lost his adult son. That was here in Branch. I investigated the case and it came to a successful close—as successful as it could be, when you've lost a child you're never getting back. We got the guy. Rand is a transplant—his sister lives out here. His wife was killed during a robbery attempt in Phoenix. They were part of a support group."

"You trust them."

"I even checked Rand's story out, just to be on the safe side. So what is this about? Do you have any idea?"

"I'm pretty sure Jace is playing around with cloaking tech. You've heard of that?"

"I've heard the term. What is it?"

"Does Rand have a 4G phone?"

"I think so."

"Ask him if we can get Wi-Fi."

Rand followed Jolie back into the cabin. "I can't get any bars here, but if we go out on the lake, we should be able to."

"Let's do that, then."

It wasn't long before they had 4G. Landry suggested using the phone as a hot spot. Rand went into his Wi-Fi settings on the laptop and connected them to the Internet. "What am I looking for?"

"Google 'cloaking technology,'" Landry said. "Select 'Images' on the toolbar."

The screen filled with photographs. A woman in her living room, cut in half by the couch she should be sitting on and the carpet where she would rest her feet. The top part of her there, the bottom part, gone. A van with its midsection gone, replaced by bridge pillars. A man, standing in a field, only his legs and his boots showing. A tank driving through the desert, kicking up dust—the entire back section gone, as if it had been cut in half. Many of the images—other than the photo of the tank—were clumsy and awkward.

"Looks like a stunt to me," Jolie said. "Freakish."

Landry pointed at the legs of the man. "The secret is to fill in the rest of these people and vehicles with your eye. Where would the man's body be?"

"He's like a jigsaw puzzle with most of the pieces missing." Jolie squinted at the photo.

Rand cleared his throat. "This kind of stuff gives me a headache. I think I'll go do a little fishing. Later I can swing by the marina and get us something to eat. You can call in your orders to me around dark, okay?"

He stepped down into his boat, pulled the cord on the motor, and pulled away from the Bayliner. The sound soon faded to a faint whine as he disappeared past an outcropping of rock and grass.

Jolie said, "He doesn't want to step in this."

"Smart."

"I don't know about that."

SPECTRE BLACK

"You already stepped into this big-time when Jace Denboer showed you his magic suit. It could be he's too dumb to know that, so let's hope it stops there."

"How'd he land on this? You think Daddy gave him his Magic Car?"

"Could be."

"Miko Denboer works with the federal government. But I thought it was agricultural. He has one of those farms."

"People are into all sorts of things. They don't need to be connected."

Jolie said, "So give me the short version of what this is about. Be gentle—I almost flunked physics in high school."

The long version would have taken too much time to explain—he'd be at it all night, and while he'd made a study of the technology, he probably knew only one percent of what really went on. The long version probably wasn't all it was cracked up to be, anyway, since the technology kept morphing.

He told Jolie that there was a standard stealth tech for hard objects—for military hardware, aircraft, and boats. The Stealth Bomber was the most obvious example. These "hard objects" were coated to fool radar and sonar. To accomplish this, the military used a special kind of paint. "Write this down so you won't forget it: carbon nanotube stealth paint."

"'Carbon nanotube stealth paint,'" Jolie said. "Is that anything like Batman's decoder ring?"

"Batman doesn't have a decoder ring."

"You sure about that?" She grinned at him, but her smile faltered. "Seriously, carbon nanotube stealth paint? Who comes up with this stuff? Is this pie-in-the-sky stuff?"

"No—you've already seen it. On Jace's car. Ultra black."

"Ultra."

"Blacker than black. As you said, his car seemed to swallow light, not reflect it."

"It looks like shit."

Landry grinned. That was Jolie—no sugarcoating it. "The paint might look like shit to you, but there are microcrevices and pinholes inside all those layers, to 'eat light.' Multiple coats of paint, building one on top of the other so it's harder to see at night. You said it looked like a chunk of charcoal. Powdery, porous—"

"Ugly."

"But also, hard to see."

Jolie nodded. She'd known that better than anybody.

Landry explained that the big players focused their military and scientific research on "metamaterial": the blackest black imaginable. This could render an object virtually invisible, depending on the circumstances.

Jolie had seen it in action, seen it for herself. Or rather, she *hadn't* seen it. "Nice trick."

"It has its uses, especially in the military. C-130s painted Spectre Black are good for flying at night, because they're hard to spot. Same with the Stealth Bomber. Three things make the Stealth Bomber virtually invisible. One is the paint job. Another is altitude—they're too high up to be seen. And third, the shape. The Stealth Bomber is built to cheat radar—it's configured like a diamond with many facets. The facets break up what would normally be flat surfaces on the aircraft. With a regular plane, its flat wing surface makes it detectable to radar—large points of the fuselage bounce back to the radar center. Radar can't reflect off the Stealth very well, if at all. The military—ours and everyone else's in the world—know that stealth is going to be more and more of a commodity as things change.

"Look at submarines. The biggest Achilles' heel for a submarine back in the old days was the noise. A submarine's worst enemy was the enemy's sonar. So they quieted their subs down, came up with nanocoding to foil sonar. Instead of engine noise or propeller noise, they used a worm drive. A corkscrew that propelled the sub smoothly, and *quietly*, through the water."

Nanotechnology was adapting and changing dramatically, every

SPECTRE BLACK

new adjustment speeding the technology forward, and farther. This was mostly due to the military.

He told her about miniature netting.

The netting was so small it couldn't be handled by human hands. A strand was half the width of a strand of human hair. It could be used to support certain kinds of material, so that you could affix that material to an object. Landry compared it to sticky-note paper. You peeled it off and pasted it on. Landry said, "You can manhandle it, roll it out on the roof of a house or the side of the car. The netting is what holds everything together—it transfers electricity. It's a conductor. It transfers electricity from the cameras to the projectors. Whatever it is you need to apply. Infinitesimal. Say you spray the adhesive on the side of the car—it's heat-activated. You can roll it out, just the way you want it, use a heat gun, warm it up, fuse it to the car's surface. Like clear coat. Clear polyurethane. Nanowire with one or two coats."

"That's not the same thing as what Jace has, right? He's just got the black paint."

"You're right. It's not the same. Different technology, same goal. That's where technology is going."

"I don't understand what Jace did. How can you see through an object if the person is standing right there? How can you see right through him?"

"You don't."

"Then how do you make it seem like you do?"

Landry said, "Remember how tiny everything is. So tiny it's just this side of nonexistent."

"I get that."

"The netting, the adhesive, the things that hold it together, that's the key."

"To *what?*"

"To the material you want to put on the netting. In this case, it's an infinitesimally small camera placed side by side with an infinitesimally small projector. Multiplied exponentially. Receiving and transmitting constantly."

"Like two beads placed next to each other," Jolie said. "Rows and rows of them?"

Jolie was a quick study.

"Like that," Landry said, "Only these beads are too tiny to be visible to the human eye. Picture two infinitesimally small beads, one next to the other. One bead is the camera. The second bead is the projector. Repeat the pattern, on and on—a camera next to a projector next to a camera next to a projector."

"That's nanotechnology?"

"One kind of nanotechnology. 'Nano' means tiny."

Jolie got it. "So—does this mean the cameras take pictures of what's behind you, and the projectors display them for you to see? Say you have a van parked outside, and behind that there's desert and mountains. If the van is wearing the cameras and projectors, the projectors are relaying an image of the desert, right? Not the van. Is that right? That's what you'd see. A projection. Like a hologram?"

Landry thought of the man who walked past him near the bridge. "Something like that."

"Wouldn't those cameras and projectors have to be on both sides of the object?" Jolie added. "So the cameras could record what's behind the object?"

"Yes."

"Judging from these photos on Google Images, they've got a ways to go. They're not very good."

"No," Landry said. "But look at the difference between the Wright brothers' plane and the Stealth Bomber. Technology is always moving. Technology evolves."

"This is what Jace's father's involved in?"

"Could be."

"Could be?"

Landry shrugged. "Maybe Jace got his hands on the Camaro another way."

"How?"

"Got me."

"So what do we do?"

"Go black."

"If you mean go into hiding, I *did* go black."

"How many people helped you get here?"

"Just two. Jerry Boam—his actual name is Jerry Bartlett, by the way—and Rand. I called you because I thought—"

"You have to go."

Her eyes turned stony. Two gray-blue marbles in her head. "Go where?" she asked. Her voice low, quiet. Contained.

"You think you're safe here? You think they're not looking for you? Jace did you a big favor, showing you that car. Now it's all out in the open. But you know what? Even if you don't know much, it's possible—fifty-fifty—that they believe you know too much."

"Because of a car?"

"And Dan Atwood."

She said nothing.

"You found him at the agricultural farm with the poplars. Isn't that Miko Denboer's farm?"

"Yes, but that doesn't—"

"They came after you once."

She opened her mouth to argue, then closed it again. He could feel her anger. It was a living thing, writhing in the air between them like an electric wire.

Jolie looked away and remained quiet. It made Landry want to tell her how he admired her, how tough she was. He had a list of reasons, all logical, for her to stand down. She was a known quantity in the town. And she'd already gone on the run. But he didn't say any of it. She would have to come to her own conclusion.

Whatever it was, he would deal with it.

At last she said, "I need to think about this."

"Think fast."

Landry heard the whine of a boat on the water—they looked at each other. The sound changed to a drone, the boat coming closer. Landry grabbed his .32 Colt. "You stay hidden, just in case," he said. The gun was small enough to fit inside his hand. He held it back and slightly behind his thigh and went above.

It was Rand McNally, holding up his branch with the blue underwear tied on. He threw the rope and Landry secured the boat. There was a grease-spotted paper bag on the bench seat behind him—their dinner—but Rand left it there. Landry could tell by McNally's face that something was wrong.

Not just wrong.

Devastating.

Jolie materialized beside him.

Rand's face was drawn in the last red light. Landry could see the sun behind him, its eye almost closed, a few plum-dark clouds above. It was like a snapshot.

A snapshot of the moment when something had changed, drastically.

Landry looked at Jolie.

She was a cop, with a cop's sixth sense.

She knew it was something bad.

Landry gave Rand a hand onto the Bayliner. Rand clutched a newspaper in his fist. His face was pale. Stricken.

"Bad news," he said. "Really bad news."

"What happened?" Jolie demanded.

"You live on Turner Avenue, right?"

He handed Landry the paper. It was today's edition. One photo took up the front page above the fold. Blackened timbers, smoke, a firefighter traipsing through a puddle. Landry stared at the address, read it over three times. It was her house—burned to the ground.

CHAPTER 14

It had been a half hour and Jolie had still not said a word. She sat at the dinette, hands clasped so hard her knuckles were white.

Landry said, "Tom probably got to them first."

"Why doesn't he answer?"

"He might be away from his phone." Landry didn't explain that the man who had flown him here was very low tech, despite his hours in the cockpit. Tom was hard to reach, because he wanted it that way. He had an abundance of caution. Landry got the feeling he let his calls pile up before answering them.

"You're sure he came and got them?"

"I told him to do it ASAP."

"There's an alarm system—"

"That was no problem."

She nodded. "I guess not. So you *think* he got them."

"I think so. But I'm not sure."

"Try your friend in San Clemente again."

Landry tried his friend Louise. This time the call went through—to voice mail. He left a message, asking her to call him as soon as possible.

Jolie said, "So he came and got them and he flew them to your friend, Louise . . . How does she figure in?"

"She lives next door. I can count on her."

"That's good, then."

Landry nodded. What he didn't say: he thought it was about fifty-fifty at best.

"They're trying to get me to come out of hiding. That's what they're doing. That they would do that to two helpless . . . They—"

She pulled the laptop to her and called the article up online. There was a photo of the house—burned timbers, part of her carport standing, firemen, hoses, water running down the street, everything in black and white. Now she saw it in living color.

She closed her eyes. "I hope your friend Tom got them."

Landry read through the article. There wasn't much there. Nothing to indicate there were people dead in the house. Nothing to indicate that there were pets, either.

"We need to make sure who and what we're dealing with. Who have you had run-ins with, besides members of your own department and Jace Denboer?"

"The sheriff, the undersheriff, some of the people I work with— at least one of my fellow detectives. I couldn't believe the corruption. It's all out in the open, like confiscating the cars. Waldrup clamped down on my investigation into Dan Atwood's death."

"How'd he do that?"

"He kept giving me other stuff to do. Busywork. He *buried* me in it."

"Why?"

"I included the Denboers in my investigation, since the kid was killed and buried on their farm."

"Did you interview Miko Denboer?"

"No."

"Why not?"

"The sheriff said it wasn't necessary. He made that *clear*."

PART TWO

PART TWO

CHAPTER 15

Jace Denboer reached up to take the joint from Carla's fingers, sucked in the smoke, and held it in as long as he could. On the exhale, he closed his eyes and smiled.

"You look like a choirboy," Carla said.

Jace knew he had an angelic smile. It had saved his ass many times. All his life, he'd been able to turn it on and off any time he felt like it. He'd been told a hundred times how lucky he was, how he'd been on the receiving end of the good looks on both his mother's and father's sides.

Those good looks pretty much eased him down any path he chose to take.

Good looks ran in the family. Look at his half sister. Carla was the hottest-looking bird in New Mexico. He liked to call women "birds" because a friend of his was English and that's what he'd called them. It sounded different from what his other friends said, and he liked to differentiate himself from the crowd.

And Carla was the only bird who could keep up with him, sexually and in every other way. The only one who was like him on this whole, fucked-up planet.

They were very similar, except that she was older than him by three years. And she was a woman, not a man. "Big differences there," he muttered. "*Vive la différence.*"

Carla finished pulling up her skirt, concentrating hard as she fiddled with the clasp at her waistband. She'd already covered up those awesome boobs with the lace bra, the one with the front catch he'd had a hard time fumbling open. She took another toke from him and sat down on the edge of the bed to pull on her boots.

Her mind seemed far away.

She spent less and less time with him. He wondered if he should feel insulted.

Outside, the lawn mower droned. He glanced out the window by the bed and watched as Hector Canazales, the groundskeeper, rode the mower across the huge lawn. The lawn didn't look real. It was as green and flat as the felt on a billiard table, shaded by royal palms on one side and a gigantic Aleppo pine on the other. The Aleppo pine had been planted when he was born. It was his mother's idea. It was the last decent thing she'd ever done for him.

As if sensing him, Hector looked up and waved.

"Why is he doing that?" Jace said.

Carla was leaning into the mirror to attach her earring. "Why is *who* doing what?"

"The grounds guy. He was staring at me."

"Paranoid much?"

"No. I'm not paranoid. There are people looking for me."

Carla turned her face to him. She wore her sad expression. "You're taking your meds, aren't you?" Her expression got sadder, like she was *bereaved*, as if she was already looking into his grave and planning to shovel the first clod of earth onto his upturned face.

That was exactly what it felt like. What it *was*. Like he were in the grave, lying in the coffin, smelling the earth, his face tickled by cobwebs, staring up at her. He'd often wondered what "dead" was like. Lying there, eyes wide open. Or maybe they were closed. It was all up to the mortician. If you got a practical joker, you would be staring up at the roof of your coffin for eternity.

SPECTRE BLACK

He caught Carla's fake-sad expression and knew that inside, she was laughing at him.

She wanted to suck his soul into herself. He was sure of that.

"Oh, you have such an imagination!" his mother used to tell him when he was little. "You are the brightest little boy!"

She lived in Cancun now.

"What did you say? You're the brightest little boy?" Carla stared at him.

"None of your business what I said, you stupid bird."

Carla laughed. She laughed loud and long. Like a clown, and then, all of a sudden, she *was* a clown. She'd morphed into the Amazing Santarini, the clown who'd performed for his eighth birthday party. Same hair, same body, same lips, that wide smile, that toothy smile and bright red lips, expanding and expanding and expanding—

He shut his eyes. Drummed his fists against his knees. He knew she would *keep* laughing at him, she always did, and why he slept with her he didn't know. His mother (if she'd had enough guts to stick around) would say it was a sin against God. But he knew there was no God.

Carla's lips widened, cracked open, and he saw squirming yellow teeth and boll weevils.

He squeezed his eyes shut, but knew it would do no good, so he opened them again. Luck was on his side. Just like that, she was his beautiful sister again. His beautiful, hot, sex-starved, half sister.

She scrutinized him. It was like she was looking at a specimen in a jar. Cocked her head. "You're not taking your meds, are you?"

"Fuck you."

"Hey, suit yourself," she said. "You're not on your meds, that's a *fact*, and you *know* Daddy will notice. You want to be committed? You want to go to the scary place with the dungeon walls and chains? Over in Albuquerque?"

"Stop that shit. There's no place like that."

"No?" She walked over to him and tapped her finger on his forehead. "You have no idea."

He knew Carla was messing with him. As she pushed through the French doors, she looked back and winked at him. He heard her high-heeled boots rap hard against the flagstone patio, smack, smack, *smack*.

The smell of sickly sweet potted flowers and rich dark earth trailed behind her. Someone had watered the plants on the patio. He knew they were for decoration, but that wasn't all. The flowerpots were bugged. His dad did it to spy on him. And to keep him from sifting through the potting soil, he'd filled the dark earth with worms.

Like the worms in that deputy's skull, poking and wriggling through his eye sockets. Pushing through the loose dark earth of the bean field. That was pretty cool.

You killed him, remember? His dad's voice. *But you're not going to jail. I'll make sure of that. You're the one who's responsible for this, and I'm the one who will protect you, as long as you keep your mouth shut.* You *killed him.*

He remembered. Once he remembered, once he *knew what he'd done*, he'd gone back three times to check. (He wasn't supposed to. He was supposed to forget it.) He always went at night. He drove with no lights except for the infrared on the Camaro's windshield, and even though sound carried, no one was way out there at the farm at night.

The deputy was always there—he wasn't buried all that deep. Jace hadn't been back since the sheriff announced they'd found him. There had been stories on the news and stories in the paper and stories on the Internet, but he'd ignored that, because he knew the deputy was still in the grave, despite what his dad said, despite what he'd seen on the local news or read online. He *knew* he was still there.

Carla had shown him the front page of the newspaper. There was a photograph of heavy equipment, some guy bending over an empty grave. But that was a lie.

SPECTRE BLACK

People made things up all the time. You could make anything look real—they did it all the time. Faked things. Especially online. All sorts of crap that wasn't real.

The body was still there—he knew it.

And that was what scared him. The corpse might reanimate, and come after *him*.

It was like those horror stories he'd read as a kid. Maybe the corpse would be washed up by the spring rains that filled the irrigation ditches like chocolate milk, or maybe it would just worm its way up out of the earth.

The stench!

He knew at some point, Atwood would come for him. The corpse would reanimate. And the only way he could escape was to pile his stuff in the Camaro and take off.

The good thing about the Camaro, it was fast. Another good thing about the Camaro:

You couldn't see it.

He had the best car in the world.

But he wondered . . .

He wondered if the deputy's corpse had X-ray eyes.

He'd noticed, these days, a lot of people did.

CHAPTER 16

Landry reached his neighbor Louise late in the day. He nodded at Jolie and gave her the thumbs-up. Handed the phone to Jolie. They talked for a bit, mostly about the dog and cat and their adjustment to a new place. The Rottie had settled in fine and was playing with Louise's schnauzer. Rudy was another story. He'd stayed in the cat carrier for a couple of hours, before slinking out to hide under the couch. "He's still there, but I'm not worried," Louise said. "He'll get hungry eventually."

When Jolie disconnected, her relief was palpable. "Thank God. Thank *you*."

Landry gave her a nod. He didn't like to be thanked for something he would have done, anyway—SOP. Compliments were superfluous. But having been married for many years, having raised a daughter, he knew that women liked to bestow compliments and it was best to accept them with grace.

Then she launched into his arms and held him so tight and for so long, he got a crick in his neck. But he didn't complain. He had learned to love the way Jolie pressed her body to his.

Rand ducked outside to watch the sunset.

They could not stand another moment apart. Pulling at each other's clothes, casting them away, kissing and molding hands to every place they could think of. First time through was a brush fire. Second time was slower, a long and flowing river with interesting things to see on both banks. It had been a long time, and now they were rediscovering what they already knew about each other. She tucked in against him and fell asleep, and he could see that everything that had weighed her down over the last few months had vanished, at least in sleep.

Jolie awoke an hour later. He was still holding her, stroking her dyed-black hair, thinking that she looked good with that color. With *any* color. She opened her eyes, tipped her solemn face up to him. "I don't know where we go from here, and I don't care. But. I *need* to be *part of this*."

- — -

As much as it pained him, Landry told Jolie about his assignation with Carla Vitelli. He didn't make excuses because excuses wouldn't wash. She was there, he was interested, it happened. Regretting it didn't change the story.

"I don't own you."

Landry sensed, though, that she was hurt. If not hurt, offended. Landry had adopted one way of dealing with both. "It happened and I can't change it now. We good?"

"Of course we are. I have a friend, Vicki Dodd, a detective in sex crimes. Sometimes our cases overlap, and sometimes she or I, we get territorial. We end up making the case bigger than it is. So we have this saying: 'How big is King Kong?'"

Landry wasn't following.

"Think about it. King Kong was on the big screen throwing airplanes around like javelins, but what was he, really? He was a puppet. A puppet that was moved this way and that. Yeah, he climbed up a miniature Empire State Building, but how big was *that*? So whenever one or the other of us ran into a seemingly impossible case, we'd cheer each other up by saying, 'How big is King Kong?'"

"Interesting," Landry said. "Do you know Carla?"

"I know *of* her."

"She was the FBI agent assigned to your case. Your disappearance."

"Didn't do a very good job, did she? Except for interrogating you at length."

Jolie could nail you to the wall when she wanted to. He couldn't help but smile at that. "So what do you know about her?"

"Just the common knowledge stuff. She's Jace's sister from another mother. There's a rumor going on that she's banging her own half brother. How'd she latch on to you?"

Landry told her about his arrest and subsequent grilling by Sheriff Waldrup and Carla Vitelli. He thought she had targeted him from the beginning: a stranger in town who spent his time hanging out in a cop shop.

"Not a lot to go on," Jolie said.

"No, but her instincts were good. She was right about me. Either that, or she really did have the hots for me and stalked me because I'm so good-looking."

"That's a bit of a stretch, don't you think?"

"That hurt."

Jolie thought about it. "She must have had some idea about you, maybe put it together that you were looking for me."

"Probably."

"What happened in the jail? You think it was her trying to get you killed?"

"It was a damn good imitation of it if she wasn't."

"But then you were released, no charges."

"Someone else got me out."

"Why?"

"To make it look like I shot Rick Connor at the checkpoint, and then went after the two witnesses."

"The sheriff?"

"The sheriff."

"For a man who's used to staying under the radar," Jolie said, "you could give a billboard competition. So they wanted to frame you for the deaths of those militia members, but lacked evidence? And maybe throw in Rick Connor? They set you up."

"They did. Carla thought she found the perfect suspect."

"Why do you think Rick Connor was killed?" Jolie asked.

"I don't know. But everything they did since was to cover it up, including killing the witnesses."

"Maybe we should check out Connor."

Jolie still had a few tricks. She still had access to databases. She looked for Rick Connor in wants and warrants. Found seven of them. "That could be our guy," she said. But there were plenty of Rick Connors in the southwest. Hundreds of them. Expand it out to half the country and you had thousands of them. A needle in a haystack.

"It could be an assumed name," Jolie said. "Rick Connor. It even sounds made-up."

"It's a common name, too. You could tie yourself in knots looking for him."

"Let's look up his buddies. 'The Right Hand of God Freemen's Militia.'"

A click or two and there it was.

"Jesus," Jolie said. "All these groups have names like that. It's like they sit in a circle and toss out words that sound good. God, Freemen, Patriot. It helps with credibility—at least for the people who join up. What they are to law enforcement—might just as well call them 'The Pain in the Ass Militia.'" She thought about it. "But maybe that's not true. The worst thing for the sheriff is the Feds. He probably likes having the militia around. I bet from his standpoint, they inoculate the sheriff's office against the Feds."

"You mean the Feds don't want to come around here? Because they're worried about a range war?"

"Never start a fight you can't win," Jolie said. "You saw what happened in Nevada. The photo that went viral, right? A guy on a bridge with a sniper rifle, drawing down on federal agents. Guy should have been tossed into a prison hole so deep he would never be able to crawl out, but there were no arrests. They won that one."

"Where'd the sheriff come from? Before he was here?"

"Albuquerque. He's been here seven or eight years."

"Ever wonder why they hired you?"

"I think it's because of the bank robbery—when I shot those guys. That should have been a warning bell right there. It says something about the sheriff if he wants headlines and a hard-ass cop. Back then I was his flavor of the month. He called me Little Miss Sure Shot."

"Annie Oakley."

"What?"

"That was what they called Annie Oakley."

"By the first week I knew I was just window dressing. By the second week, I knew this department had its fair share of thugs. Some of the bad apples who were fired out of Albuquerque came down here. What does that tell you?"

"The car seizures," Landry said. "Sounds like a free-for-all."

"Not just cars. Boats, houses, real estate. Some of the higher-ups have some nice stuff."

"Why are you still here?"

"Good question. I don't know the answer to that. Except I want to stay a cop."

"Why didn't someone tell Dan Atwood not to confiscate the kid's Camaro?"

Jolie shrugged. "Another good question. I've asked it myself on a few occasions. I've been thinking. What if one of us went undercover?"

"As what?"

"A militia member. Not you—everyone on God's green earth knows about you by now . . ."

"The only militia members who saw me are dead."

"You said even your own mother won't recognize you. Can you do that for me?"

"For you?"

"Yes. I think it's more believable if we go as a pair."

"No. You're a known quantity. People are still looking for you."

Jolie looked like she was about to argue, but then gave up on it. She saw the logic. "What about ID?" she asked.

"I have plenty. The best money can buy."

"You know, even though I make fun of them, these guys are the real deal. They have a network—they will check you out in a New York minute."

"The reason you can't come."

"I get that. You don't have to rub it in. I'm saying don't underestimate them just because a few of them look like all they do is eat MoonPies and watch reruns of *Honey Boo Boo*. You know how to disguise yourself, and so do they." She added, "I belittle them—I have to, for my own sanity. But every time I see one of these guys on the street I'm back to being the little girl who's afraid of the monster under the bed. Some of these militias' networks, their tentacles are even into government—it's enough to freeze your blood."

Landry nodded. "I'll watch my back, stick as close to the truth as possible. I'm former military—elite. You can't fake that. I've worked security for a company that's now defunct. All that's true. I can even give them a name. Whitbread Associates."

Jolie smiled but her smile was thin. "You haven't exactly been keeping a low profile. The whole thing about the white car."

"That was bad luck."

"Yes, but—"

Just then Rand ducked in and Landry said, "I need to get back. Would you drive me?" He said to Jolie, "I can arrange for Tom to fly you to San Clemente. He's under the radar and he's good. That way you can be far away if it hits the fan. You can stay in my house."

"I'm staying," she said. "You never know when you might need me."

- — -

Landry and Rand left the lake and drove to the Big 5 sports store in Las Cruces. Landry bought a couple of pairs of camo pants, three extra-large black-and-Army-green tees, some jeans, a couple of dark knit shirts, and desert boots. He went next door to Walgreens and bought a packet of razors, a cheap pair of earrings shaped like a cross, and some aviator shades.

He excused himself and went outside to call his friend Eric the Red. Eric answered on the first ring.

"Hey. You want to do some damage?" Landry said.

"What's the op?"

Landry told him.

"Be there with bells on—where do we meet?"

Landry gave him the name of a motel in Lunaria, the neighboring town to Branch, where he'd bought the red Forenza.

"You gonna pay me? I wouldn't bring it up, but things are a little tight."

Landry sympathized. Since the recession, personal protection and special op training businesses had taken a big hit. Combat training for personal security was at its lowest ebb. The recession had made it tough for expert combat instructors—police forces decided that money couldn't go two ways, so they scrapped the tactical training and just took all the military surplus goodies from the Feds—free stuff that a lot of them had no clue how to use, like the MRAP he's seen driving down the main drag in town.

Eric ran a training center specializing in tactics, SWAT training, hand-to-hand combat, and a side business in personal security, but his clientele had slowed to a trickle.

Now the big worry was cybersecurity.

"Sure, I'll pay you," Landry said. He was okay for the foreseeable future, but the small fortune he'd amassed wouldn't last forever. He hadn't been able to invest it, so his money sat in a few banks and many more drop spots throughout California. Because he relied mostly on cash, his personal wealth was beginning to look a little skimpy.

Things were tough all over.

They arranged for a meet.

"Dress former military," Landry said.

"That'll be easy. You want to dress up, I've got a whole case of Mehron stuff. Wigs, makeup, all sorts of shit. Enough to turn this into an early Halloween party. You want biker? You got biker."

"Former military *and* biker. There's a mono vault on the road up above my town house in Lake View Terrace. It's sunk into a pullout on the right-hand side of the road, right where it gets steeper." He gave the GPS coordinates. "Inside are a couple of identities. One is Sean Marcus Terry. It's solid." He mentally ran down his wish list. "Also pull out the parabolic mic and send it to me overnight." He gave the address. "Can you pick up a truck when you get here? I'll reimburse you."

They arranged where to meet. Eric thought aloud. "For this op, we go badass. Black Dodge Ram, two to four years old, am I right?"

"Sounds good."

"Monster truck tires?" Eric laughed. "Just jerking your chain."

CHAPTER 17

The headquarters of The Right Hand of God Freemen's Militia was located in an RV park in the low hills just outside Branch city limits. The RV park and a few other businesses were cheek by jowl up against forestland. A former ranch, the campground was set back from the winding dirt road that hosted a cluster of small businesses: a filling station and minimart, a shooting range-slash-petting zoo (fortunately these two attractions were on different ends of the property) and the RV park itself—the last outpost before US National Forest land.

While Landry waited for Eric the Red, he set up surveillance on one of the hills, having followed a track above the scattering of houses and cabins. He was high up, concealed in a copse of scrub oak.

The blacktop wound through the canyon. A quarter mile before the general store, the road forked. The left fork led an eighth of a mile to the Pine Cone RV Park, and the right fork went through forestland, all the way to the main highway. The few homes scattered along the road ranged from ramshackle miner shacks to newer ranchettes. Anyone wanting to drive through the canyon had to pass through a militia checkpoint. Landry parked at a trailhead four miles distant and hiked in cross-country rather than risk being seen by the militia members. He did not want to make his presence known until he and Eric showed up on their doorstep, looking to join.

SPECTRE BLACK

It had taken a full day for Landry to figure out where the militia stayed. He'd been looking for RV parks and trailer parks and campgrounds, mainly because places like that offered a constantly changing population. People camped for a day or two and moved on. Some stayed longer—for the winter. But the transient nature of a campground made it easier for the militia to remain hidden in plain sight.

That was, if you didn't notice the bikers, rough characters, paramilitary weapons, and swagger. If you didn't notice the posted signs—KEEP OUT, like something from a kid's tree fort. If you didn't see the big trucks, or notice the counterculture appearance of some and the paramilitary looks of others. Or the armed sentry.

Landry watched their comings and goings. At first, they were as indiscriminate as ants in his binocs. But after a while, he saw the pattern. Cars and trucks going out at specific times. Eight o'clock was one. Ten thirty, another. He wrote it down. Punctual, like the military. Cars and trucks going in and out in an orderly manner. The sentry saluting. Landry guessed they were either going for supplies, or to a checkpoint—their day job.

He set up the parabolic mic.

There was no one out and about, so Landry fixed the GPS position, saved it to his phone, and sketched a map of the compound. Jotted a few notes in a memo pad. Sometimes the most obvious and outdated method worked better than fancy equipment. He'd learned long ago that if he had a chance to write his thoughts out, he assimilated them better and deeper than any other way. This was a time to get a feel for them, to begin to figure out the hierarchy. This would take hours of just watching them, and eavesdropping with the mic.

The outskirts of the place looked like a cross between a gypsy camp and a junkyard where cars and appliances went to die. Maybe because the riverbed was lined with rusted car hulks, some of them dating to the twenties. Protection against the river flooding its banks. There were operational vehicles, too; three trucks and a couple of cars.

The RV park itself was a sprinkling of travel trailers and campers under a row of Aleppo pines. Some of the trailers and campers were in pristine condition and some were falling apart. Tent trailers, travel trailers, trucks with camper shells, two older motor homes. And one standout: a top-of-the-line Mercedes/Airstream motor home.

Landry photographed three buildings: a house made of cinderblock, painted yellow—someone's domicile, a camp store with attached restrooms, and a small, one-story building that would have been right at home on a western movie set. The yellow house held down one side of the campground, and the western building, which he labeled "Bunkhouse" in his notes, was on the other. Not far from the bunkhouse was the whitewashed camp store. It too, had a low wooden porch, and offered up an ice machine and a soft drink machine. Another sign on the big cottonwood shading the building said, "Sewer Dump Station."

The entrance to the property was a cattle guard between two posts. Four-strand barbed-wire fencing stretched into infinity on either side. It wouldn't stop attackers, that was for sure. The militia could have gone one of two ways: "impenetrable," or "hide in plain sight." They'd chosen the "hide in plain sight" model.

As Landry watched, a man exited the motor home and walked over to the old west shack. Sound in the mountains carried and he heard the screen door slap to.

Landry waited for the man to reemerge, which he did, a few minutes later. He was spare—no fat on him—and wore a cowboy hat that reminded Landry of the old westerns from the sixties. The kind of hat with a triangular crown. Because of the man's hat and the confident way he walked, Landry labeled him TV Western Hat. Other than the out-of-place cowboy hat, he was dressed in jeans and a western, snap-button shirt. But Landry couldn't shake the feeling that there was something, for want of a better word, corporate about him.

SPECTRE BLACK

Landry remained where he was as early morning turned to late morning, and then to noon, jotting notes on the memo pad. Anything and everything—no matter how small or seemingly unimportant. The parabolic mic wasn't effective because no one spoke. All he heard were birds.

He noted the times people came and went. He noted who went into which building, a quick description, trying to keep it down to one or two words. Like Lion Mane—a short, tough, wiry individual with blond hair that would have looked appropriate on a surfer circa 1970. Landry didn't make any value judgments, just observed. At times like this, it was best to think clinically.

He had looked up The Right Hand of God Freemen's Militia, and seen Lion Mane featured in a news article. His name was Jedediah Kilbride. He and TV Western Man were similar in build. Landry wondered if they might be brothers.

Kilbride didn't reveal much about his militia, wisely using jargon to say very little. Lots of references to God and Country, Freedom, Liberty, and trampled rights. The usual. If you wanted to obfuscate, hit them with a flood of words and lofty rhetoric that couldn't be pinned down.

Whatever was going on, the main crew was gone. Landry assumed they were manning their checkpoints around the small city.

He wanted to get an idea as to how professional they were. It didn't matter how they looked. It was how they worked together, how they achieved their goals. It must be cleaning day. Women did that work, one of them buzzing from one outbuilding to the other with a vacuum cleaner, another taking out the trash and heading into one place with an industrial squeeze mop and bucket. They spoke a few words to one another in Spanish, and Landry got most of it. Stuff like "I'll do that house, you do the other." One was a thin woman with long black hair. Maybe Hispanic, maybe not. Her movements were languid, verging on sexy. The men he saw going about their business spent a good deal of time shooting the breeze with her. Another woman, also with black hair, was shorter and softer-looking. But she was a dynamo, a hard worker. She was definitely Hispanic. Some just had walk-on parts, but Lion Mane, the blond surfer man—Kilbride—gave the orders. He carried himself importantly, as if a spotlight were always following him. But he didn't overdo it, and his voice was quiet. Landry could barely hear him.

He remembered an old TV commercial. "If you want to catch someone's attention, whisper."

The remaining four men looked like central casting had sent them over. Three of them wore green Army tees, camo pants, and Kevlar vests. They were youngish men, playing soldier. They might be former military. Two of them were bulky but not big, and one was lean like a sapling. He was a kid but Landry sensed he had more on the ball than the others. For one thing, he often lifted his binocs to scan the area. He was alert but not hypervigilant. He looked like he'd be able to swing into action instantly, if need be. He had restless eyes, and when people talked, he was not among them. He was constantly taking in his surroundings, shading his eyes and scrutinizing the hills.

The parabolic mic captured their voices, but it needn't have bothered; it was all small talk.

Landry concentrated his binocs on Kilbride. He looked to be in his mid-fifties. Probably dyed his hair. The other two were sloppy and lazy. One of them leaned against a post holding up the porch. Physically lazy, but also, he might have problems. Back problems, maybe, or the knee. Musculoskeletal problems.

The other shifted from foot to foot, also uncomfortable. Hand shading his eyes against the sun. It seemed to Landry his attention wandered. He'd nod as if he understood, then he'd shift his weight, put his thumbs in his belt. "Yes, sir," he'd say, and then his gaze would wander away again. Attention deficit disorder, in the flesh.

"Quite a team you've got there," Landry muttered.

He reminded himself that he could not underestimate the spear-carriers. Lazy men, inattentive men, bored men—they were the dangerous ones. They could be surprised. They could be frightened. They could react unpredictably. With Lion Mane, Landry had a pretty good handle on how he would react to any situation. He'd tighten himself up. He'd be ready. He was short, probably a former Navy SEAL. Most of Landry's fellow SEALs were short and compact. Kilbride would keep his eye on the prize. And so would the kid.

So there they were: Lion Mane, Western Hat (who had since disappeared), the young guy Landry thought was on the ball, and the two spear-carriers in this opera. And the two women—one who seemed preoccupied with her looks, and the other, stouter woman, who was no stranger to work.

Landry had the luxury of watching them interact most of the afternoon. One of the spear-carriers started digging postholes. The other drove off the property in a GMC Suburban. Landry recognized the Suburban from the checkpoint. Navy blue, almost black, dented and floured with dust. The guy gunned it out of there—macho.

Landry focused on the women. He knew that women in militias were mostly hangers-on. Most, but not all. Many came with their boyfriends or husbands, but every once in a while you'd run into a tough nut, a GI Jane. Neither of these two fit the bill. The slim, beautiful one was clearly with Lion Mane. The shorter one, the dynamo who worked efficiently but thoroughly—Landry put her into another category. She wore a gray T-shirt with a navy blue logo on it, and he saw now she wasn't fat, but muscular. Short-waisted, yes, but strong. He pegged her as former military.

He took photos of them all, but mostly, he memorized them. The way they moved—for instance, how Lion Mane walked with his arms swinging at his sides but slightly out from his body, as if he'd spent a good part of his life hefting hay bales. The gray-shirted woman—every movement she made was economical and effective.

Western Hat might be the boss, but Landry couldn't get a read on him. Too short an exposure to him. The guy had walked from the motor home to the outbuilding and back again, and that was it. He could well be calling the shots. But calling the shots wasn't always the best barometer of effectiveness. Of a potentially worthy foe.

For now he would focus mostly on the formidable ones: Lion Mane, The Kid, and the Short Woman.

He waited a while longer, but it must have been siesta time. No one was out and about. No trucks or cars drove in or out.

He'd come back tomorrow.

He had some time.

By the end of the second day, he knew them cold. He caught only bits and pieces of the story with the parabolic mic, but he had a good idea of their operation—who was assigned which checkpoint, what worried them, and what they could not care less about. Who you could count on and who wasn't up to snuff. The shock of losing three of their own—there was plenty of talk about that. Plenty of blame to go around, too. Who would hang tough, and who was the weakest link.

CHAPTER 18

At five thirty in the morning Cyril Landry awoke to the sound of a big truck engine idling past his motel room window. He left the light off, peered through the narrow seam between the curtains and saw the Dodge Ram.

The Dodge idled, the big engine shuddering—still cold. The Ram was black, late model, but not new. Eric Blackburn sat in the driver's seat, window rolled down, massive arm cocked on the door. The exhaust burbled, gray in the near dark. The motel was shaped like an L and Landry saw a drape twitch in the window of the room across the way. Landry fumbled for his phone, found it, and hit Eric's number.

"I hope you're buying me breakfast."

"Roger that."

"Room Six."

Landry stood in the doorway and watched as the taillights came on and the behemoth truck backed up. He could hear the squeak of the suspension from here. Eric parked beside Landry's Forenza and killed the engine.

"Nice piece of shit you got there," Eric said, jumping out of the truck and nodding toward Landry's car.

"It's served its purpose. You can't get more under the radar than that. You brought your bike."

"I brought *a* bike. It's cheaper than mine, but not by much. I figure if I wrecked it you'd pay me what it's worth. And if it comes out okay, I'll give it to my kid. One of those offers you can't refuse. Let's go get some breakfast and have us a powwow."

- — -

The Busy Bee Diner was just a greasy spoon, but there wasn't much else in this town except Mexican food places, and even a dedicated Mexican food fan would want a little variety now and then.

Eric leaned back and crossed his arms across his massive chest. "What's the planistan, Stan?"

"I forgot how cheery you are in the morning."

"I'm a regular Kris Kringle."

"You bring the stuff?"

"Yeah. Right here." Eric reached down, unzipped his run bag, and let Landry get a glimpse of his biker outfit. Leathers, jeans, chains: the usual.

"The girls are gonna love you." Actually, Landry thought they'd be repulsed—or at least intimidated. Either one was good. He wanted the two of them to join the club, but make people uncomfortable enough in Eric's presence that they wouldn't stick around to chat too long. It wouldn't take much to make the women uncomfortable. Eric had a lascivious smirk that would scare anybody. "You grew your hair long."

Eric fluttered his eyelashes. "You like it?"

"It's all good."

"Yeah, I'm just a former Navy SEAL turned biker turned patriot." He slid his wallet across to Landry. Landry pulled it down under the table and checked the driver's license. "The ID is solid?"

"Oh, yeah. Speaking of which, here's yours from the mono vault. Good to meet you, Sean."

Landry took the zippered pouch and looked through it. "Sean Marcus Terry."

SPECTRE BLACK

They kept their voices low and conversational. It was a busy Saturday morning and the babble was continuous and loud. Mostly they ate their breakfasts and joked a little. They knew what to do—both of them had gone through intense psych training, where you learned and practiced ways to put yourself in other people's shoes.

In this case, they had to reflect—and embody—the qualities of the militia members. They had to be ready to take on that persona, and wear it.

They had to tighten up, willfully change their mindset, from belittling the weekend warriors in the militia to becoming one *of* them.

Walk a mile in their shoes.

There would be militia members who actually *were* clowns and wannabes, but many of them were serious—and smart. It would not pay to underestimate these men; some of them could catch on if there was even one wrong note sounded.

For all of Landry's belittlement of the militias privately, he knew they were dead serious. They had money, they had soldiers, they had commitment, and the group was naturally wary of strangers. If your ID didn't pass muster, you could end up with the door shut in your face, or worse—

Much worse. Some of these groups were disciplined and professional, and had a lot of money behind them.

The trick was to think like them. That was number one. And that started with respect.

"So," Eric said, "how is this gonna look?"

"The obvious? They'll try to test us, see if we're really former military."

"The guy who tests me will need new dental work."

"Also, we're both tall."

Eric smeared the last of the egg on his plate with some rye bread. His eyes on Landry's. "Yeah," he said. "They'll have to look up at us."

It sounded like a joke, but height was a valuable tool.

People relied on first impressions, and generally stuck with that impression. Two tall guys, former military, professional—that was what most of them would see. They would do background checks because it was policy, but they would accept who they were.

Talking to tall men required the converser to look up, not across. Holding that position required the person looking up to tighten the muscles in his neck and back. Tendons and muscles bore the brunt of keeping the head tilted upward. This was not a comfortable position for very long. It was harder to assess someone new when part of your mind was concentrating on holding your head in an unnatural position. So the key was to keep their new pals standing as long as possible, forcing them to look up as they gathered their initial impressions and made their first judgments. Because sooner rather than later, they would have to adjust their necks, lower their heads, just for a rest. They would see less, and maybe even hear less.

Yesterday, Landry shaved his head. He'd adopted a gold cross earring. He wore the uniform—the T-shirt that showed his musculature, the camo pants, the boots. He and his buddy would show up in the big black Dodge Ram.

Subtlety was not called for. They weren't trying to join a group of linguistics professors.

"I expect you'll be flapping your jaw," Landry said.

One thing Eric had in abundance was the ability to talk bullshit. He could talk about anything and make you believe he'd been there, done that. Landry, too, could hold up his end in a conversation, but he'd be more of a silent party. You have two people, one is the conversationalist, and the other is less so.

First impressions would be spoon-fed to the militia leaders right off the bat. They needed to mirror the people they were talking with and make sure there was plenty of common ground. They couldn't just act sincere; they had to *be* sincere.

They had to practice what Fort Bragg called Mental Transitional

Necessity and put themselves in their new partners' shoes. Find sincere common ground.

And since both Landry and Eric had learned this and used it many times, it was like putting on an old, soft, comfortable shirt.

- — -

From there they drove into Las Cruces, which hosted a gun show on the weekend. While Eric was all set, Landry needed a sniper rifle. He'd been meaning to find himself a semiautomatic, and this would be the perfect time.

They strolled around the show until Landry saw what he wanted: an H&K G3 semiautomatic sniper rifle, .308 caliber. The rifle was known for incredible long-distance accuracy—and, also important—dependability. The guy, a cricket of a man with a military haircut and goatee—so red it was almost orange—didn't do much of a sales job. He didn't need to. He just took Landry's measure and mentioned the rifle was good at the very least to a thousand yards or three-fifths of a mile, however he liked to think about it.

"You could make ten headshots in twelve seconds!"

Landry sighted through the scope.

Eric said, "Hon, it's so *you!*"

Landry thought about kicking him in the balls but he was too concentrated on the rifle.

"I'm a Christian, but I don't judge," Red Beard said. "I can throw in some armor-piercing bullets, too," he added.

He knew he had a fish on the line and didn't give a damn about Landry's sex life. He probably wouldn't care if Landry were an aardvark, if he had the money to buy.

"I'll take it," Landry said.

On their way out, Landry's eye was drawn to a table that sold a number of crazy things—posters like "Guns Don't Kill People, But if You Don't Get Out of My Way, I Will," and beer koozies with the legend "FROM MY COLD DEAD HANDS." But what caught Landry's eye was a small cardboard box of tin stars and badges. Most of them were silver in hue, but a couple were the color of cheap gold. Some of them looked real. A round gold badge caught his eye. On the top it said "DEADWOOD"—the Deadwood of gunslinger and TV series fame. The gilt was a little hard to read, but Landry liked it, so he bought it for twenty-five cents.

"What'd you want that for?" Eric asked.

"It might come in handy."

"Damn, sometimes I wish I could figure out what was inside that brainpan of yours."

From there they drove out to a deserted stretch of desert, turned off the highway onto a dirt two-track until they were far away from any farms, outbuildings, or livestock. Landry set up on a dirt berm populated by stunted mesquite and yellow bunch grass.

He took a prone sniper position, lying flat and belly-down on the berm. The bipod was mounted underneath the barrel of the rifle, and all he had to do was push the legs out and down until the H&K was ten inches off the ground.

He took several shots. Then, taking pity on Eric's abject and piteous expression, let him try a few. Twenty minutes later, Betsy II was not only baptized; she was zeroed in.

Or as Eric said it, "Betsy's one hot babe, and now she's ready to rock 'n' roll!"

- — -

Back in the Travelodge, Landry stared at himself in the mirror. His head was smooth as a cue ball, and the gold cross earring looked right at home. He thought he looked like a younger, buffer Bruce Willis.

SPECTRE BLACK

A fist rapped on his door. He peered out the window and there was Eric: ponytail, naked chest complete with tattoos, motorcycle boots, leather vest, and eye patch.

"You think this is Halloween?" Landry said. "Ditch the eye patch."

"Just fucking with you," Eric said. He pulled the eye patch off and shoved it in the pocket of his soiled-looking jeans. "Gonna actually wear a shirt, too."

"For a minute there, I thought this was going to be a *Treasure Island* revue."

"Give me a kiss and I'll take you away from all this."

"Only if you make an honest woman of me."

"Hey, you play tennis now?" Eric said, walking toward Landry's open run bag.

"They're special balls."

"I've heard that before. In fact, I've *said* that before."

"Whatever you do, don't hit one of those balls with the racket that goes with them."

"How come?"

"Boom."

"Boom?"

"As long as they don't interact at a certain velocity, we're all right. Or so says the guy who sold them to me."

"You believe him?"

Landry shrugged. "I'm not going to try to find out right now."

Eric the Red placed the ball back into its carton like a nature hiker returning an egg to a nest.

Landry contemplated the gold paint for his tooth.

"Seriously, bro," Eric said. "You think maybe we're trying too hard? A little over the top?"

"Yeah. There might be some real guys in there who are former military. Maybe too much camo."

"Jeans, knit shirts or tees, boots, and our watches," Eric said. "You're right. We don't want to overwhelm them."

— · — —

There were probably ten or twelve bars in Branch, maybe more. They chose the bars from the cars and trucks out front to the people they saw going in and out, visiting two the first night. Went in, ordered drinks, played pool. The first place was dead, so they went to the second. Much better. More of a crowd—a down-at-the-heels group. The place was smoky, dark, and verging on rowdy. They played pool with some of the locals, boasting about how good they were, but mostly losing. Gave their new friends the upper hand. They joshed each other mercilessly about their rusty pool playing, drank a little more, got a little louder, came on to the ladies. Ended up closing the place down, sitting at the bar trying to impress young women, reminiscing about the good old days in Fallujah. Neither one of them had to make up a thing. They just recounted the stories they knew by heart, stories that had gotten laughs in other bars in other places. As the night wore on, Landry and Eric appeared to get drunker. Not stinking drunk, but looser. Friendlier. More apt to talk to the people at the bar with them. Not as wary as they were when they came in. Not as tight.

But still, impressive. Two big strong guys, former military, letting go and having a good time. Looking for work here and there, they said, just seeing the country, how bad it had become, and maybe they should do something about it.

At the second bar, a guy Landry got into a conversation with told him he knew some people who felt the same way.

And Landry said, blowing a big burst of beer stink on the man, "To tell you the truth, that's one reason I'm here. My friend and me. Heard there was a militia out here, standing up for the average guy, you know—right with God. We're planning to look them up."

The guy grinned. "I'm Clint. If you want, I can introduce you."

Landry smiled blearily. "Sounds like a plan." He stood, unsteady on his feet.

"Wait until tomorrow. You want to be sober when you meet the boss."

CHAPTER 19

Landry and Eric the Red rolled into the Pine Cone RV Park around eleven a.m. They drove through the campground to the yellow cinderblock house Landry had spotted earlier. This time, two Dobermans prowled the chain-link fence enclosing the house and about a three-acre area. A sentry manned the gate—someone new to Landry. He was young, in his early twenties. Short red hair, olive drab tee, ARMY stenciled on the front, jeans, desert boots. Not too young to have served. Peaches-and-cream complexion turning red in the broiling New Mexico sun.

"What is your business, sir?"

Landry said, "I met Clint at The Cavern last night. He left his credit card behind—thought he'd want it back."

"Oh, wow." The kid blushed a little. He stepped back. "He's gonna be happy to see that."

"That's what I figured, son."

The kid opened the gate. As Landry drove through, he saluted.

They parked between a late-model black Humvee, polished to a gleam, and an old Dodge truck with mismatched fenders. Two vehicles, different ZIP codes.

Landry heard the door to the house squeak and a man stepped out onto the stoop. Youngish guy, dressed like the kid manning the gate. "Who're you?" he asked.

"Name's Sean. Sean Terry." He motioned to Eric. This is my buddy, Mark. Is Clint around?"

"Yeah." The man leaned in through the doorway and yelled, "Clint! You got visitors!"

Clint came out, a little green around the gills. He'd had a lot to drink the night before. He seemed confused for a moment, but then his face cleared and he smiled as he recognized Landry. "Hey."

"Hey, man, how you doing?"

Clint held his head. "Not too good. You here to talk to the boss man?"

"Yeah, thought I might. You remember Mark, right?" Motioning to Eric.

"Kinda." Clint sat down on the top step.

"You left this behind." Landry held up the credit card.

"Oh, shit!" He grabbed at it and Landry handed it to him. "Good thing you were there."

"Yeah. I went outside to flag you down but you were already gone."

Clint put his head in his hands. Landry was prone to headaches, and he knew how bad they could be. He sympathized, but he also had business to conduct. "You looking for new guys?" he asked.

"I said so, didn't I?" Still rubbing his temple.

Landry waited.

Finally, Clint stood up. "First, you gotta meet the boss man."

- — -

They trooped over to the building on the opposite end of the compound, the one marked "OFFICE," near the sewer dump.

The bell on the door rang as they went in.

The place was small and cramped, a minimart with limited shelf space, selling mostly camping supplies like small jars of mustard and medium-size bags of charcoal. The focal point of the place was the Coors waterfall sign on the wall behind the cash register.

The air conditioner must have been on the fritz. It was hot and stifling inside, and dark.

"Wait here," Clint said. He walked to the back door near the beer and soft drink cooler and disappeared.

The guy who had been watering plants on the porch came inside and stood behind them. He had been completely silent. Landry made note of this and took a closer look.

He was short, compact, and muscular. Landry didn't see him yesterday. Maybe he had been out manning one of the checkpoints.

"It's gonna be a while," the man from the porch said.

"Fine by me," Landry said. He shoved his hands in his pockets and looked around the store, taking note of everything. He said nothing. Eric said nothing. They stood there.

Awkward.

Finally the man from the porch said, "Why do you want to join us?"

"Are you the boss?" Landry asked.

"No."

"I'll tell the boss."

The guy gave him a dirty look, but didn't take the bait.

"Where'd you serve?" Landry asked.

"Afghanistan. How about you?"

"Afghanistan and Iraq."

"What detachment?"

Landry said, "Not your business."

The guy stared at him for a moment, seemed to take that in, and then relaxed. Landry realized it wasn't relaxation so much as recognition. Recognition, and respect.

"What about him?" the guy said, nodding in Eric's direction. Eric was spinning the revolving rack of paperbacks, seemingly preoccupied.

"You can ask. He speaks English."

The guy looked away. They waited in uncomfortable silence. The door to the back opened: Clint. "Come with me," he said.

"Where are we going?" Eric said.

"Like I said. To meet the boss."

- — -

The door to the back let out to a short hallway, leading to an office. Nice view of the hills. The window, though, was reinforced by bars. Landry recognized Lion Mane.

Seeing him up close, Landry thought: *pink and yellow*. The man's face was deep pink—sunburn or high blood pressure, or both. And his hair was even more yellow than he'd thought—unnatural-looking, but Landry knew it was real. He had sandy brows to go with it. A tiny scar cleaved one side of his upper lip.

He wore a bulletproof vest under his blue work shirt. He was armed with a Heckler & Koch 9mm—shoulder holster.

Watery blue-gray eyes assessed first Landry, then Eric.

Since the man was approximately five feet eight, he had a distance to look up. "So you're interested in joining our little band of patriots."

"That is the plan," Landry said.

The man said nothing in reply. His watery orbs were like searchlights piercing the gloom. First it was Landry's turn. The man showed no discomfort in their looming presence. With a lesser man, looking up like that, there would be discomfort by now, but he kept Landry in his sights, as if it had turned into a battle of wills. Finally, he transferred his gaze to Eric—boldly assessing him. Eric, being Eric, boldly assessed him back.

Finally, the militia leader nodded. He reached out and shook hands with them both. A strong handshake, but Landry sensed he had steeled it—he'd felt a slight tremor. "Jedediah Kilbride's my name. Call me 'Jed' for short. Have a seat, gentlemen."

They did.

He looked from one to the other. "What do you think we do here?"

Landry crossed his arms over his chest and stretched out his legs. "I think your primary mission is keeping the peace."

Kilbride's face remained impassive. "How so?"

"To my way of thinking, the sheriff's office is undermanned. There's an influx of people coming up from Mexico, from Central America, more every day. That means more people, and the people of this area, the people who *live here*, are underserved. I see your group as a necessary adjunct to law enforcement." He added, "I think of you as an extension of the sheriff's office, only independent and far more flexible. The very definition of a militia—boots on the ground at a moment's notice—that's what it means to be 'keepers of the peace.'" His gaze held fast to Kilbride's watery eyes. "Am I wrong about that?"

Kilbride said nothing. He was still assessing Landry and Eric. His eyes missed nothing.

So Landry gave him nothing.

"Sir." Eric leaned forward, his expression earnest. "We want to do something. We've both been in the military; we're useful guys. I fought for my country and protected my country, and I plan to *keep* protecting her. Whether it's with you here or with another militia, I want to serve. I want in."

Kilbride tapped his fingertips on the desk. He was thinking seriously about them. Landry noted that he was also unconsciously leaning forward, engaged. "Why us? Why here?"

Landry shrugged. "It's as good a place as any. I have family here."

"Whereabouts?"

"Hobbs."

"That's practically in Texas." He leaned back and assessed them some more. "How about we do some shooting?"

Landry shrugged. "Suits me."

They went to the range that had been set up a quarter of a mile away from the campground.

Spent a couple of hours shooting, everything from handguns to sniper rifles. Landry set up his new sniper rifle: Betsy II. Made one shot.

It was a good one.

They walked back toward the main house.

"We don't have any room here," Kilbride said, "So you'll have to commute. We're ten minutes from town. This is a volunteer position, so you rely on yourselves to tighten up, and when we need you, we'll need you ASAP. Drop whatever you're doing, got me? Justice and the security of this country never sleep. I'll have background checks done on both of you, just so you know." He reached into the pocket of his jeans and pulled out two wafer-thin cell phones, threw one to Landry and one to Eric. "Don't call me unless it's important. The number can*not* be given around. It's for your own personal use. You're on call twenty-four-seven."

"Yes, sir."

"Just so you know what we do. We're like an auxiliary force: we patrol the area. Much like the cops do—we're looking for trouble. We want to keep this area, this part of the county, *safe*. That's why we have two checkpoints, on the road into Branch and the road out. There's a lot of illegal activity, and a *lot* of illegals. Our job is to assist the sheriff as much as we can. Now," he added, "I know you served in the armed forces, and that's a fine thing to do. The best men come from that training, that *experience*. But we are patriots here, and as much as I revere the United States of America, this here is a sovereign entity of its own—We are, and so is New Mexico. We give our allegiance to the sheriff of this county first, and to New

Mexico second, and to the United States of America, which has been badly corrupted and weakened by the current administration, third. Understood?"

"It's the way it should be," Eric said. "That's the way the Founding Fathers planned it. The sheriff is the law here."

"Damn straight." He looked at them both. "Take off your sunglasses."

They did.

"Good. You're good men. I can see that. You have served your country. Now you will serve this state, this county. You will assist the good people who need protection from the interlopers and those who would interfere with our sovereign rights.

"This can be a boring job. I know you are warriors, but you need to understand this. Mostly, we stand at the ramparts. We stand at the ramparts and watch. Because if we don't, who will?"

"No one, sir!" Eric said.

Landry wanted to pummel him.

Fortunately for them, Lion Mane didn't have a good ear for irony. He accepted Eric's gung-ho attitude at face value.

That was his first mistake.

CHAPTER 20

Landry and Eric fell into a pattern. They showed up, did their job, were dependable. They carried themselves as the professionals they were. Within a very short time, this engendered respect. Landry and Eric were the real deal and the rest of the group (twelve men, three women) looked up to them. Often, they asked for advice, or asked about their deployments.

They saw little of the boss. Kilbride didn't live on the property but in a Mediterranean-style mini-villa in Branch, in the same neighborhood as Miko Denboer lived. The part of Branch where houses were categorized by address and square footage.

Kilbride held a party in honor of his two new members. It was a nice evening, the party outside, a fireplace surrounded by a low rock parapet to keep the evening chill away. They watched a perfect sunset. The food was excellent, and so was the wine, although Landry pretended to drink more than he did. They met all the players, including the man Landry thought of as Western Hat. It turned out that Western Hat—his name was David Bruce—was the moneyman. He bankrolled the operation. Bruce was the son of a Montana congressman who had died a couple of years before in a plane crash. Dave Bruce the younger was currently running for his father's seat.

Landry wondered what the younger Bruce was doing down here. He was far from his constituency. He had looked up David

Bruce Senior's web page and saw that he was very pro-military. When it came to warfare, he had wanted more of everything. He'd particularly been a big supporter of the Stealth Bomber.

It was a nice evening—pleasant ambience, spectacular view of the valley—but no one talked much. It wasn't a party atmosphere. The militia members were careful to watch their alcohol intake. It felt more like a field trip than a party—everyone on his best behavior.

They didn't talk much about what they were doing, possibly because they weren't doing anything except stopping people on a road before letting them continue on. They talked about the food, the guys talked about the good-looking ladies they'd seen around, they talked about their cars, and all of them talked generally about the wasteland the US had become. But there wasn't much passion to it.

They completely ignored the elephant in the room: the three militia members who had been shot to death. Landry would have thought that would be their chief concern. That there would be conspiracy theories about who had come after one of theirs. As he went from group to group collected around the bar or in knots by the fire, he thought he would hear people talking about the recent loss of their cohorts. He thought they would be talking about what they'd do if they found whoever killed them. But no one said anything about the shootings.

Landry realized they were keeping quiet because they were scared that the same thing would happen to them.

He spotted the guy he had manned the checkpoint with today, Luke, standing by the low stone parapet overlooking the town. Landry joined him. "Great view," he said.

"Yeah."

The guy seemed preoccupied—subdued.

Landry had noticed that while they were manning the checkpoint, there was a certain swagger to the militia members Landry had been paired with. But at this party, everyone was circumspect.

He got the impression they didn't want to talk too much, for fear of saying the wrong thing.

Who made them feel that way? Was it Western Hat—Dave Bruce? Or was it the head of the militia himself, Kilbride?

Landry said, "What I wouldn't do for a place like this."

"Yeah."

"You live out here, or did you come from elsewhere?"

Cyril Landry, Master of Small Talk.

"Elsewhere."

"Oh? Whereabouts? I hail from California."

Luke said, "That's nice."

"Something on your mind? You don't look like you're enjoying the party."

Landry waited for an answer. If it was "What's it to you?" or "Mind your own fucking business," he would drop it.

Luke shaded his eyes against the sunset and squinted up at him. Landry was aware of all the muscles and tendons in the neck that the man would use, expected him to look away after making eye contact. But he looked him square in the eye. "Take my advice and leave while you can."

"I just joined up."

Luke turned back to look at the valley. Mumbled something. A dismissal, Landry thought. "What'd you say, pard? I have a right to know if my buddy and I have stepped in something."

Luke turned to face Landry. One side of his mouth turned up. "Pard? Seriously?"

Landry could tell this was a smart kid. Twenty-five to twenty-eight, he thought, but he was still just a kid. "So why are you still here?"

"It's easy to get in, but not so easy to get out."

"What do you mean by that?"

"Ask Rick Connor."

"Who's he?"

"You don't know?"

"Was that the guy who got blown away at the checkpoint? You think someone's out to get us?"

Luke turned back to the sunset. His expression was bitter.

"Is that it? Are we being targeted?"

The kid said nothing.

"Is someone targeting us? Is it the police? The sheriff? The Feds?"

The kid just shook his head.

"Was it about the guy who was shot at the checkpoint? Listen, my buddy and I, we have wives and kids. I don't plan to end up like that guy. Are we fucking up here? Is this what it's supposed to be or is there—"

"Shut up," the kid said.

"Look, if you want to get out . . . we can help you."

"I doubt that."

"We're—"

"Former Navy SEALs. Yeah, I know." Sarcastic. "Why would a former Navy SEAL sign up with this bogus outfit? Seriously. Who are you guys trying to fool? Either you're spying on us or you're crazy."

"Why'd you join?"

"Because I thought the country was getting shot to shit. I thought we would be going after illegals, but that's not what we're doing."

"What are you doing?"

Luke shook his head.

"I have a right to know."

"If I said anything . . ." He shook his head once more. "Never mind."

He turned away to walk back to the party.

Landry said, "Hand me your phone."

"What?"

"Hand me your phone."

The kid handed him his phone. Landry typed in "Jackson

Automotive," and the cell number of his burner phone and handed it back to him. He transcribed the kid's number into his own phone. He handed back the phone. "Just in case," he said.

- — -

The next day, the kid was gone.

Landry was heading for one of their battered black vehicles when Kilbride fell into step with him.

"You notice there's one less member around here?"

Landry said, "The kid."

"Yeah, Luke."

"What happened?"

"It was too much for him. Most guys wash out early on—it's kind of like natural selection."

"Too bad."

"Not really."

Landry started to walk away.

Kilbride called out, "I want to talk to you."

"So talk."

"Not here." He handed Landry his binoculars and pointed in the direction of an oak-covered hill. "See that cabin up there in the trees?"

Landry took the binocs. "The cabin with the green roof?"

"Yep. There's a trailhead about a mile up the road from here, on forestland. You hike on up there and wait for me."

"Okay."

- — -

On the road, Landry walked to the entrance gate and crossed onto National Forest land. He followed the blacktop until he came to the dirt track leading up the hill to the cabin.

As always, he stayed hidden by the trees and circled the cabin, checking it out from all sides.

As always, Eric had gone ahead and was somewhere in the trees, probably above, where he could watch. He'd been put on sentry duty today, ostensibly watching over the compound. Instead, he had followed the trail into the National Forest. He would stay in touch by radio and go back to the compound if need be.

If anyone tracked them, they would know the two men had left the reservation. Eric had his story ready. He was a hunter, and he'd spotted a doe and followed her. It was out of season, but he enjoyed tracking and liked to keep his chops up.

They both knew this: Telling a successful lie was nine-tenths believing that lie absolutely.

Landry waited outside the cabin. A car engine droned down below him on the road. Kilbride's late-model Land Rover appeared through the trees.

Kilbride parked, but remained inside.

Landry waited.

Finally, Kilbride exited the Land Rover, his Ruger at his side—just in case—and looked around him. "Sean Marcus Terry!" he shouted. "Are you here?"

Landry trained his own weapon on Kilbride, just in case.

Kilbride holstered his weapon. "Sean? Answer me!"

Landry held his own weapon close to his leg and trotted down.

"You're a distrustful son of a bitch, aren't you?" Kilbride said.

"Better safe than sorry's my motto."

"I want to discuss some business with you."

"What would that be?"

"Let's go inside."

They walked up to the cabin and up the shallow steps. Kilbride showed him around. It looked like a regular cabin, but the walls were reinforced—ten inches thick all around, and bulletproof glass windows. It was homey, if you didn't notice the surveillance video monitors covering every inch of the property including the encroaching pines, comms, and stockpiles of weapons.

They sat in a small room off the kitchen where they could look out at the forest and see the road below. The row of windows was reinforced. Kilbride demonstrated the rolling metal window covers that came down with a push of the button. He buzzed it back up.

"I think we'll be okay, don't you?"

Landry shrugged.

Kilbride leaned forward on his elbows and studied Landry. Said, "I know who you are."

Landry kept his expression neutral and said nothing.

"I've checked you out. You're a former Navy SEAL all right, but you're not here to join this two-bit militia."

"I'm not?"

"You're no weekend warrior reliving your glory days. You're not like the rest of these guys, these fucking misfits. I pegged you right away—you and your buddy are not the kind of guys who play in the kiddie pool. My guess is you're under deep cover and you're on to something in this valley."

Landry said nothing.

"So you don't want to enlighten me as to exactly who you are? That's fine by me. I don't care about that. What I care about is your skill set."

A car went by down below, and both of them watched it. It kept going.

"Where were we?" Kilbride said. "Ah. Yes. I don't know what you're doing here, but you interest me."

"Why is that?"

"Because right now I've come to the end of the road with Denboer.

"His son killed three of my people. Shot my best man at that checkpoint. I figure you know about that because my people claimed it was the car you were driving."

"I didn't kill them."

"If I thought you had, you'd be dead already."

Landry smiled. "I doubt that."

Kilbride slapped Landry's shoulder. "See? That's what I mean. You're the real deal. There was a guy looked like you, saw him on the news once—must have been a year ago now. Made big headlines. But apparently it was a fake sighting. Turned out the guy was dead. Killed in a firefight in Florida."

"Oh?"

Kilbride settled deeper into his chair, leaned forward, and rested his elbows on the table. "That's what I heard."

Landry said nothing.

"You don't say much, do you?"

"Just waiting for you to get to the point."

He leaned closer, so his face was right up against Landry's. "How's this? I want you to kill Jace Denboer." He leaned back and smiled.

"Why?"

"He set you up."

"He didn't know me. He just picked a random car. I won the lottery."

"You're a funny one. Let me give you my theory. My theory is you're here for a reason. What could that reason be? You tell me."

When Landry didn't answer, Kilbride said, "Remember the guy who was in a firefight in Florida, the one you remind me of? As I recall, there was a sheriff's detective in the middle of it, a real hero. Her name was Jolie Burke. Strange coincidence that she's a sheriff's detective here in this town, and now you're here, too. If it's true, if it's the same person and she's, let's say she's missing, I can help you with that, too. I can help both her and you."

"You and *her*," Landry said.

"*What?*"

"You. And. Her. Better yet, you should say 'I can help both of you.'"

SPECTRE BLACK

Kilbride looked puzzled for a moment, then grinned. He clapped Landry on the shoulder. "You've just corrected my grammar! I'll be damned!"

"What do you know about Burke's situation?" Landry asked.

"Just that she's in hot water with her own sheriff's department. What I'm offering you is a chance to get even."

"How do you know she's in trouble with the sheriff's department?"

"You don't think I have a few people in the department that I talk to? And all of a sudden a detective just disappears? You're the right man for the job. So how about we get down to brass tacks?"

"You have me confused with someone else. I'm not a hit man."

"That's not what I heard. What about Florida? What about Iraq? What about Afghanistan? What about *Aspen?*" He let the last reference hang in the air for a moment. "Let me make this crystal clear, soldier. I know who you are. I know what you did in Aspen. I know about Florida; I fucking did my *homework*. Kill Jace Denboer and I won't say a word."

Landry looked at Kilbride and considered the offer. Kilbride watched him avidly, like a lion studying a gazelle. "Tell me what you know about Rick Connor."

"I know he was a good man. Former military, like yourself. Like me. He shouldn't have died like that."

"Do you know why Jace shot him?"

"Maybe Connor was undercover. Or maybe he was like you. I know men like you. You're not good at civilian life. You only feel alive when you're being a hard-ass. Or when you're on a mission. Which is why you'd be perfect for this job."

Landry stood. "If you're looking for an assassin, I'm not your man."

Kilbride rose and thrust his head forward, which put him approximately in the vicinity of Landry's Adam's apple. "I know who you are." He tapped his own chest. "*Inside.* I know *what* you are!"

"You've been watching too many *24* reruns."

"Maybe so, but this is a mission. You don't turn down a mission, especially when there's so much at stake."

Landry was no poker player, but he knew the man thought he had the winning hand. And he was anxious to show his cards.

Kilbride's next words confirmed his suspicion.

"Did I tell you?" Kilbride said. "I know people who have extensive ties to law enforcement—all kinds, Border Patrol, local cops, Feds—all over the southwest. But thanks to politics, a lot of hands are tied."

"So?"

"Jace Denboer, that fucking little rich kid, killed *three* of my *best people*. Maybe you don't care about my problems, but I'm willing to pay for your expertise. It's clear you can handle yourself. You know your way around an operation, and that's what I need."

Landry said nothing.

"I can pay the going rate, whatever that is these days, you just name it. I don't care how you do it but I want him dead, and I want him to know why. You with me?"

"The kid with the Camaro, his father owns the agricultural farm? I hear he owns the town, too."

Kilbride nodded. "And the sheriff's office. That's why I need you."

The man must have thought that because Landry was big, he was also stupid.

"If he owns the town, you're in trouble."

"I'll take that chance."

"I'll think about it and get back to you," Landry said.

CHAPTER 21

It had been a bad day. Not bad enough to take his meds, but almost. Jace had gone to see a friend of his, but they'd had an argument and he started seeing things he knew weren't real. Nothing crazy. Just a cockroach running across the floor and up the wall and across the ceiling.

And some colors. Dirty-colored rainbows.

Now, though, he was fine—better than fine. It was all good.

He saw the checkpoint outside Branch, and tried not to let the memories eat at him. Nothing to worry about; they always waved him through. Usually, they stood at full attention, like he was a visiting dignitary.

And seriously: Who would try to stop him?

There was a new batch of militia members today, but it didn't matter. They came and they went. Bunch of weekend warriors playing soldier, most of them giving up after a few days of boring sentry duty in the hot sun. Plenty of flies around here, too, thanks to the hog farm nearby.

He expected them to step back and let him drive through as usual. He knew they were scared shitless—for obvious reasons. They knew he wouldn't take shit from anyone. He had demonstrated that, for sure. If they didn't know it before he blew away that spy, Connor, they knew it now.

There was a car ahead of him, though, and even Jace Denboer couldn't crash through an immovable object. So he waited, revving the Camaro's engine, thrilling to the big, throaty roar, a Z28, 500-hp, 7.0-liter dry-sump LS7 V8, to be specific. That would put the fear of God into anyone! Get past this asshole and he'd be on his way, per usual.

One of the militia, though, was looking at him. Not just looking at him, but *scrutinizing* him. The tall guy with the shaved head and the tiny gold cross earring. Even though the big guy's face was impassive, even though he wore dark aviator shades, even though his arms were crossed at his chest and not lingering near his hip where his sidearm was . . . even so, Jace knew the man was drilling through him with his eyes.

He could feel it. Not just the X-ray eyes, but the man seemed to have some kind of powers beyond that. Suddenly he felt bugs crawling on his arms, up his neck, onto his face. He always sensed when he was under scrutiny. That was happening more and more nowadays. And it made him flinchy.

For a minute he thought about confronting the guy: *do you know who I AM?* But his father had told him to keep a low profile, and he understood why.

"I had to promise the sheriff's office you'd be a model citizen," his dad said.

He'd never even been charged in the shooting of the guy at the checkpoint. That was because, although there were witnesses, there were no witnesses. How about *that* for a paradox?

Still, a lot of people were after him, waiting for him to make another mistake, and there were spies everywhere.

He had to comply out of self-defense. "Walk the straight and narrow," he mumbled to himself. "Walk the straight and narrow, walk the straight and narrow . . ."

SPECTRE BLACK

But Connor was a spy—he deserved what happened to him. Didn't they *get* that? He was a goddamn *spy*. Jace had done the right thing, and if given the chance, he'd do it again.

Finally the car in front of him moved away. He'd reached the entry point.

The man stood there. His face was impassive. Like he didn't give a damn who Jace was. No expression at all. Just those crossed arms, the light gleaming on the top of his shaved head. New guy.

Possibly, bodyguard material.

Jace had to crank his head way up to look at the guy's face. The guy didn't lean down to him. Didn't wave him through, either. Just stood there, peering through the window at him, like that guy on the commercial, Mr. Clean.

The guy made a cranking motion for him to buzz down the window. The air conditioning was on, and Jace didn't feel like cranking down the window, so he just stared defiantly at Mr. Clean, slammed his hand on the horn, and kept it there. He yelled, "Get out of my way!" Once he started yelling he kept at it. Added a few choice words. Every invective he could think of, but the guy just stood there with his arms folded, so tall it was almost impossible to keep looking up at his face. He was so busy yelling at Mr. Clean, he didn't see a dark blue Suburban come around him, pull in front, flash on the backup lights, and back up to his front bumper.

Behind him, he heard another engine, and saw the grille of a black Suburban, jutting up high over his back bumper.

He was trapped.

Mr. Clean made the rolling motion with his hand again.

Jace felt the coldness in the pit of his gut. He'd been afraid of a lot of things lately, but *this!* It was like quicksilver rippled straight down his legs, making them unmanageable. His heartbeat tripled; blood pounded in his ears.

Mr. Clean was holding a tire iron. He motioned Jace to roll down the window again, make it quick—

A tire iron! His *car!*

He buzzed the window down. Stared up at the man. The man ducked his head down to Jace's level, and Jace was transfixed by his face. By his moving lips. He almost didn't hear what the man had to say, because what had once looked like Mr. Clean had become a viper's head. Not completely, but close enough. Jace could see the faint outlines underneath—what Mr. Clean *really* was.

Paranoia. Hallucinations. He should have taken his meds.

Then the Suburban in front of him pulled forward and off to the side. The viper's head receded as if it had never been there in the first place. Mr. Clean said to Jace, "You and I are going to talk, soon."

"Bullshit. No way I'm talking to a weekend warrior playing soldier."

"No? Maybe you should know that someone's gunning for you. I can help you with that." He slipped Jace a burner phone. "There's one number on here. Call it." He leaned in closer, so that his face was within an inch of Jace's startled eyes. "And don't tell your sister. She's one of the people who are after you."

Then he stood back and tapped on the roof.

"You may proceed."

CHAPTER 22

Landry and Eric the Red hit the chimichanga place for lunch, sat outside in the shade of the building, looking out at the parking lot. Landry told him about his run-in with Jace.

"You warned the kid? Why'd you do that?"

"I gave him a fair chance. Who knows if he'll take my advice? He's so full of himself and his Magic Car he probably thinks he's bulletproof."

"Why, though? Why'd you warn him?"

"A couple of reasons. Kilbride, for one. He called me an assassin."

Eric looked at him as if he were crazy. "Well, you are one."

"I don't consider myself to be an assassin. I don't kill for money. What that is, is stereotyping. You see some big guy who's former military and he can handle himself, you automatically think he's a killer for hire? Kilbride's assumption rubbed me the wrong way."

"Okay." Eric rested a size-thirteen foot on the extra chair. "So now you've set his ass up to get killed. You warn him, too? It's the least you could do."

"I did warn him."

"How'd he take it?"

"He took it like the tough guy he is. He asked me if I wanted the hit or not."

"Cold."

"I suggested that he should take off for a while and let things cool down, but he said it's the principle of the thing. He said he'd just find someone else. Said he wasn't for damn sure going to be scared off by a spoiled kid with money."

Eric removed his foot from the chair and stretched his legs out, staring into the parking lot. "Don't look now, but there's a lady who can't get enough of you."

"Behind me?"

"Yeah. Standing by a brand-new Jaguar. She's staring a hole right through you, bro. Don't look. She's hot, though. Rich, too, judging by those wheels."

"Description?"

"Slim, legs you could buy by the yard, long, dark hair but she's got those pretty blond highlights, you know what I mean? Upscale suit, matching shoes, cheekbones to die for . . ."

The wind shifted and it was chill. Landry stared into the plate-glass window of the chimi place and saw the car and the woman beside it. She shaded her eyes and stared in his direction. He remembered the last time he'd looked into a window's reflection, the day he met her. "Carla Vitelli."

"The FBI agent Albuquerque sent to look for Jolie? You have any idea what her game is?"

"She was the one who got me put in jail."

"She the one who set you up with that crazy cracker tried to kill you, Earl? That's cold, man."

Landry shrugged. Water under the bridge. "Still there?"

"Still there. She's leaning on the truck adjusting her shoe. You want me to go over and talk to her?"

"I can fight my own battles." Landry stood up and turned to face the parking lot. A gust of wind blew past, shuttling a paper cup across the pavement. Landry started in Carla's direction.

She climbed into the Jaguar, gunned the engine, and backed out of the parking space. Turned in his direction. Expensive sunglasses concealed her eyes. She drove past without bothering to look at him, her expression impassive. She reminded him of a mannequin. The car reached the street and turned right onto the thoroughfare. Eric whistled. "Cold, brother. Cold."

They gave it ten minutes before walking to the truck. Landry reached down, felt under the left rear panel, and produced a transponder.

"Cute," Eric said.

Landry leaned against the car next to the truck to check his shoe and clamped it behind the rear tire.

"What next?" Eric asked as he opened the driver's door.

"We split up."

Eric drove him back to the Travelodge. Landry would miss the plush seats and the growling engine of the Dodge Ram, but the Forenza would do just as well.

As Landry walked to his Forenza, he placed a call to the militia kid, Luke. He got a message, and left one of his own. Landry wondered if the kid was busy or if he was scared.

Twenty minutes later, his phone buzzed. The readout showed the number for Luke Winkler.

"What do you want?" Winkler said. His voice was a little on the high side; he was spooked.

"Did Rick Connor ever talk about what was going on at Denboer's farm?"

"I don't know if I should—"

"This is not going to go away. I *will* find you. The best thing you can do is give me the information and I'll leave you out of it. What do you know? What did Rick Connor tell you?"

"He told me to stay away."

"From Denboer's farm? Why?"

"I don't know why."

"He didn't say anything else?"

"He just told me to get out of the militia. That they could be in a lot of trouble."

"They could be in a lot of trouble? Do you know what he meant by that?"

"No."

"Have you been to his house?"

"Yeah. I can show it to you."

"Just give me the address. I'll find it myself. Was he living with anyone else?"

"No."

"And you were there on how many occasions?"

"Just once." Added hastily, "It was a party. For the militia."

"Did you know the other two who were killed? The man and the woman. Gary Short and Amy Diehl?"

"Kind of. I worked the checkpoint with them."

"They tell you anything about the shooting? The guy who came through?"

"They said it was some guy in a white car."

Landry and Eric had a checkpoint to man. They were relieved by the evening shift, grabbed something to eat, and drove to Rick Connor's rental house.

The house was old, probably built in the forties or fifties. And small. There was a pocket porch surrounded by arches. White stucco over adobe, Landry thought, a Bermuda grass lawn, and beds full of flowers. An enormous eucalyptus tree that would scare the bejesus out of any thinking person during a thunderstorm.

A big "FOR RENT" sign stood outside, with a notation to inquire next door.

The man who answered the door must have been in his eighties. He was stringy, as if he'd recently lost a lot of weight. Most of his weight hung down below his waist. He was tanned, with white hair and wire-rim glasses.

He showed them around. The house was dark despite the ancient dome lights set in the ceilings, and smelled of something bad. Landry thought it might be rat poison. He told the old man, whose name was Ben, that Rick Connor was his cousin. Ben wasn't too interested. He was watching *Wheel of Fortune* and he wanted to get back to it. He told them to go ahead and take what they wanted—otherwise it was going to Goodwill— and bring back the key when they were done.

Rick Connor traveled light. There was virtually nothing that gave a clue as to who he was, other than some neatly folded knit shirts, underwear, and jeans nestled into the chest of drawers. A few frozen dinners in the refrigerator, a couple of bottles of beer.

They assumed that the homicide detectives had been thorough, but it had been some time ago and the yellow tape that would have sealed the porch was gone. Landry wasn't sure if it would be sheriff's or the local PD.

He hoped the homicide detectives weren't *that* thorough.

He hoped they missed something he and Eric were looking for: a thumb drive.

They looked everywhere. Fortunately for Ben, he did not see them slit open the sofa cushions and the innards of the chairs and couches. He did not see them take the toilet apart or unscrew and remove faucets in the shower and the sinks. Or pull the old refrigerator out and go through the back.

They tried everything they could think of but came up empty. There was no thumb drive.

"His car?" Eric the Red said.

"Looks like it's been towed. We'll have to find out where."

"Let's try the front and back yards."

There was a small backyard. It felt as if they had been sent back in time to the 1950s. There was an old table and iron chairs, rusting in the New Mexico sun. Probably had the original paint on it, which was a sort of dusky rose that went well with the rust. They dug up the flower beds all the way around the house. Again, nothing.

Ben didn't hear them as they took the house apart. It must have been a damn good *Wheel of Fortune.*

"What now?" Eric said, slightly out of breath.

They were out front, just having finished unscrewing the porch light. Landry passed a hand over his brow and looked skyward. The sun was almost down. "What's that?" he said.

"What's what?"

Landry pointed to the ceramic roof tiles.

"Oh, shit. You want to look under all those tiles?"

"I don't think we'll have to," Landry said. He pointed to the third tile over. Like every other tile on the roof, it formed half of a circle, the brittle terra cotta tile creating a semicircle of negative space. Landry spotted tiny branches stuffed into the mouth.

"Probably a bird nest," Eric said.

"Or a hiding place."

- — -

A thumb drive was tucked deep inside the hollow, camouflaged by leaves and stems from the eucalyptus tree. And just beyond that was a small camera, state of the art. A car went by on the street, but didn't slow. Landry up to his shoulder in the hollow. He threw the camera and the thumb drive down to Eric, who pocketed both of them smoothly, just as the screen door to the neighboring house squeaked open and banged shut. "You boys find anything for your trouble?" Ben asked.

"No, sir," Eric said. He walked up to shake Ben's hand. Ben withdrew his hand and looked at the roll of cash. "You don't need to do this, sir."

Eric clapped him on the shoulder. "Trust us. We do. Wishing you a very good night."

On the way back, Eric said, "Let's hope it's not photos of Connor's son's Little League team."

- — -

At the Travelodge, Eric plugged the thumb drive into his MacBook Air—and swore. "The drive's blank."

"Encrypted?"

"Hold on." He tried a couple of things. "I don't think . . . What's this? 'Show Hidden Files.'" He clicked to open.

A video appeared on the screen.

It was short and went fast. One moment it was there, and then it went black.

"What the hell?" Eric ran it again—eight seconds, tops. He had to run it again and again before the pieces fell into place.

The cam was shaky, handheld. Someplace in the hinterlands, desert. A road: tarmac. Dusk or dawn. A smattering of lights blurred in the background. All of it behind a chain-link fence.

Then: three tiny jets of spray shot up from the wet surface of the road, accompanied by the sound Landry knew well: the engine of a small plane. The other noise was a rubbery chirp of tires as the plane touched down.

"Look at that," a man's voice whispered. "Virtually invisible."

The phantom plane's wheels hopped along the tarmac. Landry

could only assume that was the case, because he couldn't see the wheels. He could only see the water flung up by the tires.

He amended that: he saw only a *shadow* of the wheels. A shadow of the plane.

Like a layer of plane-shaped gauze, overlapping the scenery. Now you see it, now you don't.

The small plane whisked by and out of frame. Virtually invisible.

The handheld camera juddered up and down. "Did you get that?" the male voice whispered. "Jesus."

The video went black.

"Play it again," Landry said.

Eric played it again. And again. And again. They heard the sound of the small plane's engine, the squeak as the wheels touched tarmac. They saw little sprays of water on the hard surface as the wheels came down and then bumped up again: one, two, three.

But no plane.

Just the neutral gray of dusk in black and white. Just the feeling that the landscape beyond the landing strip seemed to scroll by, misshapen as a fun-house mirror.

What they could see. Which wasn't very much.

Dusk.

The video went black.

"You recognize the area?" Landry asked.

"Airport?"

"Maybe."

"Private airstrip."

"The buildings behind were low. Am I right about that?"

They watched the video again.

"Low," Eric said. "One long, single-story building."

"Were those trees on the right side of the frame? Just as the plane was coming in?"

They played it again.

SPECTRE BLACK

"Trees," Eric said.

"Poplars," Landry said. "There are three agricultural farms in the valley outside of town."

He recalled the three farms he'd driven past on the way to Branch. The buildings on one of the farms were beige with gray roofs. The second one he'd passed had been similar in layout; only the buildings had rust-red roofs. He remembered the white sign with the blue legend, the drawing of a bird—Heron Lake. Heron Lake Agricultural Farm.

The third farm was mostly manufactured steel buildings. Poplar trees lined the roads. Valleyview Experimental Agricultural Station. The farm also had an airstrip.

And the third farm had bean fields.

Milepost 120. That was the general starting place for the three big experimental farms. They ended by 122 at the most. There would be no trouble finding them.

"Any doubt Rick Connor was undercover?" Eric said.

"Nope."

"Connor sure got an eyeful, that's for sure. You'd think the DEA would have agents all over this place by now. But not a sign of them."

"Maybe he wasn't able to make contact with them."

"That can happen when somebody drives up and blows you to kingdom come. I bet someone would give his firstborn son to get his hands on this video . . . such as it is."

"If they know it exists." Landry thought about it. "I wonder who will turn up in town next."

"Probably, they're already here."

- — -

The next day and the day after that Landry and Eric manned their respective checkpoints. It was an easy job. Stand around, look intimidating, stop motorists, more often than not just telling them to be careful and look out for illegal aliens. Every once in a while, give some hard-ass a tough time. Show me your ID, that kind of thing. The same deal Landry had gotten when he'd gone through.

The good thing about being in the militia, all you had to do was throw your weight around, and nobody would dare stop you. Most people Landry stopped made a conscious effort not to engage. Big men in military gear who were clearly not with any government agency made the average Joe nervous, or at least contemplative. Landry would be willing to bet that anyone coming through the checkpoint wouldn't be able to remember his face. They would remember his body armor, they would remember the assault rifle slung across his back, but they would likely not remember his face. His father and mother had done him a huge favor by giving him a generic face. As an operator, he had done his level best to use that competitive advantage wisely.

One person who *did* remember him was Jace Denboer. The second time Landry encountered him at the checkpoint, Jace wanted to set up a meeting. Landry told him no, they had nothing to discuss. Then Jace dangled the carrot. He thought Landry would be the ideal man to work security for him.

Landry said he'd have to think about it.

Always good to play hard to get.

CHAPTER 23

The third time Jace asked the man he knew as Sean Marcus Terry if he would take the job as a security officer at his father's farm, Landry had already quit the militia and prepared for his next place of employment. He called the number Jace Denboer had given him and got him on the first ring. He said he'd thought it over and was interested in interviewing for the job.

They met at the entrance to the farm. Jace drove a green golf cart out to greet him, followed by a second golf cart carrying two men—part of his security detail. The golf carts were green with beige letters sporting the legend, "Valleyview Experimental Agricultural Station." He wore a matching VEAS cap, as did the two men with him.

Jace told Landry to pull his truck off to the side of the entrance and ride in with him. Landry nodded to the two muscle-bound men who accompanied him.

"Dad told me to take you on the grand tour," Jace said. "While we're cruising, we can talk."

Landry got in.

As they pulled away, Jace said, "I'm glad you decided to come aboard. We need people like you."

"I haven't decided yet."

"You'll come around when you hear the salary."

Jolie'd mentioned the kid was bipolar. He must be on his meds today. He was sound as a dollar. Behind the wheel of the golf cart, the son of the man who had built all this, he seemed perfectly normal.

They drove up the lane and hung a right, following the one-lane asphalt road past the row of poplars. Landry heard cawing.

"Fucking crows," Jace said. "One of these days I'm going to grab my shotgun and blast 'em all out of here."

"Ravens," said Landry.

"What?"

"They're ravens. Historically, this area isn't a habitat for crows."

Jace glanced at him. "You're funny! Over here, in this field, we're growing beets."

He talked about the farm, the state-of-the-art practices and layout, how the work being done here would revolutionize agricultural practices. They drove past several outbuildings, which Jace pointed out. One was a warehouse. Another was a greenhouse for hydroponic tomatoes and other vegetables that Landry forgot as soon as he mentioned them. It was all filler. Jace wanted to impress him with the breadth and depth of the operation. They drove the neat blacktop lanes from one field to another, and all the while Jace kept up the chatter like a tour guide. It was a canned speech and he had it memorized. Landry wondered if this kid really thought he could fill his father's shoes. But Landry was impressed, too. Jace had managed to swallow down his paranoid schizophrenia, at least for now. He even seemed friendly.

They stopped on a little knoll at the edge of the farm and took in the view.

Two security people drove up behind his golf cart and parked. Jace waved them away. "You guys take off," he yelled. "We'll meet you back at the main building."

They sat there for a moment. Jace staring out at the fields. Finally he said, "Did you hear about the guy who used to run the militia?"

Used to run the militia.

Landry said he hadn't. He hadn't looked at a newspaper, he hadn't turned on the news, he hadn't logged onto the Internet. But he could guess.

Jace said, "He disappeared."

"Disappeared?"

"He left town."

"When did this happen?"

Jace shrugged. "The last day or so." Right now, Jace Denboer was operating on all cylinders. Perfectly normal. Crafty, even. He said, "How would you like to be second in command, right under the chief of security?"

"How about you give me the details."

"Of course it's contingent on your background check."

"Of course," Landry said.

"You seen the big guy, Raife?"

"Did I see whom?"

"Raife. One of the two guys who was with us."

"Which one?"

"The bald one. He's the one you'll be replacing."

Landry pictured the man. Compact, former military, a head like a bullet and a manner to go along with it.

The one who gave him the dirty look. Now Landry knew why.

- — -

From there, Jace drove to the security center, which was a lot like the other security centers Landry had seen and worked in. Desks, video monitors, comms. A charging station for sat phones. The video monitors' reach was extensive. They covered every building and every field.

"The perimeter is all fields. If someone makes it into the interior—they're picked up on these cameras. There are sensors that detect anything bigger than a small animal. It's very secure."

"Secure."

"What?"

"'Secure' is sufficient. 'Very secure' is superfluous."

"Jesus, you're a stickler for shit like that."

Very calm. As if nothing troubled him, his expression passive, his face smooth. It was hard to imagine the kid he was talking to driving up to a checkpoint and shooting a man point-blank.

"What do you think?" Jace said.

"Good layout. Very secure."

"And we have a great employment package. You'll like it. If you're right for the job."

"Can we drive around some more? I'd like to see it all."

"Sure thing."

This time they drove by the hangar where Miko Denboer kept his Beechcraft King Air. A big hangar for an agricultural farm. It went with the extra long runway. And the control tower.

"This could be a small city airport," Landry said.

"We deal with people from all over the world. Growers, the United States government, small countries. Hydroponics is the wave of the future."

He sounded as if he had memorized the spiel and practiced it in front of a mirror. He stopped at a greenhouse and nodded for Landry to get out. "Check *this* out!"

Landry followed him in. He saw banana trees. Jack fruit. A host of tropical plants. But most of the greenhouse was taken up by row upon row of smaller plants, all growing out of what looked like balls of clay. Landry had read about hydroponics, but let Jace tell him about it, anyway.

"To feed the world's hungry, we'll have to go to a different system.

The real goal is to create the conditions to be able to grow enough food to feed everyone on the planet. Our plants here have all the nutrients they'd have normally." He nodded to the rows and rows of green. "People think you need earth for plants to survive. But that's not true. You need the nutrients *in* the earth for the plant to grow and thrive."

Landry wondered if Jace had learned this lecture by rote.

"So we use a gravel or a clay ball, and grow the plants that way. Liquid food is circulated around the roots with a pump—it can be simple or it can be high-tech, like ours. But really, all you need is a pump and a timer.

"Plant roots have to search for the earth to tap into them. Hydroponics delivers the nutrition right to the roots."

"Interesting."

"Hey, you haven't lived till you've eaten a hydroponic tomato. Larger, better tasting—sweet. That's our mission."

He ran out of gas. End commercial.

"Impressive," Landry said.

"Yeah, I know. Not only that, but we're currently bidding on a contract with NASA for experimental lunar plant growth."

"You mean, on the moon?"

"Eventually, yes. We're working with a graduate student at the University of New Mexico. She got a grant from NASA Engineering Design Challenge to build a lunar plant growth chamber." He added, "Of course the moon is pie in the sky but we have a lot to do right here. There's so much being done to feed the nation. Even feed the world. This farm is state of the art when it comes to produce." He glanced at his watch. "Time to go back. Dad wants to give you the time and space to think about it, and then we'll set up a meeting. I can give you our website and some other sites that feature us and what we do."

"Sounds good."

Jace took Landry back a different way, past a good-size parking lot. Closest to the main building's doors was the black Camaro.

"Sweet," Landry said.

"Uh-huh."

"Your wheels?"

"Oh, yeah. Hey. One of these days I'll take you for a spin and show you what that baby can do."

"Looking forward to it," Landry said.

He really was.

On the way back to the Travelodge, Landry stopped at a convenience store to buy a newspaper. There was a stack of them on the counter, so it would have been hard to miss the headline: "MILITIA LEADER FOUND DEAD." The subheading read, "Militias Under Fire Across the Nation."

Beneath the second headline was an inset photo of Jedediah Kilbride, and a larger photo of an SUV, door open.

"Jedediah Kilbride, the founder of The Right Hand of God Freemen's Militia, was discovered late Monday afternoon outside a cabin on National Forest land." It went on to say that the cabin had been rented to a company named Kilbride Enterprises.

There were no suspects.

Landry recognized the cabin as the one he'd visited. Kilbride was only steps away from his vehicle when he was shot point-blank. He'd been identified both by the contents of his wallet and the registration on his truck.

Another militia member bites the dust.

It was open season for anyone who crossed the Denboer family. Which meant he'd have to be extra careful.

He purchased the paper and walked outside to read the rest. Most of the article was background and filler. A ranger driving past saw the body of a man beside his vehicle and went to investigate.

There were no suspects.

But of course there was a suspect, and Landry was sure that every person in law enforcement and every person who knew someone in law enforcement knew who that suspect was. The question they had to answer: could they prove it? And if they could prove it, what might happen to them if they did?

He could see Jace Denboer going straight to the cabin and shooting Kilbride. By warning Jace of Kilbride's intentions, Landry had put that scenario into play.

He'd expected one of two things to happen. Either Jace would have Kilbride killed, or he would keep his powder dry and wait for another time. The odds were with the former. Jace had proved to be that rare bird who was both paranoid and entitled. He lived in a fiefdom where he was the prince who could do no wrong, and he'd gotten away with murder once already. Since Jace had driven up to a checkpoint and shot a man in front of witnesses—and then gone the extra mile to have those witnesses killed—Landry had been pretty sure what Jace would do.

He'd warned Kilbride to watch his back. Kilbride could have taken steps to protect himself, but apparently he hadn't taken Landry's warning seriously.

He'd pretty much told Landry that at the time.

Or maybe he did take precautions, but his people weren't smart enough.

Landry thought of it as putting two scorpions in a bottle and betting a very small amount on the outcome. He wouldn't lose any sleep over it.

- — -

Back at the Travelodge, Landry knocked on Eric's door.

"Just got out of the shower, bro!" Eric called out. "I'll be by in a few minutes."

Landry went on up the walkway to his room. Inside, he removed the stainless steel watch, a Night-Vision Spy Camera Watch he'd bought from "Gadgets and Gear" online, and set it on the bed. According to the website, the Night-Vision Spy Camera Watch had "Incredible HD 1080 Video," a built-in SGB flash memory, and a recording life of two to three hours. It boasted night vision and "Crystal Clear Audio." The Night-Vision Spy Camera Watch could also be used as a webcam, and was waterproof up to three meters deep.

$99.95 with free shipping.

He connected the watch's mini-USB to the USB port on his laptop.

A hard rap on the door and Eric came in, toweling his hair. "What you got, bro?"

Landry pointed to his magic watch, and Eric grinned. Sat down on the queen-size bed next to Landry to watch the show. There was approximately two hours and twenty-five minutes of video.

They went through the footage. The second time through Landry stopped and froze the frame at certain spots. Eric used a sketchpad to sketch the layout of the farm and would match that with the aerial view on Google Earth. "Kid sounds all business," he said. "I thought you said he was a paranoid schizophrenic."

"He must have tightened up for the interview."

"I guess so. What's the plan?"

"I'm going to take the job."

"*Hoo*rah!"

"You're awful cheery."

"That's because I ran into one hot-looking lady at the Laundromat."

"Seriously?"

"Hey, I takes 'em where's I finds 'em."

"Watch your back, brother. You can find trouble anywhere."

"Yeah, ain't *that* the truth."

SPECTRE BLACK

CHAPTER 24

Jolie Burke dreamt about the bean field where Dan Atwood was buried.

She awoke thinking about the kid, just twenty-four years old, and about his home in Sitka. She'd reached out to his parents but there had been no reply. First she'd tried calling them from the number Dan Atwood had given for next of kin, but the number belonged to someone else who had never heard of Dan Atwood. She'd gone through the phone numbers for "Atwood" in Sitka, Alaska—there weren't many—and had contacted the sheriff there to deliver the news, but she'd never heard back from him. The idea that Dan Atwood might not have parents in Sitka, Alaska, had been stuck in her head as she swam up out of sleep.

Jolie hadn't pressed the issue. There had been a lot on her mind, and she'd assumed the sheriff—her boss—would also make a call. She had been distracted by crime, and plenty of it. Homicides. Especially on the border with Mexico. Drugs, shootings, domestics.

It was still dark, so she lay on her bunk in the Bayliner and tried to figure out what it was about Dan Atwood that bothered her.

Barney Fife.

Dan had been so clueless, so gung-ho, so . . . pathetic, he was almost a stereotype.

For instance: He'd been stupid enough to seize Jace Denboer's car. Jolie was sure that Jace either killed him or had him killed, but there was no way to prove it after all this time.

But why bury Atwood in the bean field at Denboer's farm?

She sat up.

There had always been something wrong about this. Yes, Atwood had confiscated Jace's car—for about five minutes—but Jace got it back the very next day.

No one crossed Jace Denboer.

Look at Rick Connor. Jace had no qualms about shooting him point-blank in front of witnesses. He'd just done it. And what was the result?

He got away with it. Everyone knew, or at least suspected, that it was Jace Denboer who had shot Rick Connor in cold blood. But he was still walking free. If Jolie hadn't been on the run herself, she would have asked for the case and gone after him.

And very likely might have been killed for her trouble.

So, yes, Jace could have killed Dan Atwood for any reason under the sun. Confiscating his car was probably an excellent reason in Jace World.

But why the bean field?

That was what bothered her.

He either killed Dan elsewhere, transported him to his father's farm to hide the body, or he had killed him there. There at the bean field.

How would that play out? Maybe Atwood had stopped Jace Denboer and his Camaro on the road outside the Valleyview Agriculture Experimental Station. Maybe to ticket him, or even arrest him. And there had been a struggle. That was the most likely scenario.

It made sense, but something about it bothered her. Dan Atwood wasn't working the night he disappeared. She'd checked that specifically. Bad things could happen to patrol officers on shift. Police work was dangerous. There was always a chance that you could be ambushed. Always a chance that a domestic call could be turned on the officer. Always a chance that you could make a routine traffic stop and be shot right through the heart. You never knew what was coming your way.

It could have happened a dozen different ways.

But most ways wouldn't include burial in a bean field—close to the road, or not.

Maybe it was the times, but most people involved in a homicide would just point, shoot, and take off.

She didn't talk to Dan Atwood much, but he had talked to her. He would have followed her around like a little lamb if she'd let him.

She remembered him talking about Jace's car after he confiscated it. How ugly the paint job on the Camaro was.

This was long before her date with Jace, when she'd seen the unsightly paint job up close.

Dan Atwood told her something else. Something so un-Barney Fife-ish that she'd managed to discount it until now. It didn't fit in with the stereotype of the kid, so she had just . . . forgotten about it.

Atwood had told her he'd confiscated Jace's Camaro just to look at the paint job.

She'd asked him why. He'd said something about "research."

Research.

Jolie had asked him what he meant by that, and he'd shrugged and said it wasn't important.

She remembered other things about him. One time she'd come around a corner and he was talking to someone she didn't know. What had struck her was the difference in his demeanor. He didn't come off as clueless, or hapless, or accident-prone, or fumbling. He'd sounded like one professional talking to another.

Now that she was actively searching her memory for examples, Jolie realized there were other things. Phone calls that ended abruptly when she came into a room. Usually he'd say good-bye to his mom, his dad, or his sister. She'd wondered why he spent so much time calling home. But she'd figured he was young—a raw rookie who was homesick.

And there were times when she'd tried to reach him by radio, and he hadn't answered.

She remembered that the sheriff himself didn't like him. It wasn't just that he didn't like him, but he didn't seem to trust him. He would call on-the-spot meetings, and would find a way to exclude the kid.

Thinking about it, Jolie realized the sheriff had tiptoed around, had practically *avoided contact* with—

Barney Fife.

Jolie remembered an old saying: don't pay attention to how a person acts, but how other people react to *him*. She'd learned that from a psychiatrist friend, who'd described what the hallmarks of sociopathology and psychopathology were. "Look at how people are around that person," he'd told her. "That will tell you what you need to know. A sociopath always affects someone negatively. There's always something there, even if it's minor. Something bad there."

Maybe that was it. Maybe Atwood was a psychopath.

Or maybe, he was something else.

Possibly, he was undercover. An undercover agent? Maybe DEA. Or maybe he was just someone who'd gotten in over his head and paid the full price for it.

She had no way of knowing. Not from here.

Dan Atwood—and Jolie was sure as shit that wasn't his name—could be anything.

CHAPTER 25

The next morning, Jace Denboer called Cyril Landry's cell.

"So, you want the job?"

Landry said he did, but told Jace he needed a week before he could start. "That going to be a problem?"

"Nope."

"Good."

"So that would be next Monday, right? Come in around eight and Gary Stella—he's head of security—will make sure you're all set." He paused, and Landry could hear him swallow. "Thanks again for what you did. Telling me about Kilbride."

"I take it your troubles are over."

"I'm good." Jace laughed. His laugh was a little off, but what could you expect from a paranoid schizophrenic? The kid was working to hold it together, probably every single day of his life.

"Glad to hear it," Landry said.

There was a pause. Landry thought Jace would fill in the silence and he did.

"You heard, right?" Jace said. "Kilbride got himself killed."

- — -

Landry would start in a week. He didn't know if he'd need the whole week, but it was better to be safe than sorry. He'd need that time to put everything into place. The first thing he did was contact a soldier pal of his he'd befriended during the Iraq War—one of those people you could always count on. Jeffery Briggs was not a SEAL, but an Army signal corpsman. They'd forged a friendship in the hot wind and blowing dirt of Iraq. Landry's unit relied on the corpsmen many times for their comms.

Jeff Briggs had the highest security clearance available—he was an SC-16.

Anything above SC-12 was not just good, but stellar. An SC-16 had the best security clearance imaginable. Even the FBI went from only an SC-9 to SC-13. So Jeff Briggs's designation beat the crap out of the FBI. Classified at that level, you could pretty much go anywhere and do anything you wanted.

Landry and Eric the Red had checked out the agricultural farm's phone line to see if they could tap in, but they could not—and that was why he needed Briggs. He'd seen the farm's system up close—sat phones for each of the crew—six in all. Landry and Eric had gone out in the dead of night to see if there was a way to break into the telephone junction box above the ag farm, but soon realized there was no way in. The farm's security was as good as it got, a sophisticated system that made tapping in impossible. The communication was airtight. Airtight, and scrambled.

So Landry made the trip east.

Jeff was stationed at Fort George G. Meade in Anne Arundel County, Maryland. The Defense Information Systems Agency was located on the grounds of the US Army post. Fort Meade was a heavy hitter as far as Army installations went; the fort housed the Defense Information Systems Agency and the National Security Agency. The Defense Information Systems Agency was located underground.

Fort Meade also happened to be close to Laurel Park, the racecourse where Landry's older brother stabled his horses. The day before his meeting with Jeff Briggs, Landry watched the races at Laurel. He wished he could see his brother, but he couldn't. Wished he could spend time on the backstretch the way he used to do, inhaling the scent of hay, horse, manure, and dirt, walking a couple of hots on the shaded lane, observing horses working and galloping, topping off the day with a great steak dinner out with the family. But those days were gone.

He was a ghost.

- — -

When Landry got back to his room at the Days Inn, he put in a call to Jeff Briggs and they arranged for breakfast at the Country Inn the next morning.

They got in their catch-up time, breakfast disposed of and three or four coffee refills later, got down to talking good times—and bad.

Landry said, "Is this a good place to talk?"

"If you're asking what I think you're asking," Jeff said, "there's no problem."

Landry agreed. The place was full, mostly Army families and servicemen. The restaurant seemed to float on the babble of many voices. Jeff was dressed like someone on his day off—because it *was* his day off—the usual uniform of a knit shirt and khaki slacks, a belt. Landry wore something similar. They'd found a small alcove inside the restaurant, back to the wall, and kept their conversation low but casual.

Landry said, "I'm doing surveillance for a friend. Her husband might be into something that could ruin her life. I told her I'd check him out, but you know how it goes—I ran into a brick wall. Guy's former military, high up, has clearance up the wazoo. Between you and me, I'm worried he's been talking to someone who might do him and his wife some serious harm."

"Harm, huh?"

Landry nodded. He knew that Briggs's own daughter had been used as a punching bag by her husband. He knew that Briggs had a talk with the husband, and the husband had wisely decided to give his wife a divorce—including a generous settlement. Not too long after that he had been transferred out, after he recovered from the injuries he'd sustained in an accident at his home.

Briggs, who had been enjoying his omelet, set his fork down. "Serious harm?"

"The guy I'm talking about, he's the vindictive type. He's been harassing her—calling and hanging up, but now it's turning into threats. I'm thinking he's using a sat phone from his place of employment. He works at an agriculture farm." Landry pushed the phone number across the table. "I've tried to get in to see what he's doing, so I can help her, but the phones there are scrambled, and I can't listen in on the conversation. She thinks he's trying to set up something unlawful, with bad people."

Briggs leaned forward. "Like what?"

"She won't say. He's a sneaky bastard, that's all I know. And I know Cindy is scared shitless."

"Is that why you came out here?"

"That and to watch my brother's colt run." Landry shrugged. "Thought I'd kill two birds with one stone. I understand if you can't—"

"I'll see what I can do." Jeff took the slip of paper with the number on it, slipped it into his wallet, and stood up. "I know a couple of guys who wouldn't be around if you weren't in Iraq. Tell you what. I'll take care of this . . . when do you need it done by?"

"Wednesday would be fine. Just let me know. You have my number."

Jeff nodded.

They walked outside into the milky sunshine. Maryland smelled fresh and sweet compared to Branch, New Mexico. Beautiful trees, green grass everywhere. A great day on tap.

They said their good-byes and Landry got into his rental car and drove back to Laurel Park to watch the races. Musing that if things had turned out differently, he'd have been a racehorse trainer like his brother.

Too late now.

CHAPTER 26

Landry started work the following week. A sport jacket over an open-collar shirt and slacks—"casual dress"—was required, as well as a laminated ID card clipped to a ribbon around his neck. An H&K 9mm and a holster to go with it was issued to him as well.

There were plenty of rules, everything from where he could park and where he couldn't, to the length of his two short breaks and one half-hour lunch, to the places that were off-limits (there were several areas like that) and a list of policies he was told to memorize.

Landry was a good employee. Mainly, because he knew he wasn't going to be stuck in the job forever. If at all possible, this would be a get-in-get-out kind of situation. He would concentrate on being a reliable security guard but not a great one. When in doubt, stick to the middle of the road and don't stand out in any way. The only drawback in this regard was his height.

He learned about the phones first off. There were seven sat phones set into a four-point charging station—five for security and two for higher-ups, including Miko Denboer himself. Landry was intimately familiar with sat phones from the military. They looked like black bricks with telescoping antennas, and were nearly as heavy.

Landry was briefed by the chief of security, a beefy guy with a red face named Derek Talbot, who demonstrated how to use the phone.

"Be sure to pick a different one each time," Talbot said. "Even Mr. Denboer switches phones, so you make sure you do, too. We really like to change them up."

Smart.

"You keep your phone overnight, then bring it back in to be charged first thing in the a.m."

"Yessir."

"Recharge it every day."

"Yessir."

"Former military, right?"

"Yes *sir!*"

He nodded curtly. "Good. You'll toe the line, then. You come in by seven a.m., on the dot, no slackers here, and you put that phone into the charger. It takes three hours for a full charge, but you can use one if you need to after the first hour and a half. Don't let it get away from you, do you understand me?"

"Yessir."

"Good. You listen to instructions and you do your job to the letter, and you won't get any misery from me."

"I understand."

"Where did you serve?"

"Iraq and Afghanistan."

He kept his face level with Landry's but Landry thought his gaze slid away—no more than a micro-eyelash—as if he couldn't look Landry fully in the eye. It was the same exaggerated behavior a dog would exhibit to its better, just short of slinking. "Good for you," he said curtly. He paused, about to add something. Landry guessed it would be an explanation why he didn't serve. But his face hardened up again and he said, "Be sure to recharge every day. And always choose a different phone. The number is here, on the bottom."

"Yes sir."

The man cleared his throat and walked away.

— · —

Landry spent a couple of days learning the ropes and observing the people he worked with.

Two of the employees were excellent—top-notch. He would have to be careful around them. The other four were average. They did their jobs, but they were either lazy, uncertain, or downright hostile to work. Landry didn't take any of them for granted.

The first thing he did was become a person to all of them, a guy they could get to know. He stuck to the truth as much as possible. His interests: football and handicapping the ponies. He mentioned an ex-wife and daughter who lived in another state, which was not only close to the truth—it *was* the truth. This, Landry knew from years of training and experience, was the key to lying. Stick as close to the truth as possible, and use situations and certain turning points in your own life. Those memories were easy to remember in an emotional sense. Do it that way and you didn't have to rummage through your memory files. The memories were already there, baked into the cake.

Landry also made sure that he seemed smart enough, but not too smart. Just an average everyday Joe Blow doing his job and trying to do it well. Likeable but not too chummy.

When he had learned the routine, he called Jeff Briggs at Fort Meade.

"How's it going?" Jeff asked. "Did you get everything you need?"

"To be honest, I could use your help. You know what I was checking out? Now it looks like there are some bigger implications here."

"Elaborate."

Landry said, "I think I stepped in something big. From what I'm picking up, this could have national implications. I can't go into it on the phone."

"I understand."

"You remember Fallujah."

"I do."

"So you know my word is my bond."

"Tell me what you need."

He told Briggs he needed a powerful parabolic mic and a couple of operators with Briggs's unit. "Can you dispatch a crew?"

"I've got two in your area. Albuquerque and El Paso."

"El Paso would be faster."

"You want this ASAP?"

"Yeah. If this is nothing, no one will ever know. But if it isn't . . ."

"I understand."

"This won't be a problem, will it?"

"No way. They go where I tell them to go. They listen in on what I tell them to listen to. If it's a dry hole, it's a dry hole."

"This won't be a dry hole," Landry said.

"I'll see who I've got and I'll deploy. It will be no later than tomorrow morning."

"I can send you satellite images of the area—"

"No problem. Our guys know how to hide in plain sight. Just make sure the signal isn't scrambled. We can't tap in if it is."

"Roger that."

- — -

Every day at eight a.m. on the dot, Miko Denboer drove his dark blue Jaguar XJ sedan to the entrance of the main building, handed the keys to one of the security guards, and walked inside the main building, which held his office. The main entrance was a box, mostly plate-glass on two sides with a long standup counter, a couple of desks behind that. There were also plants, a couple of western art paintings on the wall—a welcoming introduction to the maze of hallways and larger buildings beyond. The kitchen, complete with a long table, was off to the right. Denboer always went straight to the charging station to pick up one of the phones. The charging station was in a recessed alcove off the hallway, one door down from the kitchen. Denboer was careful to look at the number—the habit of a man who left nothing to chance.

On the morning of the conflagration, Landry came in early, around a quarter to seven in the morning. Fifteen minutes ahead of the others. Denboer wouldn't be in yet—you could set your clock by him. Landry was grateful that Denboer was a creature of habit. He sat in the kitchen area and watched as his fellow security guards deposited their phones in the charger. The sat phones were on a "trickle-charger" and took approximately three hours to achieve a full charge. The security team would let the phones charge partway before going on their first rounds around eight, then return the phones to the base for a full charge.

Landry checked one of the phones for warmth. It was now partially charged, good enough for the first inspection of the grounds. He made his rounds and came back fifteen minutes early to return his sat phone to the base. From here on he would need to move quickly and efficiently. He had fifteen minutes before his fellow security guards trickled back in.

Landry walked into the break room dining area again, selected a powdered donut, and sat at one of the rickety tables near the window. He looked over the local newspaper as his fellow guards stopped at the quad charger to return their phones before heading in for their morning coffee and breakfast rolls. There was a knot of guys sitting at a table some yards away from Landry. He had yet to prove himself. As it stood right now, he was the New Guy who had replaced a pal of theirs. At the moment, they largely ignored him. It would take time for them to thaw—he knew that—and as far as he was concerned it was the best possible situation. He went

SPECTRE BLACK

to one of the coffee urns, filled his coffee cup, and added cream to it. The cup was not one of the ceramic mugs sitting facedown on the table beside the urn. This was Landry's cup, which he'd picked up at the dollar store in town—a cheap china cup sporting a gold-painted decorative ring around the rim. Landry shuffled over to the microwave and placed it inside, setting the timer for ten minutes.

He went back to his rickety table and cleared up the mess—napkins, crumbs from the donut, paper plate—then headed for the restroom off the break room. And waited.

Inside the microwave, the coffee cup was heating up and so was the gold ring. The coffee would evaporate and one of the resulting sparks on the ring would blow the cup apart—shards of china would go flying. Likely, this would disable the microwave. Smoke and the burning stench of fried coffee and china would ensue—

He heard a loud *whumpf* as the cup exploded. The smoke billowed black. The fire alarm went off, so loud you could barely think. And then he heard the sound of the sprinkler system coming on. He heard voices, shouts, footsteps running. "Over here!" someone shouted. "Grab the fire extinguisher!" Some people running to the kitchen, some running out the door to the outside. There might even be a call to the fire department, although Landry wasn't sure if Denboer wanted that kind of scrutiny, not for a microwave mishap. Landry headed back to the alcove where the quad charger was. The alarm was deafening. Everyone ran in one direction or the other. But nobody watched him. He was just another shocked employee distancing himself from the explosion.

He had a guaranteed ten minutes, fifteen at the outside.

All the sat phones were seated in their base.

Landry knew the backs of the sat phones were held together with Torx heads. He inserted the right size Torx screwdriver blade and tightened it. He removed the six screws on the back of one of the sat phones, removed the back, and split the casing with the screwdriver.

He broke one of the wires inside, snapping the casing before plugging it back into the phone. The phone would sit there, looking as it always did, and no one would be the wiser that he'd just unscrambled the frequency. He quickly moved on to the next and the next after that—thirty seconds to each phone—until all seven were done.

In the course of that time, a few people funneled out of the break room but barely registered his presence. When he heard footsteps, he stood with one of the phones, looking confused, a man wondering what he should do in this situation. One of the guys just shook his head and kept going, his personal cell phone to his ear. He could have been calling the fire department or he could have been talking to his wife. Whatever it was, the man appeared to be completely absorbed.

The guy with him didn't even bother to look in Landry's direction.

Landry turned back and finished what he was doing. Every time he heard footsteps and voices, he put on his worried face, looking focused as he held one of the phones to his ear. "Don't put me on hold! We need—" He stopped. One or two people ran by him but barely noticed him. The noise, the smoke, the smell of the burned coffee and the shrieking of the alarm shattered normalcy.

He got to all seven phones.

No one would suspect they were tampered with. The sat phones were now unscrambled, and no one but Landry, Eric, Jolie, and Jeff Briggs's crew knew about it. Pretty soon the mess in the break room would be cleaned up, the kitchen area back to normal except for the burning smell and perhaps a simple remodel. There would be a new microwave, definitely. And now Landry's friends in the satellite van would be able to listen in to everything that went on at the ag farm.

As he waited for the satellite van to come in from El Paso and move into place, Landry spent the rest of the day playing security guard. Which mostly meant poking around some more, looking for anything unusual. Jace had made a big deal of the hydroponic plants. That was what he wanted the new hire to focus on. But there were a lot of buildings on the property, and sooner or later Landry planned to visit all of them.

Security guard work was a lot of walking around, driving around, and sometimes, sitting around. If there were visitors, he would escort them, on occasion. But mostly he was either driving a go-slow or checking buildings. There was a little talk about the fire in the break room, but the compound had an excellent air-filtering system, and after a mop-up there was very little damage.

Miko Denboer stayed until early afternoon. He looked nervous. The day had started out wrong and continued on that way. That, in itself, could throw some people.

He saw Landry and nodded to him. "What say you drive me to Hangar B? My knee is acting up again."

"Yessir."

Miko climbed into the cart Landry brought around from the side of the building.

"How'd you like the excitement?" Denboer said as they drove down the asphalt lane between buildings toward Hangar B.

"It was that, sir."

Miko looked sideways at him, as if seeing him for the first time. "You former military?"

"Yessir. US Army infantry."

"What did you do?" Miko stared out at the field to their right. He seemed distracted, but Landry wondered if he was trying to get information about Landry or just wanted to talk.

"Transport. I drove a truck."

"Jace said you were in the militia, is that right?"

"I was, sir."

"Jace told me you warned him about Kilbride. Is that right?"

"Yessir."

"How'd you find out about the plot?"

The plot.

"I went out for a smoke and heard Kilbride telling someone about it."

Landry was aware of the man staring at him. Landry met his eye. "I couldn't just keep that to myself."

"Some people would have. Let's pull in here," he added, pointing to a side door to Hangar B. "Thank you."

"You're welcome, sir."

"Did you . . . hear anything else?"

"Like what, sir?"

"Anything about me. Did you overhear any conversations about me, other than the one possibly touching on Jace?"

"I didn't hear anything about you."

"What about here?"

"Here, sir?"

"Yes. Your coworkers."

"No. I hardly know any of them."

Yes, the man was definitely nervous, and possibly paranoid.

Or just worried.

"If you want me to keep an eye out, sir."

"That might be good. I've got local law enforcement covered, but I can always use a sharp eye."

Landry nodded.

"I want to thank you for what you did for Jace. I'm glad to have you onboard. Now, you walk on back and I'll keep the cart. Okay?"

— — —

Landry walked back to the offices, thinking about their conversation. The dialogue between them had been nothing much. But

SPECTRE BLACK

Miko Denboer was afraid of something, or someone. He'd hidden it fairly well, but he was shaken by the fire in the break room.

Maybe he thought it was more than that. Maybe he thought it was sabotage. Or a diversion. Or an attempt on his life. Landry decided to let the idea roll around in his head for a while. But he was thinking about something else. Hangar B.

Hangar B was off-limits to everyone except two guards. Landry rarely saw them, but he knew they were there. Landry pegged them as former elite military. There was no way you could mistake them for security guards. There was no casual dress, no golf carts, no shooting the shit in the break room. These men were operators. Whatever resided in Hangar B was in good hands.

Landry thought Miko had an office inside Hangar B.

He thought that Miko had his regular security guards, but also, an inner circle. The few men he could depend on. Hard men. Former military, no crybabies need apply.

These were people you couldn't scam. These were guys you couldn't get around. These were guys who could drop you like a bag of rocks. And they were posted at Hangar B.

This made him all the more interested in what was inside Hangar B. It probably had something to do with stealth technology. It was easy to draw that conclusion, considering Denboer's son drove a black Camaro with the paint job from hell. Stealth technology was a hot item, particularly as a way to level the playing field for many smaller and poorer regimes. He thought cloaking technology—depending on how far along the developer was in the process, and what they wanted to sell it for—would be worth a lot of money to the right person. Or the right small country.

From the farm Landry drove around the back roads, looking for the satellite van. He found it, situated in a pullout under a massive cottonwood tree, a quarter mile away from the Denboer farm. The road was two-lane blacktop and passed between fields, windbreaks, and the occasional farmhouse.

Landry pulled to the side of the road and got out. His eyes were hidden by his sunglasses. Landry had been in the military and he had also, off and on, worked for other agencies in the government, so he knew how to approach them.

One of the guys was sitting on the step of the van, eating a sandwich. He looked up as Landry approached. He eyed Landry's black Dodge Ram, and nodded.

As Landry walked toward him, he let his hand brush back his jacket, just a quick peek. What one of the surveillance guys termed, "The slow lifting of the kimono." Just a tiny peek.

The guy stood. His face changed. He had clearly seen the badge hooked on Landry's belt, even though it was just a glimpse. Having dealt with law enforcement often, no doubt he was used to the casual nature of the reveal. When cops were dealing with fellow cops or government people, they didn't flash their badges.

Landry said, "Hope you guys are finding everything okay here."

"Pretty good so far."

"Just coming by to tell you we appreciate what you're doing—it's going to be a big help, believe me. If you need anything . . ." He let the offer trail off.

"We're good. You DEA?"

"Yup." He glanced at his watch. "Gotta take off. Good to see you're here, and thanks again." He nodded to him and headed back for the truck.

Inside, he glanced at the guy in the rearview mirror. The guy didn't seem to be impressed or unimpressed. He'd just gone back to his sandwich.

Now Landry had put another face to the mission. Just another leg on the stool they'd created from nothing.

SPECTRE BLACK

- — -

Back at the Travelodge, Landry took a dip in the pool. It was surprisingly quiet in the late afternoon.

His cell rang; Jolie's number on the readout.

"I think I need to go someplace else," she said without preamble. "I can be much more help if I have resources. Being on this boat is impossible."

"Where do you want to go?"

"San Clemente."

"My house?"

"If it's okay with you. That way I can be with my animals, too. I need to have resources, and the Internet on this boat is spotty. I need a sports car and I'm sitting in a covered wagon."

He saw her point. "We'll have to coordinate on when you go and how. Tom can fly you from Las Cruces."

They agreed on a tentative schedule and Landry disconnected. The truth was, he could use all hands on deck, and Jolie was good at being a cop. She sounded like one because she was one, and had all sorts of contacts outside her own agency. Not only would it be safer for Jolie, it would be best for their mission. He called Tom and arranged for the flight, then called Jolie back.

"Day after tomorrow, two in the afternoon. All Rand has to do is get you to the Las Cruces International Airport, and Tom will take it from there. You can get a rental car at LAX and drive straight to San Clemente. Louise next door knows where to find my extra key."

"Under a rock somewhere?"

"No. It's in a safe deposit box."

"You don't leave anything to chance, do you?"

"That's why I'm still alive and kicking. If you need another name, I have one for you: Barbara Kay. I've put together a few things. She's about the right age for you and all you'd need is a photo. But it's up to you."

"Might be a good idea."

"And a burner phone, too. Tom will have everything you need when you get there. License, passport, if you need them. We good?"

"We're good."

He heard the smile in Jolie's voice.

She liked this cloak-and-dagger stuff as much as he did.

CHAPTER 27

At LAX, Jolie picked up the car Tom had rented for her and drove south to San Clemente. She encountered the usual: smog, multiple lanes of traffic that ebbed and flowed and sometimes stopped, the odd super-expensive sports car dodging in and out of traffic, missing her bumper by a hairsbreadth. LA drivers—they were nuts. The only way to deal with LA drivers was to drive as erratically and as fast as they did. Dodge in and out of lanes, close enough to take the paint off.

But there was something about LA—Energy. She realized that living in that Podunk town with crooked cops and Miko Denboer's Mordor just up the road was really not for her. She loved wide-open spaces, but she also knew that she could dodge and dart her way out of this city and end up in some beautiful places in no time.

Plus, there was the ocean . . .

As she turned off at the exit for San Clemente, everything slowed. Literally. She was behind seven or eight cars waiting to go through a stop sign. But if she had slowed to a stop physically, she'd also come to a stop mentally. The spinning hamster wheel in her head slowed to a stop.

There was the beach. Ahead, where the street trenched between the rooftops. She smiled when she saw that faint blue bar of ocean.

Ocean! She buzzed the window down.

The air! Mild, cool and yet warm, welcoming. As if it wrapped around her instead of assaulting her.

For the first moment in a long time, she could relax.

Not let down her guard. Oh, no.

But, she could relax.

It took her two trips up and down a winding road and a stop to ask directions at a Chinese-owned convenience store to find Avenida De La Estrella, the street that meandered back up the hill. And there was Landry's rental, up a flight of terra-cotta tile steps, above a rolling garage door that opened up to the street. An envelope was attached to the waist-high wrought-iron gate. Inside were the keys to his house and a note from Louise, Landry's next-door neighbor. She walked up the steps and turned to the left—Louise's house. Heard deep-throated barking within. Big, scary barks.

Rottweiler barks.

The door opened and a slim woman with a beautiful smile and blond hair loosely held up by a Japanese stick barrette stepped outside, holding onto the collar of the straining Rottie. She let him go and he launched toward Jolie, wriggling and slobbering and whining—before racing around the pocket yard. Then back again, rolling on his back, wriggling some more.

"Rocky!" Jolie said.

"You must be Jolie," Louise said.

"In the flesh. I don't know how to thank you for taking care of these guys."

"Well, that's one portion of the welcome wagon. Get out of the way, Nikki," she said to the barking schnauzer.

Jolie followed her inside. A tremendous view from the plate-glass windows—you could see a little of the waterway down the hill, that same hazy bar of ocean. But on the couch right in front of her was Rudy, curled up on a chair cushion. He opened an eye and looked at her. Yawned, stood up, and stretched. And curled up again.

"I see these guys are right at home here," Jolie said.

She felt at home here, too.

- — -

Jolie moved Rocky and Rudy to Landry's place. There, she checked her e-mail. She'd changed all her passwords the moment she'd plugged the thumb drive into Rand McNally's computer. Now she configured the new laptop the way she wanted it, and moved all her files from the thumb drive.

Whatever documents Jolie had left behind in her old computer were likely to be in the hands of the enemy.

Jolie had no doubt that if someone had actively tried to track her movements, they would have found her if she'd stayed on the lake much longer. But she guessed that the sheriff's office had other problems. Like, for instance, their own little crime wave in Tobosa County. In a short period of time, Rick Connor was shot to death at a militia checkpoint, another two militia members killed a few days later, and now the head of the militia had been found murdered on National Forest land. Being a militia member was a good way to get killed.

Since Kilbride's murder had taken place on National Forest land, Jolie was certain there would be an investigation by the federal government.

And of course there was her own homicide case—Dan Atwood.

And her own disappearance.

If all this didn't bring the Feds, what would?

In the meantime, she wanted to clear up the one thing that truly nagged her: who killed Dan Atwood, and why?

Did Jace kill him for confiscating the Camaro, or was it the fact the hapless deputy was poking around the ag farm that led to his death?

The theory Jolie was operating under at the moment was that Atwood was undercover. She'd tossed around the idea that Rick Connor had been his replacement, that they'd both been DEA agents. From Cyril, she knew Rick Connor was with the DEA, but did that mean Dan Atwood could have preceded him?

He might have just been a wannabe. By now, whatever he'd been investigating—*if* he'd been investigating anything at all—would be hard to reconstruct. She didn't have access to his notes, his files, his laptop. Whatever he'd had was gone, either packed up by family, or, worse, packed up by the sheriff's department.

Was Dan Atwood a dead end?

Probably.

All she could do was keep at it for a while longer.

But first, she'd take Rocky for a walk down to the pier.

CHAPTER 28

Cyril Landry drove into town for lunch. He stopped at the McDonald's on George S. Patton Boulevard. It was the noon hour, prime time for McDonald's customers, and the place buzzed with conversation. It was a regular zoo. The level of babble was at its high-water mark—exactly what he wanted. He sat at a table in the corner closest to the restrooms, and rested a fast food bag on the postage-stamp-size table.

Eric came in and sat down opposite him. "Hey, bro," he said.

"How's your van? Sound system okay?"

"Yeah, but you know music these days," Landry said. "Not a whole lot of good stuff out there. How you doing?"

They talked about various things. Wives, kids, football. What the traffic was like on Route 38. Eric balled up his Big Mac wrapper and shoved it in the bag, held up a finger, and groped around in his pocket for his phone. "Gotta get this," he said. "You go on ahead."

Landry nodded, picked up the bag, and crumpled it into a ball. "You up for some pool later?"

"Yeah, I want to check out Dos Cabezas."

"Stupid name for a bar, you ask me."

Eric nodded, but it was clear he was busy on the phone.

Landry walked past the garbage can and pushed his balled-up napkin and butcher paper through the small swinging door, but pocketed the bag.

He drove back to the motel. Inside, he checked everything twice—Santa Claus had nothing on him—and went into the bathroom, closed the door, and turned on the fan. He also turned on the shower.

Only then did he put in the earphones and listen to the recording. He started just short of forty minutes in.

The conversation was short—terse, even—between Miko Denboer and someone named "Randall."

It soon became clear that Randall was high up in the Drug Enforcement Agency in Washington, DC. Landry took note of Randall's phone number the old-fashioned way: by writing it down on a notepad.

Randall wasn't convinced that Miko Denboer knew nothing about the death of his undercover agent, the man who went by the name of Rick Connor.

"This has really fucked us up here, do you know that?"

"I told you not to send him out here. It was an accident and that's—"

"An accident? It was your kid who shot him. Point-blank!"

"He's a paranoid schizophrenic."

Landry got the impression that Miko Denboer had said this about a thousand times during his life—or at least in the last five or six years.

"Is that what I should tell the family?"

"He knew the risks. DEA agents are an endangered species. You know that. I told you we had everything under control."

"I think we're done here."

Denboer said, "No, we're not."

"I haven't seen one damn thing—"

"You saw the video, didn't you?"

"Yes, but—"

"But what? You think we faked it? Do you want to get on a plane and come out and see what we're doing here? Talk to the guy who built this?"

"I thought he went back to Pakistan."

"Yeah, but I can have you talk to him."

"How would I know he is who you say he is?"

"You could trust me," Denboer replied.

"We have a long way to go for me to do that. I need to go. We'll be in touch."

The man on the other end hung up.

"Don't wait too long," Denboer muttered.

Then there was a dial tone.

Just then, there was a knock on the door. Eric came in. "Where are you, dude?"

"In the bathroom."

"What—?"

"Quiet."

Eric joined him.

A few minutes later Denboer made another call. The phone on the other end rang and rang before picking up.

Dead air.

Someone on the tape said, "Shit!"

Landry recognized the voice. It was one of the Army guys with the satellite van—his name was Mark.

A voice in the background said, "What?"

"I can't get a reading. There's no way I can pinpoint where he's talking from. No location here."

"What?"

"What I said! There's no location *here*. In the *US*. No way to find them."

"What the hell?"

"Shitfire! It's a Dead Site."

"Dead Site? What are you—?"

"The number," the first Army guy said. "We traced the call to this number—it's legit."

"So?"

"The number is in New Guinea."

"New Guinea?"

"Papua-New-Fucking-Guinea!"

Eric looked at Landry. "What was that about?"

"Sounds to me like the call was rerouted."

"On purpose?"

"What do you think?"

"They know we were listening in?"

"Maybe they're just being careful—on general principles."

"Or they know the United States *Army* is listening in." Eric whistled. "What was *that* all about?"

Landry said, "Looks like Miko Denboer's playing both sides of the street."

CHAPTER 29

Jolie woke to a stomach upset. Maybe it was the food she'd had at the little cubicle of a Chinese restaurant she'd visited last night. Queasy, she decided to take it easy and hang out with the two beasts on the couch watching movies. But her mind kept going back to Dan Atwood.

More than one detective she'd worked with had called her a dog with a bone.

She realized she needed to think about Atwood in another way. *Any* other way. She'd been fixated on Dan being some sort of undercover agent. It fit neatly enough that part of her wanted to believe it. Dan Atwood was interested in the Valleyview Experimental Agricultural Station, Dan Atwood had confiscated Jace Denboer's Camaro, and Dan Atwood was found buried in a bean field at the farm. All of it fit perfectly. But maybe she was making too much of him. He could have just been a deputy who had crossed the wrong person and ended up in the bean field. A traffic stop gone wrong, maybe.

But where was his car?

She'd been through the file before. Atwood did not check out a sheriff's unit the night before he failed to show up for roll call the next day. His shift had been during the day, not at night. Whatever

Dan Atwood did, he'd used transportation other than his department vehicle. Jolie had looked him up in DMV when she got the case. He owned a green 2008 Ford Escape SUV with a New Mexico license plate number, which Jolie had duly recorded and logged a few hours trying to track down. She'd put in time checking car ads, craigslist, police and sheriffs' databases, tow companies, and junkyards, but the whereabouts of Dan Atwood's Ford Escape remained a mystery. Like his family background and next of kin.

She'd operated under the theory that he'd left town for some reason—possibly because he'd been threatened by Jace Denboer. That was before his body was found in the bean field.

Someone had killed him and buried him there. But Jolie was no closer to figuring it out than she had been when she had the official information sources at her fingertips.

A great, big goose egg.

She'd been through every salient piece of paper, every contact, official and otherwise, every friend (all three of them), every ex-girlfriend (she'd driven to El Paso to talk to her), and had mined every little piece of information she could beg, borrow, or steal. She'd hoarded that information like a raven salting away shiny things in its nest. She had been thorough; she had been *beyond* thorough. Tireless. Obsessed, even. But the case petered out, anyway. There were no leads.

None.

She drifted off to sleep and woke feeling much better. The TV was still on, *Inside Man*, on CNN.

Morgan Spurlock. The fast-food guy who did investigations into certain businesses and companies.

Here in the west, "The Inside Man" had a different connotation. "Inside Man" was the serial rapist who had wreaked havoc in three, maybe four, states. He had escalated to killing his latest victims.

Jolie had worked the case with Vicki Dodd, who worked sex crimes.

SPECTRE BLACK

It occurred to Jolie that neither one of them had looked at the web pages of the victims. Well, maybe Vicki had.

She called up Vicki.

To say Vicki was surprised was an understatement. "What happened?" she asked. "Where'd you go?"

"I had to get away."

"Yeah, I know. The stress."

Jolie accepted the gift she'd been given. "The stress. I couldn't deal with it anymore. To be honest, I kind of . . . lost it. I'm trying to get the nerve to come back, but I need more time. Can you keep this a secret?"

"Sure I can."

Jolie was fifty-fifty whether or not she believed her. But what was Vicki going to do? Nobody liked making waves there. Especially not the female deputies and detectives. She'd sensed that she wasn't the only person who was uneasy about things in the department. There was a cadre of guys who had the sheriff's ear, and the rest were merely rank-and-file employees.

Jolie said, "Did you ever look at Karin Stokes's web page? Did she have one?"

"I think I *did*. It was a while ago, though."

Jolie sensed uncertainty in Vicki's tone, along with resentment. Jolie could hear muted clicking.

Then: "If she had a page, it's been taken down. Let me look . . . nope. There's nothing there . . . wait."

"What?"

"This is weird."

"*What?*"

"It says, 'The Diary of Karin Stokes.' I'm gonna open it up."

Jolie typed in the same sentence.

A website came up, but it was blank. Everything had been removed. Erased.

"Nothing," Vicki said.

"I guess that's it, then."

"I guess so."

"So it's like King Kong."

She could hear the smile in Vicki's voice. "How big is King Kong?" She answered for herself. "Not as big as people think he is."

They disconnected.

Jolie stared at the Google URL window on her laptop screen. Her idea didn't work.

She tried Carla Vitelli.

There were several references to her as an FBI agent—testifying in court cases, articles on busts, etc. Jolie went through them but found nothing of interest at the moment.

One thing she'd never done was try a Google search for Dan Atwood. She typed his name into the box and hit "Return."

There were a number of Dan Atwoods to choose from. She tried a shortcut, hit "Images" under the bar and suddenly a sea of faces came up. Most of them were other men. One, a good-looking thirtyish man, dominated the page. But there was Dan Atwood, *her* Dan Atwood, *just one image*, among the better-known Dan Atwood and his other namesakes.

Her Dan Atwood held up a trout in front of a lake. The photo looked recent. He looked like himself. Impossibly young. Wet behind the ears. Almost goofy. He wore a striped T-shirt and held the trout high above his head.

She clicked on the photo and got a larger view. Beside it was the legend "Visit Dan Atwood's Page."

- — -

Jolie typed in the URL and a page opened up. There was nothing on it except another hyperlink.

The hyperlink said, "Guests."

Jolie clicked on the link.

A page opened up. There were three more links embedded in the web page. One said, "Erin Locke." Another link said "Anita Loyoza." And the third said, "Carla Vitelli."

Jolie hit the link for Carla Vitelli.

Carla's face filled the right-hand side of the website's banner. It was sunset, and her complexion took on the glow of the orange rocks around her. Her long, gold-streaked hair was ruffled by the wind, and a perfectly manicured hand shaded her eyes against the dying sun. Her stunning eyes, in this light, were the color of amethysts.

In Jolie's inexpert opinion, this was a professional photo. She thought that Dan Atwood must have found it elsewhere and co-opted it for his banner.

Jolie opened up another page, Googled Carla Vitelli, and once again hit "Images." There were numerous photos of her. She must have done some modeling—many of them were professional photos. They didn't look too old, either. She certainly wasn't dated by her hairstyle. Jolie quickly found a shot of Carla among the sandstone rocks at sunset.

Jolie scrolled down. There were a few entries, many of them describing Carla Vitelli and her job as an FBI agent. Photos of recent busts, photos of her cool and beautiful in jewel-colored suits in courtrooms, and photos of her house.

Her house in Albuquerque.

From across the street.

And there she was driving by in her car—

From the street.

And several photos of her with men. In restaurants, on the street, in their cars or hers. On her balcony, sitting around a garden table. Food and wine.

Plenty of men.

But no photos of Carla Vitelli and Dan Atwood together.

Jolie went back to the Dan Atwood page and opened up "Anita Loyoza."

The page filled up with photos of a beautiful young woman whose face was familiar.

Jolie knew why. Anita Loyoza was the young mother from Tucson who disappeared and was later found buried in the desert.

This wasn't a harmless crush. This wasn't even stalking.

This was a freak page.

She'd seen them before. Of women who had been raped, or killed, or were targeted by someone. She'd seen a few serial-killer freak pages in her time—people getting off on the murders of women, mostly.

Jolie could well imagine the people who dropped in here.

Dan Atwood.

She saved the page and went back to Carla Vitelli.

There was the street view of Carla's house. And an aerial view of Carla's house. Zooms of her windows, her yard. Photos of her walking to her car. Different outfits, different weather. Spy stuff.

Actually, the tipping point was that a whole web page was devoted to Carla Vitelli.

She went back to Loyoza's page. The same thing. Many photos of her, taken, no doubt, from a telephoto lens. Many photos of her grave in Evergreen Cemetery. Many photos of the mourners, also from a telephoto lens.

The same with the third victim, Locke.

Dan Atwood wasn't a victim.

Dan Atwood wasn't hapless.

Although he *was* careless. A lot of predators were. It never ceased to amaze Jolie how few serial killers bothered to cover their tracks. So many of them got tripped up by something mundane, or downright stupid. But even then, thanks to the random nature of their

SPECTRE BLACK

predation in a country jammed with people—many of whom wandered from place to place—serial killers got away with their crimes for years. Some of them were never even discovered, let alone caught.

He was either the guy who killed these women, or the pal of a guy who killed these women.

- — -

Jolie took another walk with Rocky down to the pier to clear her head, but her head wouldn't clear. Dan Atwood had fooled them all.

Or at least he had until he'd run into someone stronger and more dangerous. Whether or not that was Carla Vitelli, or her brother, or both, Jolie had no idea.

She wondered if Dan had "loved" Carla from afar or if he'd actively tried to date her. If he'd harassed her, if he had tried to make her a victim, he should have known what was coming. He should have done a little more research on the Denboer family.

Jolie called Cyril Landry, got his voicemail, and left a message. He called back immediately. "What's going on?" he asked.

"I just found out something about Dan Atwood." She filled him in on the website Atwood had put up, devoted to Carla Vitelli. How he had stalked her. "It was more than just a crush. There were . . . production values. I'm sending it to you now."

"The webpage?"

"Yes. Take a look at it. I'll wait."

Silence on the other end. Then, "This is bad. Jesus, what was he *thinking*?"

"It explains why Dan Atwood ended up in the Denboers' bean field," Jolie said. "One theory, anyway, but the one I'm going with. Atwood also had websites for two other women. Both of them are dead."

She let that sink in. "That makes three big dots, and they're all connecting. This—what he did with Carla—is classic stalking behavior."

"He confiscated Jace's Camaro," Landry said. "Why would he do that?"

"Maybe he was doing it because he could. In your face, you know? Maybe to enjoy the moment, piss Jace off. The only question in my mind is when Carla found out she was getting that kind of attention."

"That's not the only question."

"You're thinking she killed him, right? Carla or Jace?"

"Makes sense to me."

"Carla isn't the kind to be a sitting duck. If she knew about the website, if she thought he was obsessed with her, she would have done one of two things. She'd either bring all the weight of her position down on his ass and put him in federal prison where the sun don't shine, or she'd take care of it directly."

"From my experience," Landry said, "she's hands-on."

"In more ways than one."

"The lady likes control. She hates rejection. She likes to—"

"Mess with people?"

"Yes. Another thought. She wouldn't want to draw any attention to the farm."

"But why go after *me*?" Jolie asked. "I'm assuming she and Jace were together on that. Maybe it *was* all Jace. I still don't know why Jace came after me. Maybe it was the Dan Atwood case. But I wasn't getting anywhere. Not even close."

"She knew you wouldn't quit."

"She was right. I'm still not done with them."

"Carla knew that. But if she could rattle you, find a way to get you out of there . . ."

"There are other good detectives besides me."

"But she got you out of the way."

Just then she heard the blast of a horn. The Amtrak train came hurtling past. "Talk later," she shouted.

SPECTRE BLACK

She got you out of the way.

Jolie stood in the lurid red blur of the sunset and watched the train arrow past, the shapes of people in lighted windows whizzing by, and thought: *You only thought you did.*

She had more work to do on the man who called himself Dan Atwood. Jolie didn't give a rat's ass about Dan Atwood himself—or whoever he really was—but she did care about his previous victims. She'd found freak sites for Anita Loyoza and Erin Locke, but hadn't located one for Karin Stokes. Maybe it had been taken down. Maybe Atwood hadn't gotten around to putting one up. But she now knew he was her killer.

The families of the victims should know that the man who had stalked these women and killed them was now dead himself.

If it were *her* loved one, Jolie would want to know.

In fact, she'd be glad to hear he was dead. She would dance on his grave.

That call, though, would be up to Detective Vicki Dodd.

Jolie punched in Vicki's extension; she answered on the second ring.

"I'm sending you some more links," Jolie said. "To websites. We're a long way from proving anything, but it could clear the Stokes case, and probably some others. You can contact the detectives in Tucson and Albuquerque for the other two."

Vicki thanked her. "I can get a subpoena for these sites. This could be big. Atwood could be 'The Inside Man.'"

"Could be," Jolie said. "I hope it is."

She knew Vicki would reap the reward for this, and that was fine with her. Anything to be away from that corrupt bottom-feeder of a county sheriff.

They ended up talking about politics at the sheriff's office and Detective Frankel, whose wife just had a new baby. And then Vicki asked her the million-dollar question. Was she coming back?

Jolie said, "Maybe for a visit."

"I'm sorry to hear that," Vicki said. "Well. Wow. Thanks, for this. I'll talk to whomever you want me to talk to, if you find a job—"

"It's probably best if you don't."

"But you're a cop. How are you going to get another job if we don't clear this up?"

"I'll think of something," Jolie said. She realized her voice was too bright, that she sounded just a wee bit on the manic side. Time to cut the cord. "Just make sure the survivors know what happened to their loved ones."

"You know I will."

"Yes, I *do* know you will. Thanks again, Vicki. It's been . . . good."

She disconnected. She felt the sadness pulling at her the way the ocean had pulled away at the sand around her feet when she stood in it yesterday. Whittling it away from under you until there was nothing left to stand on.

The train was gone. It was time to go in and feed Rocky and Rudy, maybe make a little dinner for herself while she was at it.

On her way back up the beach, Jolie removed the SIM card from the burner phone. She chucked the phone in one garbage can and the SIM card in another.

Ten minutes later she bought another phone in the drugstore on the corner, and transferred the very few important phone numbers from her thumb drive.

She also had Cyril Landry's and Eric the Red's numbers on her new phone.

They were all she needed for now.

CHAPTER 30

Middle of the night in his room at the Travelodge, Landry woke up. What woke him was the sound of not one, but two tractor-trailer trucks driving by.

He checked his watch: three minutes past two a.m.

Landry pushed back the sheets, stepped onto the cool tile, and went to the window. He peered through the gap between the curtains, saw the taillights of the second rig swaying past.

No writing on the back, just double doors. The rig looked like every other semi truck he'd ever seen. A dull silver or pale gray, double doors from top to bottom, mud flaps, round red taillights on both sides. He hadn't been able to see the top of the cab—it was just a blur in the darkness.

This was the main route through town, and tractor-trailer trucks went through all the time.

Still, he waited, expecting to see more of them drive by.

None did, so he went back to sleep.

PART THREE

PART THREE

CHAPTER 31

In the morning, Landry went to work as usual. He was driving the crimson Forenza now, which seemed to fit his station in life. He drove along the road past the spot where Dan Atwood was buried and likely met his end, and turned in under the arched wrought-iron gate to the Valleyview Experimental Agricultural Station. He followed the pristine blacktop to the employees' parking lot and parked, even though there were only two other cars in the lot. One belonged to Denboer's personal assistant. The other belonged to one of the farmworkers who tended the hydroponic plants.

Landry checked his watch—seven thirty. Time to make his first round of the property before charging his sat phone.

Usually, the lot was about a third full by this time. Landry had grown to recognize the cars and had matched them to their owners. The lot usually held midsize, midpriced cars: Fords, Dodges and Chevys mostly, and a couple of Kias for the freethinkers. And trucks, the most popular choice among the maintenance crew. Now there were only two. Three, if you counted Landry's Forenza.

A tall chain-link fence decorated with concertina wire surrounded the maintenance and heavy equipment yard beside the parking lot. Usually, there were a number of vehicles in the lot: tractors, graders, dump trucks, service vehicles, go-slow carts, the water truck, a Kawasaki Mule. But today all the equipment was gone. The lot was empty.

Landry stood in the bright light, feeling the heat bear down on the top of his head. Birds were singing. A grackle's loud whistle grated on his ears. He felt a buzz in his gut.

The sprinklers had been on during the night or very early morning—he could smell it on the grass, could see the drops like sequins in the sun. He stared at the pavement leading up to the front of the main building. Stared at the double entry doors to the glass box.

No one was around.

No noises. No tractors. No cars. No voices.

Nothing.

Landry stepped off the asphalt and followed the patch of lawn around the building to the right. He circled the entire building. Then he approached the front from the left side. Cop-like, weapon drawn.

He was ninety-nine percent certain that he wouldn't need his weapon. But all his life he had been trained to rely on more than just one layer of protection. Aside from combat, there was no reason to meet trouble head-on. Operators learned early on that it was best to think a couple of steps ahead, to work out a plan that might or might not be fail-safe, but would have enough layers and options to give him choices.

He heard the hiss of car tires on the road across the fields: commuters driving past, toy cars on a conveyer belt. But there was nothing here, except for the birds.

The place felt deserted.

He reached the glass doors to the front building and gripped the handle. He had been certain the door would be locked, and was surprised to discover it wasn't.

Landry knew the moment he opened the door that the place was empty.

Not just empty. It had been cleaned out. The counter separating the office from the public had been cleared of computers and other office equipment. Two desks remained. The western art was gone from the walls. The potted plants, gone. The posters, gone. Every piece of equipment, down to every cord and plug, had been cleared out. The break-room-slash-kitchen had been dismantled. The chairs gone. The little square tables gone. The burners, the microwave, gone. On and on, every piece of equipment, every stick of furniture: disappeared. The quad charger. The sat phones. The light fixtures.

Julia, Miko Denboer's personal assistant, came to the front desk. "Mr. Denboer told me to tell you we won't be needing you for the foreseeable future." She smiled and held up her hands. "Actually, we won't be needing anyone. We're in the process of remodeling."

"Remodeling?"

"Yes, redecorating. He's tired of the way the place looks."

"He's not here?"

"No. Mr. Denboer's at home, handling all inquiries himself. For the foreseeable future," she added. She used the words "foreseeable future" like a tire iron. She smiled, but Landry could tell she was worried. He glanced at the ceiling. A few twisted wires stuck out where the overhead light panels had been.

Julia shouldered her bag. "I'm going home. Not much to do here." Her voice full of false cheer.

Landry nodded.

"Make sure to lock the place when you leave," she said. Then she walked to the double doors and pushed through, her heels clacking on the flagstone floor.

He was left alone with the emptiness. He checked Denboer's office. Same thing. As if the place had just been built. Good-bye to the plush Chinese carpet, the mahogany desk, the Tiffany lamp, the expensive western art, the potted plants, the large screen, the file cabinets, the computers, the extra chairs, the wall safe. The polished hardwood floor remained, but that was all.

He spent the next hour and a half checking the farm. Every sign of human habitation, of the business—was gone. Not a tractor to be found. Not a plane in the big, voluminous hangar. The tractor-trailer trucks that moved vegetables and plants had disappeared. The sprinkler systems, inside and out, gone. The planes, gone.

Only one thing remained: the hydroponic plants in the greenhouses. The hoses, the lights, and everything else had been removed.

Landry walked back into the empty airplane hangar. It was dark and cool. The light fixtures didn't work and he could see only due to the ambient light from the few windows. From there he walked on to Hangar B. The keypad needed to enter the hangar had been torn out—there were just a few wires: red, yellow, black. So who would stop him? There was no lock on the door.

Hangar B was empty.

But he did see something. Now that the planes were gone, he saw lines grooved into the floor. Long, straight, precision lines. Three sets of them. Each set of lines formed a long rectangle. Another line bisected the rectangle down its length, exactly down the middle. Landry walked over and paced one of the rectangles. He remembered the two rigs that rocketed by his motel last night. The outline on the floor was large and long enough to support a semi. Landry eyeballed the other two. All of them were exactly the same size. Three of them, side by side by side, divided by approximately ten feet. He'd never been allowed in this area, so this came as a surprise to him.

A metal cabinet stood inside the door—a control panel. He walked over. There was a padlock but it had been bent, hadn't completely closed on the latch. Landry managed to work it out of the latch and pulled the door open to reveal a row of switches inside. Three switches in particular stood out. "A," "B," and "C."

He pressed each of them in order, but nothing happened.

Drug operations could pack up everything in an astonishingly short period of time. Minutes, not hours. Fifteen minutes, tops. They always had a contingency plan. If there was a threat, if law enforcement was on the way, they went to their battle stations. The whole thing was coordinated. They could pack it up like a circus in the night and be gone. Gone without a trace.

Landry had seen an article about places like this. A warehouse in Barstow, California. It had belonged to a drug crew that had to leave fast. They'd taken everything down to the screws that fell on the floor. The place was a big factory, but after they were gone, there was nothing left but dust. Dust. Lots of it. Powdery dust that made the factory look as if it hadn't been open in years.

And a rusty padlock on the door.

But there had been vehicles going in and out at all hours. Big semi trucks. Expensive cars.

And there had been levers in the wall. The levers were gone but the wires had remained, and the recessed vaults remained. The levers triggered hydraulics that raised the vehicles to floor level when needed, up through double doors that opened outward. They could then be driven out of the building. When the FBI agent pulled one of the levers, the joint in the middle of the floor buckled upward and opened wide, two long doors that opened to reveal an oblong vault. And just below the top edge of the vault was the top of a tractor-trailer rig.

And once it had been raised high enough, it could be driven right up a short ramp and out of the hidden vault.

No way to know if that was the case here, but Landry guessed that it was.

Once again he thought of the two rigs that woke him in the middle of the night.

They could have been regular tractor-trailer trucks en route to their next stop, or they could have been Denboer's trucks.

Whether or not he'd seen the actual truck or not, he knew what had happened. Denboer and his crew had left like the circus in the night. They were in the wind.

CHAPTER 32

Landry called Jolie. She'd contacted him yesterday and given him a new number, and now she answered on the first ring.

"Can you come out here?" he said.

"When?"

"ASAP."

Silence on her end. He didn't blame her. He added, "Denboer's going down. They all are. But I need you."

"Why me?"

"I need three bodies."

"Bodies, huh?"

Semantics. "I mean three good operators, if that makes you feel better."

"I'm a cop, not an operator."

"All the better. You'll know the laws."

"What do you need me for?"

"As I said, I need three people. Three people I can trust. One is me. The other is Eric. The third is you."

"And what do you want me to do?"

"I want you to pick a port of entry and watch the border."

A pause. Then, "Is this about the Denboers? Is Denboer going to make a run for the border?"

"I think he's going to make a trial run. In fact, he might make three trial runs. Possibly, they'll try at each border crossing, which is why I need three people."

"You really think he'll divide it up?"

"He's got three semis," Landry said. "He might just choose the best place and send all of them through one point of entry. But we've got to at least scout all three."

"Which is where I come in."

"I need two people I can depend on. What do you know about the border crossings?"

"Not that much," Jolie said.

"You still probably know more than me. Three ports of entry: Antelope Wells—"

"Columbus, and Santa Theresa. I've been to two of them."

"That's why I need you."

"It was a long time ago. I can't remember much about either one of them."

Landry said, "What's the best way to move drugs or other contraband across the border without getting caught?"

"In the old days, it would be to drive it across the border—head for open land. The fence is pretty much everywhere now, though, but that doesn't mean you can't get through. All you need is the right kind of saw and someone who knows what he's doing."

It was a sophisticated operation. The bad guys would load the trucks, preset the GPS travel point and meet up at the rendezvous point.

"Border Patrol goes through every thirty minutes. Trucks are turned off, lights off. They saw their way through the fence, wait for the next patrol to pass by, and the truck goes through. You can set your watch by it."

"You know a lot."

"I went out with a DEA agent a couple of times. He told me a ton of stories. He gave me a primer on cartels. One of the biggest in this part of the world is Alacran, headed up by Felix Alcala. *Bad guy*. His lieutenant is a guy named Hector Zuniga. Rumor has it Hector collects heads."

"Heads."

"On the plus side, if there is a plus side, one of Felix Alcala's horses won the All American Futurity. Looks like you two have something in common. So how much stuff do you think these guys are moving?"

"There are two theories about that."

"Oh?"

"One, they're not moving anything. It's a shakedown cruise. And two, they're moving something else—guns, maybe? To make the trip profitable?"

"What do you think?"

"That's what I'd do."

"So Miko's running guns?"

"I think so, but that's not the primary reason."

"You mean he's shipping the technology. Cloaking technology, like the kid's car?"

"And stealth. The semi trucks could be cloaked." But Landry didn't know if he was even close. He had never seen the big trucks. Now he thought the trucks he had seen go by the motel the night before were just your average, run-of-the-mill semis. He doubted they were related to this situation at all. But seeing them had informed his subconscious. He took revelations where he found them.

Denboer had cleared out the farm, except for the hydroponics and the fields. Whatever he was planning, it looked to be a big score.

Jolie said, "Maybe they could smuggle those trucks past, but it would be taking a big chance. If they're invisible at night, then they're extremely valuable. So why are we targeting Columbus, New Mexico, and the other two instead of the miles and miles of empty land in between?"

"Because they're towns. If you look at the map of New Mexico and the border, you'll see there are no roads outside the populated areas—not across the border. The fence blocked them. Most of them were farm roads, dirt roads. There's not a hell of a lot outside the towns, except for farm roads. Now you see them peter off on the satellite map. But there are a few blacktop roads here and there. Near the towns. They just stop at the fence. They're cut off."

"Or," Jolie said, "they're shunted onto the cross street that runs alongside the border fence. That's what I recall, the few times I've been to these border towns."

"What we need is a good graded road or, better yet, a paved road, that goes up to the border on both sides. It doesn't matter if they're cut off by the fence. It would only be . . ." He did the math in his head.

"Thirty, forty yards?" Jolie said. "Less than thirty yards?"

"Fewer," Landry said.

"What? Oh for fuck's sake, you've really got to stop doing that. It's like Tourette's syndrome. It wouldn't be a pleasure cruise but it's doable. Old asphalt, or maybe the asphalt's been torn up and it's dirt. Potholes, maybe. But not impossible. What about the sound, though? People would hear a semi driving by."

"Sure they would. But if it's an area where there are trucks—and there are plenty of trucks going from the US to Mexico and vice versa—people would be used to the sound."

"The sound of commerce." She sighed. "So when do you want me?"

"I told you. Get out here, ASAP."

"You get Tom to fly me out and let me know where to reconnoiter." She added, "Damn it, I'm going to miss my animals."

- — -

At the motel, Landry watched Eric give his Dodge Ram a bath. Eric asked him to look in the glove compartment for the tire gauge, and Landry complied. He leaned into the truck, pulled out the tire gauge, slipped the recorder Eric had used to record the conversation the Army guys had received at the satellite van into his pocket.

Back in Landry's room, they listened.

One voice was definitely Miko Denboer's. The other voice was male, ranging in age between twenty and forty. Anglo. The guy said, "I got the tickets."

Denboer's voice: "You know I want us to get there in one piece. None of these short hops, right?"

"No worries. It's nonstop all the way."

"So the flight's full? I was hoping to bring a friend of—"

"Sorry, no can do. It's tourist season, remember? You'll have to wait for the next one if you want to bring somebody."

"All right with me. We've got a choice, right? Two other flights?"

"That we do."

"Three choices. Anything else?"

"Arrival time in Spain is three a.m. That would be Monday."

"And the reservations? You sure you verified them?"

"What do you think? Of course I did. We're good. You worry too much."

"Hey, thanks for helping me out with this."

"No problem. That's what I get paid the big bucks for."

"Yeah, right!" Laughter. They disconnected.

Eric burped. "I ate too much, gonna walk it off. You wanna come along?"

"Sure."

- — -

They took a walk. No one would be able to hear them.

"So," Eric said. "You thinking what I'm thinking?"

SPECTRE BLACK

"Code?"

"Yeah, a simple one. Three a.m. in Spain translates to eight p.m. Sunday, here."

Landry said, "Early."

"Just after dark. On a Sunday. Maybe it's the best move. It's unexpected. They've got Stealth. You think it's legit?"

"Sunday. Eight p.m. New Mexico time. The flight is full."

"Yeah. About that 'the flight is full.' I thought they would be empty. A dry run."

"Why would they do that?" Landry said.

"If they're caught—"

"If they're caught going dark they're in deep shit anyway. Might as well make the ride down pay for itself. Besides, whoever's driving will be expendable."

"Greedy motherfuckers."

"What other kind of motherfuckers are there?"

"So what do you think they're moving on the run down?" Eric said. "Arms?"

"Semiautomatic rifles are very popular down there."

"Wish they'd mentioned which part of Spain they were going to," Eric said.

"We're going to have to cover all three."

"If they're going Sunday, we have three days. We'll need someone on each entry point."

"They'd probably send their crew down the day before. Maybe two days."

Eric said, "It's a long way between the three crossing points."

"Maybe the satellite van will pinpoint the place."

"Maybe."

Toward evening, Landry picked up Jolie at the Las Cruces airport. The drive back started contentiously.

"You notified the authorities?" she asked him.

"It's too late for that."

"The DEA—"

"It's not up to me to do that—it wouldn't work. They'd write me off as a nutcase."

"What about the Army? The guys in the satellite van? They've been listening in, just as we have."

"So?"

"What do you mean, 'So?'"

"They're not going to help us."

"What do you mean?"

"They're not going to help us."

"It's just *us*? That's crazy."

Landry glanced at her. "They can't help us even if they wanted to."

"They're the US Army."

"The US Army can't initiate a military action on American soil."

"Contact the ATF then. Or the DEA."

"You can try. How do you think that will go over?"

Jolie opened her mouth, then closed it again. She knew how things worked. She was a cop. She'd encountered red tape and stonewalling as much as the next guy. *More* than the next guy.

Actually, she wasn't even a cop anymore. Jolie was a former cop. She had no standing. And even if she had standing, the DEA would not mobilize on her say-so. The DEA was like every other bureaucratic agency in the modern world. It took a while for the machinery to get moving, and that was dependent on the notion that they even *wanted* to act on the intelligence.

Denboer had friends in the DEA. But he was playing both ends against the middle, so he wouldn't be communicating with them.

SPECTRE BLACK

"If it's El Paso," Jolie said, "there's the Army base right there. The guys in the surveillance van are Army."

Landry could tell that Jolie knew, the minute the words left her mouth, that her theory wouldn't fly. "The police are a paramilitary organization," he said. "And you know how the military is.

"These are good men, but the guy in the surveillance van is still Army. In that way the armed forces—any branch you want to name—aren't so different. You know what he'd say. This is not their mission. I can hear him now. It would go like this. One of his guys says, 'Hey, we've got to help.' And the sergeant says, 'We can't without proper authorization.' And the gung-ho guy, he'll say, 'They could mobilize from the Army base in El Paso.' And the sergeant would say, 'By the time it went up the chain of command, it would be all over anyway.'"

"But—"

"And the gung-ho guy would say, 'But there are three American citizens putting their lives in danger.' And the sergeant would say, 'Son, do you want to be the soldier who executes a military action on American soil?' He'd say, 'Do you want to be on TV for that? You know that we aren't authorized for that kind of operation. We can't, anyway. It's impossible.' And that's the Army."

Landry added, "And then he's saying that the US Army is not a law enforcement agency, that all they can do is pass along what they know. By then, it's going to be too late. Even if they notified the proper authorities—and they'd have to contact a commanding officer with some pull, somewhere on some military base—you think they're going to flood the Mexican border with military and start an international incident?"

"No," Jolie said. "I don't."

"And the last thing the satellite van guy would say is this: 'We can't do anything. We're not even supposed to be here in the first place.'"

Jolie had checked into the Holiday Inn in Las Cruces. Eric and Landry checked in as well, all three of them at different times of day and using different aliases. Eric's room was across the common area, closer to the pool. Landry was on the other side. Jolie got a room halfway between. There were a lot of people staying there, which provided them cover.

Their first bull session was in Landry's room.

They had done their homework. They'd studied physical maps but mostly relied on Google Earth for terrain and ease of use.

They needed to anticipate what Denboer and his crew would do. Fortunately, they had the timeline, thanks to the coded language Landry and Eric had intercepted. They knew when they would transport the trucks, but not where they would cross the border.

Since Denboer had cleared out of the farm and put the trucks on the road, there must be another hiding place. It would stand to reason that it would be somewhere fairly close to the Mexican border. There were three border entry stations, and the land in between was vast and inhospitable. But somewhere they would find a barn or a structure large enough to house the three trucks.

If there *were* three trucks.

"This is all supposition," Landry said. "The best we can do is put ourselves into their shoes and imagine what they would do."

They looked at the three ports of entry.

Antelope Wells, New Mexico, was a long way down over rough roads. Pro: there were places to pass through the fence without being seen. Con: it was a very long drive through the interior of Mexico on inferior roads. The closest town in Mexico was almost ninety miles away. Antelope Wells just wasn't doable. It wasn't cost-effective.

There could be access to an airstrip long enough to accommodate a cargo plane, deep in the interior of Sonora. A few years ago, they would have taken that into consideration. But now they had

Google Maps. There were no airstrips of that size. There were hardly any airstrips at all.

They did not have access to the latest satellite photos, however. All things were possible. But were they *probable?*

Columbus, New Mexico was a small town with a sleepy crossing. The official Point of Entry was staffed. Columbus might be small but several roads on the US side fed into roads opposite them on the border, even though the border fence had cut them off. Most of the corresponding roads in Mexico were dirt, but there were a number of places to hide the trucks in plain sight; plenty of businesses required semi trucks. Produce, for one. And all sorts of goods that came through the border area.

Santa Theresa, near Sunland Park and off to the side of El Paso, was the biggest. Once through the border crossing, there were many feeder roads into Mexico. It was the fastest way, freeways all the way down, and many places to cross. There were also plenty of industrial areas there, which would require semi trucks. But this was the major artery and port of entry, and it was policed heavily.

Landry thought the wise move would be to take the middle road. In addition to having all the desirable qualities for moving trucks through, Columbus was the closest border crossing, and it was reached by an empty highway: a straight line between two points. Even the highway, State Route 1, no longer held the designation of a state route. It was now Highway 11. There was access to dead-end roads on the other side of the Mexican border; plenty of semis passed through legitimately.

Columbus was Goldilocks – just right.

"They had to leave earlier than they expected to," Jolie said. "The way they packed up the farm. I've heard of that before—some of these big organizations can be packed up within fifteen minutes, like they were never there. The first thing we need to do is find out if the trucks are still hidden there. Something spooked Denboer. Otherwise, they would have kept the semis hidden inside the hangar."

"So we look for structures," Eric said. "Something big enough to hide three semis. Some place remote."

"It's remote down there."

They went to Google Maps again.

There were a few farms on Highway 11. Two of them had large barns. One looked abandoned. They focused first on the abandoned farm.

Jolie said, "We know the time and date they're planning to go—unless that's changed. How far is the farm from the port of entry?"

"Thirty-five miles," Eric said.

"I think it's this place. It's the best guess we have. We have infrared scopes—we can tell if there are people there. We need to take turns watching."

It was decided that Jolie would go early, set up, and watch the barn. The other barn was farther away from the border and looked new. "We should check that place, too," Landry said.

"I can do that," Eric said. "If they're there, we should blow them up. End problem."

"The technology," Landry said. "Good or bad, the technology is cutting-edge. I want to see them for myself."

"If we blow 'em up there, it's the endgame. It's over."

"I'd rather neutralize whoever's guarding them and see what these things are like." He looked at Jolie.

"I want to see them, too."

"Neutralize, or kill?" Eric said.

"Depends, as it always does. We can't take any chances. We can't take prisoners, either. So we'd have to secure them."

"Secure them," Jolie said.

Eric looked from one to the other. "Okay. It's your funeral."

Added under his breath, "And probably mine."

CHAPTER 33

Landry and Jolie went car shopping in the want ads. They bought a 2008 Dodge Challenger that had been souped up. The owner was happy to sell it for cash.

Eric took the truck, and Landry and Jolie followed in the dark gray Challenger. Eric kept going, but Landry and Jolie turned off at the first of the two farms they'd spotted on Google Earth. Both of them had barns big enough to conceal a semi truck or two. And both of the farms were not far from the border with Mexico.

The first was a stud farm, "OAK TREE QUARTER HORSES: Racing, Breeding, Pleasure Horses." Landry and his "wife" Jolie rumbled the Challenger over the cattle guard to inquire within.

The owner was a woman in her late forties. A good-looking woman who would have been spectacular if she hadn't spent the majority of her natural life in the New Mexico sun. Landry could tell she didn't give a rat's ass about her complexion—she was having too much fun following her dream. Her long, dark brown hair was pulled into a ponytail. She wore a pistol in a paddle holster clipped to the belt of her jeans. As they parked, she walked out to greet them. Friendly, but all business. Sizing them up for riding horses.

Landry asked if she had any off-track thoroughbreds, and nodded to Jolie, who slid out of the passenger's seat and walked over.

The woman, Jeri, said she had a couple, and offered them a tour of the farm.

Landry thought the horses were pretty good. He'd heard the names of the forebears of the two stallions in residence. Well known in quarter horse circles. And the thoroughbred stallion, Archangelico, was a looker.

Jeri led them to the barn. It was like a hundred barns Landry had seen before. Open doors on both ends. A row of four stalls on one side, and three stalls and a tack room on the other. The stalls on each side were grouped together, making for a wide central aisle.

The barn was massive and very old, and had been modified to stable horses—a relic from an earlier era now utilized in a different way.

The stalls were pipe fence construction. The floor was concrete and covered by a thick layer of raked dirt sprayed down with water.

They walked back outside after the short tour. The house must have been built about the same time as the barn. Old, stuccoed adobe. A late-sixties-model Chevy Malibu, primer-gray, sat next to an eighties-model Ford truck. The Chevy had new tires, a yellow front fender, and was jacked up just a little in back.

"The Chevy run?" Landry asked.

"Nope. It's my brother's car—he's thinking of selling it." She eyed the muscle car, decided she might have someone on the hook. "You interested? It would be worth a lot if it was cherry."

"No."

They talked horses for a bit. Jeri handed Jolie her card, telling her how well one of her stallions had done at Sunland Park. She concentrated on the woman because it was usually the woman who one, loved horses and two, made the big purchases. She told Jolie how exciting it was to get into racing. Nothing like it, she said. Jeri was sorry she didn't have any horses to meet their needs. Racing was their emphasis, but most of these horses were trained for riding.

"One down," Landry said as they drove away.

The second ranch was abandoned. Since the last Google Earth shot, the roof of the farmhouse had caved in. Not only that, but it was too small to hide an underground vault for three semis inside.

The barn was equally impossible—filled to the brim with rubble and junk. Someone had shuttled half a house into the barn and left it there.

"Makes me think of farmers leaving the Dust Bowl back in the thirties," Jolie said. "Snake eyes. Now what?"

"They've got the trucks hidden somewhere," Landry said. "Maybe they're still in Branch."

"Where they always were. Inside those vaults in Hangar B."

Landry thought about the levers that had been removed out of the cabinet at Denboer's farm, the loose wires. He didn't think there was any other way to open up the doors to the vaults.

But maybe they'd had a second junction box. Someone could do it from a distance by punching in a code.

Jolie seemed to read his mind. "No matter how you slice it, they had it covered. I hope we didn't miss them—I'd really like to see what they're like."

"We will," Landry said. "All we have to do is wait."

"Yeah. *If* this is where they're headed."

CHAPTER 34

Landry and Jolie drove down through the town of Columbus, New Mexico, before hitting flat desert again. They reached the outskirts of the other, smaller portion of Columbus, this one situated right on the border with Mexico. They met up with Eric at a rest area a half mile from Columbus.

The rest area was no more than a picnic table chained to a garbage barrel, a healthy-looking yucca, and a shack marked "WOMEN" on one side and "ME" on the other—the "N" was gone.

"'Me,'" Eric said. "Nice of them to make it so exclusive."

"Very funny," Jolie said, "Better keep your day job." She consulted her phone.

"What are you doing?"

"This is the time to alert the Border Patrol," she said.

"I wouldn't," Landry said.

"We need to. For one thing, if they see a gun battle on the border, how are they going to know who the bad guys are?"

She had a point. Landry said, "What if they see us engage and they think we're the bad guys?"

"I flash my badge."

"You think they're gonna wait for you to hold it up?"

"They'll know I'm there. Or I could meet up with them ahead of time."

Landry shrugged. "Then you tell them what to look for and let them handle it. I don't want to be part of a free-for-all. Everyone shooting at everyone else. That's a good way to get killed."

"I'll tell them who we are."

"And who is that?"

Jolie had no answer. Finally, she said, "I don't mention you."

"Which will make us sitting ducks."

"They should be there. It's their job. Whether we contact them or not, they'll be there. They're right on the border, they patrol it day and night."

"Okay," Landry said. "We'll monitor the situation. Where will they be?"

"I'm assuming right on the border. A show of force."

"The runners will spot them. They'll just turn the trucks around and go back. Wait for another time."

Jolie had no answer to that, either.

But she was a cop, first and foremost, and so ultimately, she made the call. She used her burner phone. Gave her badge number and her real name. Told them she had reason to believe, from a CI she'd been working with, that three or more semis would try to penetrate the border into Palomas carrying arms. She gave them the approximate time range.

"Think they'll respond?" Landry asked when she ended the call.

"Oh, they'll respond, in one manner or other. Either with a show of force or with one car. But we can't leave it to them—if the agent talks to the Branch Sheriff's Department, all bets are off."

"What I was thinking," Eric said.

"Look at it this way," Jolie said. "It's their job to take care of it. Which means we won't have to."

"*If* they take care of it," Landry said. "We'll still have to be there to see that they do."

Eric said, "No matter what, we make our own plan."

Landry said, "Agreed."

From here they would split up. Jolie would go with Eric—it was a two-man job to find the right side street—while Landry scouted a place to set up his G3. It would be difficult, because the land was as flat as a Monopoly board. Looking for high ground was pointless.

Once he found that place, he would come back to the highway and watch for the trucks to come through.

He drove into the truncated version of Columbus. He looked at Google Maps and put himself in the place of Denboer and his crew, and immediately saw the best way for the trucks to get through. The second option wasn't even close. Landry needed a spot where he would have a clear shot at the area along the border fence. He'd need elevation.

After driving around for a half hour, Landry found the only good place to set up: a well-water-pipe access shed caged by a chain-link fence. The shed had a mild pitch to the roof, which would be useful. The slope of the roof would conceal him from the border fence.

The watershed was deserted, as these sheds usually were. Landry easily defeated the padlock holding the chain to the post and the gate, and clambered up onto the roof. He rested the tripod of his sniper rifle on the down-slope of the roof, looked through it. A clear shot. The shed was ideal. It was approximately eight hundred yards from the most likely access area—no problem for his G3.

That done, Landry returned to the rest area. He needed to be there when the trucks came through. One, to see who was escorting them, and two, to take out one or more of them if he could.

He knew that by now, Jolie and Eric would be in position. In an ideal world, Landry would manage to leave them with nothing to do. Either the Border Patrol would take care of it, or he would. But if he couldn't get his shot, if the Border Patrol didn't come, Jolie and Eric could handle the situation.

They had surprise on their side.

Back at the rest area, Landry stood by the side of the road and glassed the highway between the north section of Columbus and the section of Columbus on the border. So far, it was empty. There had been very few cars.

This was the first place to engage.

He glanced around, looking for places to mount an ambush. There were a few low bushes but they were burro brush, small little clumps close to the ground. He drove the Challenger around back of the restrooms, parked, and waited.

Forty minutes later he heard cars coming. Not just cars: the mosquito whine of dune buggies, tearing across the desert. And big engines on the road. He knew what they were: runner cars. They were there to protect the trucks: the three big semis barreling down the highway to the border. Landry stepped behind the restrooms, trained his binocs on one of the cars—a beater with a big engine. Still far out but noisy as hell.

They would run interference with anyone or any entity in their way. By attracting attention to themselves, creating diversions, or—

Ready for an outright gun battle.

The road cars zipped by, but returned a few minutes later, heading back in the direction they'd come from. The dune buggies circled back around, too.

Soon even their sound was gone.

For a while, there was quiet.

But Landry knew the trucks would be coming. They weren't all that far down the road.

It was late afternoon now. The grassland here was studded by low bushes. From a distance, a prone human would not be seen. A head and torso could easily be mistaken for a small bush. They would be round, dark shadows dotting the grassland, just like every other round, dark shadow out there.

No cars at all, at the moment.

Landry decided to cross the road and scout for a better position to engage the caravan that was most certainly coming. The opposite side of the road was the ideal place to shoot from because at that point, the highway bent in a westerly direction. Anyone driving toward him from either direction would have a hard time seeing—the sun would be in his or her eyes.

The grassland was tinged gold but would soon turn to gray.

He looked in both directions, saw nothing, and walked to the edge of the road. He kept his weapon at his side, always looking to blend in, just a guy walking across the road, maybe to look for a place to take a few pictures of the desert. The sun's red eye seemed to burst behind his eyeballs. In this light, the sun would be in the driver's eyes. Anyone coming down from the north would have a hard time seeing him.

But just as he stepped onto the verge, a gust of wind hit him.

CHAPTER 35

Landry stepped back—almost as if he'd been pushed back by the blast of warm air.

He had the sensation of something big rushing past—

Then it was gone.

He knew what it was.

He'd recognized the sound of the big rig's engine, if not the intensity. They must have found a way to muffle the noise.

He squinted in the direction the truck had gone and thought he saw a tall oblong that could have been the landscape but was slightly out of kilter, moving independently from the grassland and road around it—defined by negative space.

Like a mirror made of old wavy glass walking itself down the road.

It receded into the red haze as if it wasn't there at all.

By the time the second semi blew through, Landry was lying flat on the dirt by the side of the road, sheltered by a clump of burro brush. This time he had already been looking north, but saw nothing—

And then, mud flaps, slapping in the wind of the semi's passing, right past his ear. The high-pitched drill of big tires on the pavement, chains rattling and swaying on the chain-hangers.

He did not move, remained prone. Waited for the third rig.

And waited.

Ten seconds.

Thirty seconds.

A minute.

The third one was late.

This was good.

He went around the restrooms and started up the Dodge Challenger. He patted the steering wheel and said to the car, "I hate to do this."

It was hard to see, but his binocs locked on something. Coming. Like wind pushing down the highway. Impossible to see from this distance, but the runner cars were back—a dune buggy driving the desert on one side, and another car opposite. He could see the dust billowing up behind them.

Running interference.

He had to go by the runner cars. They would be his signal. But they weren't here yet.

Landry had to time it perfectly.

He measured the distance between the cars and where he was. They would be abreast of the invisible semi truck.

If he went too soon, they would be able to stop the truck.

If he went too late, the semi would bulldoze into him and turn the Challenger into a crushed tin can.

He revved the engine. Drove onto the verge. Waited. And waited some more. They had reached the place where the road bent toward the west, into the eye of the sun.

This wouldn't work if they saw him.

Landry had utilized the knowledge more than once during his time in Iraq: It takes a loaded semi truck driving sixty-five miles per hour under ideal conditions approximately 316 feet to stop completely. Nearly the entire length of a football field.

As the runner cars and the virtually invisible truck approached, Landry counted down in his head. One-one-hundred, two-one-hundred, three-one-hundred.

The runner cars keeping apace. Landry had to get past them, and hope they were still abreast of the thing he could not see.

The smallest mistake, and he was a dead man.

Now!

His foot jammed the gas pedal hard to the floor and the Challenger slewed onto the road. Slammed on the brakes, dead center, the grille on one side and back bumper on the other. Pulled on the door handle, shoved the heavy door open, and dove out of the car.

A little bit of a slope on the other side—

Rolled.

Right into a bush. Skidded down past it and lay on the ground like a lizard flat to a screen door.

He heard the hiss of air brakes, the stuttering screech of rubber as the semi stood on its tires, the cars out in the desert driving diagonally in the road's direction, slewing through the dirt, fountains of dust shooting from under their tires—

Destruction in slow motion.

- — -

Landry's mind ticked through the phases.

The truck would skid. The truck box would torque sideways, arresting forward motion. It would try to topple on its side.

Landry peered through the brush. He was right about that. The truck, barely visible, seemed to tremble in the air like a rectangular heat wave, canting to the right, the mesh of screaming metal and crunching truck body sounding like the death throes of a dinosaur. It was monumental.

The box toppled and slid, skidded the few feet to smack right into the cab, ramming into the back, crushing the life out of whoever was within.

Landry didn't wait to see the leviathan come to rest. He was already halfway up the low rise on the other side, keeping low and to the bushes, rifle slung over his back and his H&K in his hand.

By the time he reached his new hiding place among the burro brush, he could look back at the chaos.

More cars slewed to a stop near the big rig. Landry watched them through his rifle scope. Recognized the chase cars: a jacked-up four-wheel-drive truck with KC roof lights.

And a souped-up primer-gray car.

The car was a 1960s-era Chevy Malibu complete with a yellow-painted front panel.

Landry watched as the driver got out and walked over to survey the damage along with the rest of them.

Slim figure. T-shirt, jeans, running shoes. Attractive.

Long brown hair in a ponytail.

Jeri.

It all clicked into place: the temporary pipe fencing in a barn that in retrospect seemed way too big for its function; the concrete pad covered over with a thick layer of dirt; the primer-gray car with the yellow fender panel.

The horse farm.

The semis had been hidden right under their feet. If he'd paid more attention, if he'd kicked up the layer of dirt from the cement floor . . .

Regrets never got you anywhere.

He called in to Jolie and to Eric.

"We're down to two trucks now," he said.

- — -

"Two trucks," Jolie said to Eric.

They were sitting in the Dodge Ram truck, one among a handful of cars parked in the Columbus Port of Entry lot.

This side of the border was virtually deserted. There was a small neighborhood north of the port of entry farther north on Highway 11, but the area on the US side of the border was sparse. No way they would miss any vehicles coming their way. The trucks might be invisible—it was dusk now and hard to see—but the runner cars around them would soon have to use their headlights, or at least their parking lights. They were counting on that.

Every second that ticked by brought them closer to darkness. In this case, darkness was better.

Their theory was that the trucks would turn west on the road bordering the north end of the port of entry parking lot.

"See any Border Patrol?" Eric asked.

"Just those two in the parking lot." Most of the Border Patrol cars had peeled out twenty minutes before, after the collision on the highway. Landry was keeping them informed.

It hadn't just been Border Patrol. It had been Luna County Sheriff's. It had been Columbus PD municipal cars and emergency vehicles of every stripe—

Although they were few enough down here.

"Their attention will be on the truck," Eric the Red said. "Every emergency vehicle for miles will be drawn to the scene."

"Leaves it to us," Jolie said.

He made a noise in his throat—agreement.

"Except for whoever's patrolling the border," Jolie added. Border Patrol trucks patrolled the border area every thirty minutes. You could set your watch by them. One Border Patrol agent to a car, Jolie thought, although it was getting too dark to see.

It was *some*thing.

But for real dependability, she had the man beside her and Landry up on the roof of the water facility, covering them.

The place was quiet. Dead. The sky had gone from red to purple, and now it was near dark. Sodium arc lights came on in the parking lot, first glowing a pale sapphire blue, and then orange and finally, gold.

Cars went through on the main road into Mexico, but not many. Jolie could see their taillights as they stopped and then were waved through. Fewer cars came up from Palomas, and took longer to come through and past them.

There had been a lull, though. No vehicles other than a Border Patrol truck had appeared going either way for at least twenty minutes. The border was dead tonight.

Eric straightened, looking at the rearview mirror. "Cars coming," he said. "From the north."

One car drove straight to the port of entry. But the two cars after that turned right on the road behind them.

When they did, their lights went out.

"Is that what I think it is?" she asked.

In the last light of day they could see the cars, although they were indistinct in the gloom. Between the first car and the second, there was negative space.

The negative space wasn't really negative. Something was passing by, but it was impossible to tell what, because no light reflected off its surface. It was like a blank space, only Jolie could see the ground scrolling through it, just a shadow of the ground, the dry grass, the weeds. And way in the distance, the pinprick lights of Columbus—the larger part of Columbus to the north. *Something* sliding past, virtually invisible.

More cars turned onto the road. Followed by another space that wasn't a space.

The faintest growl of an engine.

A semi's engine.

"That is some kind of spooky," Eric said. He donned his night-vision goggles, and handed Jolie her pair. *Then* she saw the driver of the semi truck. A flare of color.

Two of them. Two semis.

Two, because the third one had been wrecked on the highway.

SPECTRE BLACK

A half hour earlier, before the sun went down, they'd driven this road, little more than a dirt track for Border Patrol trucks. There were two places where Denboer's trucks could go through. The first was very close to the border crossing. Neither of them thought Denboer would risk it, even if the vehicles went stealth. The road, a sixteenth of a mile from where they sat in their truck, looped into a turnaround for big trucks. On the Mexican side of the border fence, the ground in that spot was hardpan, solid as concrete, and could support a truck of that size. And near that was an east-west road on the Mexican side that ran along the border. A couple of north-south streets intersected with the road. Since the fence was built, those roads had no place to go. Still, it was the best possible place to cross—if you didn't take into account its proximity to the border crossing.

But there was another place, virtually identical, approximately four miles farther to the west.

"If it was me, that's where I'd go," Eric said, as the runner car in the lead turned on the road parallel to the border and the others followed. They watched through binocs, following their slow progress as they bumped along the road. Lights out for everyone, but there was still some ambient illumination.

"Twenty bucks they'll go straight," Eric said.

"I'm not taking that bet."

But she should have, because Eric was wrong.

It was getting hard to see, darker by the minute, the cars running lights-off, jouncing slowly along the rutted road, but they could see the taillights when the vehicles braked. They could see them turning.

Then they heard a truck starting up.

Jolie recalled seeing a truck parked beside a building across the short expanse of desert to the north. Now it drove in the direction of the caravan.

"Shit! What's *that?*"

"Jace." Jolie recognized the engine noise. She heard it peel out and go. Definitely a muscle car, that deep-throated grumble, the sound she'd heard the night she had hidden outside the Circle K about a thousand years ago.

"So much for stealth," Eric said.

The Camaro, which would have been invisible except for its lights, shot past them on Highway 11. With a shriek of brakes, the car nearly stood on its front wheels before slewing into the port of entry parking lot, going south. Heading for the port of entry itself.

"What's he doing?"

"Donuts," Eric said.

The noise was incredible. The car shrieked like a wounded dinosaur. Lurching, stopping, backing up under the sodium arc lights, speeding forward again, stopping, tires squealing, tires *smoking*. Backing up in wild circles before straightening out and stampeding forward again.

People ran out of the building and stood on the walk, helpless and scared. The engine revved. The tires squealed. Suddenly the headlights went out just as the screaming car hurtled forward again, scaring them back indoors. Around and around, carving out space in the parking lot. Pedal to the metal.

Border Patrol agents bolted from the booth. One ran for his car, and was nearly hit by the rogue Camaro.

"A diversion," Jolie said.

They got out of the truck, having already been careful to turn the door light off. Guns at the ready, moving fast.

"There they are," Eric said, nodding toward the cars and trucks driving down the access road.

"Right in the Border Patrol's backyard." Jolie looked back at the port of entry. Couldn't see the car at all, now. But she sure could hear it.

CHAPTER 36

Landry watched the Camaro squeal out of the port of entry parking lot, nearly sideswiping another car before hitting Highway 11 going north. *Audacious*, he thought.

He followed the car through the G3's scope. Thought about taking him out, but the kid's job was done. He'd created the diversion, but Landry had to keep his eye on the ball.

Jace Denboer was the Border Patrol's problem.

But he was wrong. Ten minutes later he heard the muffled sound of an engine, a big engine. He couldn't see the Camaro, not now, but he could hear it.

Jace had created his diversion and was coming back for the finale.

Landry trained his eye on the caravan headed for the border fence.

Shakedown Cruise.

All along, he'd doubted the trucks were empty. Customs had drive-through X-ray machines, but these trucks would have the technology to blank out their X-ray, making the inside of the truck box appear empty. Yes, the BP had dogs, but dogs couldn't sniff out weapons—guns were just metal and oil. And if the scanners were aced out . . . no problem at all. It was the unexpected thing: they weren't so worried about contraband being smuggled out of the US into Mexico. But it would be better to go through the fence. It fit with Denboer, who was greedy.

He didn't want anyone to see his magic trucks. Or even get wind of their passing.

Unfortunately for Denboer, one truck had already crashed. That set the parameters for what came next. Two choices: abort, or keep going, full bore.

The Border Patrol and other cops converging on the scene must be wondering what the hell they were looking at. Landry understood Denboer's audaciousness in going through with the run. Once the trucks were in Mexico they would stand a better chance of going undetected—especially if Denboer's people had already chosen a warehouse on the other side to hide them.

He checked in with Jolie. She answered immediately, her voice low. "Looks like they're taking the easy route. We're on it. We're right here. Can you see us?"

"Roger that."

As they spoke, the lead car went dark, and so did the others. The place was ideal: a dark spot, no lights, no contrast.

A truck engine started to life. Landry focused on the direction of the sound. A dirt lane, little more than a chicken scratch, ran perpendicular to the road along the border. Headlights came on about a half mile up that road. It was dark, but watching through the night-vision infrared scope he could see the vehicle as it jounced down the lane toward the border fence.

A tow truck.

The truck halted a couple of car lengths from the border fence. Two men jumped out of the cab. They were fast and good, used precision tools to cut grooves toward the top of the iron fence—eighteen feet between them—working from opposite sides with plasma cutters shielded by what Landry knew would be lightweight steel shields—a little circle around the nozzle of each gun. Otherwise, the light would be seen for miles.

SPECTRE BLACK

Miko Denboer jumped down from the passenger's side of the lead semi, and stood watching the men as they started to work. He held a Heckler & Koch MP5 at his side.

"Good choice," Landry muttered. The most reliable submachine gun on the market—the same make and model of the gun he'd brought to New Mexico.

It would take them all of five seconds to cut and drop the fence. When the trucks were through, they'd use the tow truck's pulley to replace the fence and tap weld it here and there to make it seem as if it had never been cut.

The lead semi, which had been idling, shifted gears. In another moment it would nudge the fence so that it would fall flat. And then the semi would roll over it and into Mexico.

Time to stop it.

And that was when Jolie and Eric stepped out of the dark. Jolie held her badge up under her weapon. Eric aimed his G3 at Miko Denboer.

The two men who had been cutting the fence used the opportunity to scurry away into the dark.

The empty tow truck blocked traffic access to the fence.

Denboer's chief of security jumped down from the cab with his M-16 and waved it around. Started firing indiscriminately.

Jolie and Eric hit the dirt.

Time stretched, as it always did in these situations. Landry was a half mile away, easy. But his rifle was zeroed three power to 55 power. Which meant he could see a wide field of terrain from a great distance and at the same time concentrate on his target up close and personal.

His peripheral vision was stellar, and he had all the magnification he needed.

Suddenly he heard a whoop of a siren.

Border Patrol.

Eric was fast. On his feet in seconds, he used the surprise factor—and the butt of his G3—to knock Denboer's security chief down.

More Border Patrol vehicles coming, a caravan of them, still a couple of miles away, but coming fast. Dust rose in a scrim around their headlights.

Landry peered through the scope. He had Miko Denboer in his sights. He could squeeze, just the slightest pressure, and blow Denboer to kingdom come.

He wanted to. He was trained for it. He had the man, owned him. It would take the lightest bit of pressure—

But he didn't.

He stood down.

Then everything changed. Oblivious to the Border Patrol cars, Miko Denboer raised his submachine gun and trained it on Jolie.

Landry took his shot.

CHAPTER 37

Denboer dropped like a marionette that had abruptly lost its strings—straight down. The MP5 slipped out of his hand and bounced once on the ground beside him. Landry had made the kill shot dead center in the "death triangle": the area between the eyes and the bridge of the nose.

The world had telescoped down to one small area to Landry. He had the power here. He could choose his shots.

An engine screamed—the muscle car was coming back. The sound so familiar it had ingrained itself into his psyche.

The Camaro roared up the road and skidded to a stop, generating a massive cloud of dust. In the infrared scope Landry saw two men running for the car. One was one of the fence cutters, but the other, Landry recognized. Small, hunched, a monkey of a man. Landry had seen him in another venue, the Tobosa County Sheriff's Office. Sheriff Ron Waldrup reached the Camaro first, dove in, and closed the door behind him, leaving the fence cutter behind. The Camaro slewed around in the dirt and took off.

Landry was about to take him out when he saw something else to the left—a man leaning on the hood of one of the runner cars, raising a submachine gun. Pointed at Jolie.

Easy choice.

Landry put him down, then turned his attention to the Camaro. The dust along the car's dead-black paint job was just enough to screen the car.

Landry could have still made the shot if he could see the Camaro, but the dust along with the car's dead black paint job was just enough to screen the car. He aimed for what might be the back window. The window exploded. By then, though, the Camaro had traction. Engine screaming, the car slewed onto the border road, fishtailing in a fountain of dust. Jace overcorrected, banged off one of the iron fence posts, straightened out, and accelerated away.

But the gun battle was still raging, and Landry had to take out whoever was still shooting. He dispatched two other shooters, but let the two fence cutters run off into the desert.

Thinking: that was one fast damn car.

- — -

Landry drove north on Route 11. His passengers were both quiet. Jolie stared at the road ahead, but Eric, in the back, was asleep.

Landry kept to a steady fifty-eight on the two-lane road. He didn't want to attract any interested parties. Like the New Mexico State Police, or worse, the sheriff's office. As it was, he'd had to drive through three jurisdictions to get to Branch.

The night was bright with stars. Grassland stretched to low mountains on either side of the road like a black ocean. It was quiet.

Jace Denboer had a good head start, a fast car, and a fire under his butt the size of a rocket-propelled grenade. Landry was pretty sure where he'd go. The only question was which Jace would he encounter? The crazy Jace or the normal Jace? He was betting on the crazy Jace.

SPECTRE BLACK

Eric opened one eye. "Are we there yet, Daddy?"

"Almost."

Eric closed his eye again. Like any good soldier, he could fall asleep anywhere.

Jolie said, "You think Jace would go straight to his father's house? He'd be that stupid?"

"We'll find out," Landry said. "He could have Waldrup with him. We should be prepared for that."

"I guess it's just the three of us," Jolie said.

"What about the Branch PD?"

"That's a no go. I wouldn't know who to trust over there. A lot of those guys are in thick with the sheriff."

"The chief of police?"

"He's poker buddies with the sheriff. Quite a few of the higher-ups in the police department have themselves some brand new cars, too."

"One big happy family."

"We stopped them from getting those trucks across," Jolie said. "At the least, they'll have to regroup. I've been asking myself: why don't we just get out of Dodge? While the getting is good. All the way up here, that's what I was thinking. Just . . . go."

Landry said nothing.

Then Jolie said, "But I like it here." She stared out the window at the low, dark mountains. "I like my job, I like being in homicide."

She lapsed into silence.

Not long after that, he saw the lights of Deming. It wouldn't be far, now.

- — -

In Branch, Landry turned onto the drive up the curvy road that led to the Denboer place. Taking the corners, enjoying the ride, filing the carnage away as he always did. He could keep his thoughts to himself because no one felt like chatting.

Jace was still on the loose. And so was the sheriff of Tobosa County.

— — -

Landry turned onto Jacarunda Drive.

CHAPTER 38

This part of Branch reminded Landry of California. Green, dewy lawns, sprinklers shooting out arcs of spray. Although there was a moon, the night had muted color. But Landry knew that every house up here was either white with red tile roofs, beige with red tile roofs, or brown stucco pueblo style. All of them surrounded by gardens that would shame Omar Khayyam's poetry. Fruit trees aplenty, hedges to hide the sprawling properties, tall eucalyptus and Aleppo pines. Behind clipped hedges he glimpsed the occasional swimming pool or tennis court.

The rich *are* different.

They came around a turn and nearly ran into Jace's Camaro.

It was parked haphazardly, having come to rest against one of the pillars marking the entrance to the Denboer estate. Dark, bulky, the ugly paint job swallowing light. The right fender was crumpled—not bad, just a minor fender bender. The kid had misjudged the distance between his car's bumper and the pillar. But it was enough of a bump to deploy the airbags. Two of them. They looked like a couple of Pillsbury Doughboys, chef's hats and all.

The driver's door was open.

Reflection from a streetlight picked out a river of antifreeze trailing down the road.

A blood trail wandered up the steep incline to the house. Not a lot of blood, just splotches. Maybe one of them had been shot.

Two people. Jace and the sheriff.

Landry nodded to Jolie and Eric, reached into the car and grabbed his MP5. He shouldered his duffle, and started up the drive.

"What's in the duffle?" Eric asked.

"Tennis balls."

"Oh. Planning on a match?"

"Grudge match, maybe." Landry winked at Jolie. Her face remained composed, but he could see that she was having a good laugh inside. He secured the duffle to his back. It wasn't perfect, but it would do. He really didn't want to leave behind his secret weapon.

Halfway up, they encountered a bloody sock and a running shoe. The footprints continued on, up past the cactus garden and the privet hedge and the lawn as smooth as the felt on a pool table.

The night sprinklers were going.

Landry glanced back at the crumpled-up car. Jolie was right about the Camaro. It was one of the ugliest things he'd ever seen.

They approached the door to the manse. Two doors, actually, opening inward; massive stained-glass doors set into heavy timber. One of the doors stood open, leaking out light. More blood splotches. It was easy to track Jace—like following Hansel and Gretel's trail.

The three of them watched one another's six. Landry went in first, low, aiming the MP5 this way and that.

The house lit up like a Christmas tree.

The foyer was empty.

Landry had never owned a foyer, and this one did little to convince him he needed one. They covered all four directions in turn. And the balcony.

More blood had been mashed into the oriental carpet that covered most of the Mexican tile floor.

The room was huge, the furniture large and heavy. Spanish stuff, boxy and dark. The two-story-high foyer dwarfed all of it. The word for it was "grandiose," someone's idea of a powerful room. On the right was a curved staircase against blindingly white walls. Railed by wrought iron. Landry saw blood on the first step, so he started up, careful not to mire his shoes in the sticky fluid.

Eric covered him.

He came out on the balcony, which circled the foyer below.

Gave the all-clear signal, Jolie and Eric followed him up.

He followed the bread crumbs some more. They split up, Jolie and Eric on each side, Landry in the middle, clearing the balcony. They did it fast, working together like a well-oiled machine. Amazing how that happened.

There were probably a dozen rooms. Landry lost count after six. It was almost like a hotel. The doors were closed but not locked. He looked in the first two and saw magnificent bedrooms. Empty. All the rooms had full-length windows looking out onto the grounds. Landry walked across the thick carpet to the windows and looked down. More billiard-table grass. The huge expanse of acreage was hemmed in by an oleander hedge probably ten feet high. Tennis courts to the right under bright lights. Landry thought their electric bill must be astounding. A pool to the left, lit from within. Flagstone paths meandering through cactus and flower gardens.

The pool resembled a Mickey Mouse head without the features. It was as big as a hotel pool. There were ramadas. Thatched roofs, a wet bar at one of them, and another structure that Landry took to be cabanas. Chairs, tables, and big umbrellas by the pool. To Landry's left was another two-story wing. The first story faced out onto a colonnaded walkway.

Through the arches, Landry could see three sets of French doors to what he took to be three separate rooms. The third set of French doors was different. One of the doors stood open. Parked inside the walkway was a golf cart from the farm.

Landry hand-signaled the other two.

Gun at the ready, he moved at a quick shuffle-walk, pivoting to the right and left at each door, weapon eye level, clearing as he went.

But there was nothing. Just the night shadows and the three of them.

The blood trail stopped at an elevator. Landry knew what had happened. Whoever was wounded had gone upstairs. Judging from the open French door below and the lamp glow coming from the room up here, it was likely he was inside. Likely, but not definite.

Eric and Jolie had cleared the other side and gone back downstairs. He waved to them, pointing down and to the left. Landry took the stairs down.

The three of them worked their way toward the open doorway—a pincer movement, with Eric and Jolie coming from the opposite direction. They had to run across an open area, Landry coming from the direction of the main part of the house and Jolie and Eric from the other side. Landry covered them, aiming at the open doorway, waiting for someone to pop his head or weapon out.

Landry followed the colonnaded walkway toward the door. He kept his weapon leveled down the walk, concentrating on the open set of French doors. The golf cart parked out front was still empty.

They approached the door from either side. Heard arguing. Landry recognized the voices: one voice belonged to Carla Vitelli and the other to Sheriff Waldrup.

"What about you?" the sheriff was saying.

"What *about* me?"

"Your involvement!"

"What involvement? I had nothing to do with any of this. If you remember, I warned you that you were playing with fire—"

"You and your talk about clean hands. Is that really how you want to play it, Carla? What about you and Jace?"

"What about us?" She sounded cool. Cool and collected, as if chastening a child.

"Who killed my deputy? Just who was it who killed Dan Atwood?"

"*What?*"

"You heard me. Who killed Dan Atwood? Was it Jace? Or was it you?"

"That's the stupidest thing I—"

"Funny thing about being sheriff. People come to me with all sorts of shit. You knew all about Danny Boy, didn't you? Dan Atwood the fresh-faced serial killer?"

"What's that got to do with—?"

"The night before Dan didn't show up for work, someone complained about a loud car racing around that area. Really putting on the afterburners. You know what else they heard? A backfire. At least they *thought* it was a backfire, but I have another theory about that."

Landry could hear most of the conversation, but not all. Some of it was muffled. But fortunately, Denboer must have added this wing on later, and used cheaper materials. Landry could hear enough. He motioned to Jolie, who quickstepped over to the other side of the door, gun at the ready. She leaned close to the wall and listened.

The sheriff said, "Someone might think it was a gunshot they heard, not a backfire. And the way that kid takes care of that Camaro, I don't think he'd let it get into that kind of shape, do you? Maybe someone was shooting out there. First, there's the sound of shooting, and then there's the sound of a muscle car. Maybe somebody who couldn't sleep at night, someone across the highway, maybe that somebody heard gunshots. Maybe the sound woke him up."

"No one reported it."

"No? And how would you know that? You have no idea what comes across my desk that never sees the light of day."

"I don't think—"

"Are you sure that nobody reported it? They wouldn't report it to the FBI. They'd report it to me. *My* jurisdiction. The Tobosa County Sheriff's Office."

Jolie, standing on the other side of the door and holding up her weapon, nodded. She could hear them going at it, as well. Her lips formed the question, *Jace?*

Landry shook his head. Jace didn't appear to be part of this.

"What if I could prove you were there?" the sheriff was saying.

Carla: "No one was—"

"You think you're so smart. You blow into town every once in a while dressed to the nines and you think you're the queen of the county!"

"Are you recording this? If you are, what you're doing is against the law. Give it to me! *Give* it to me!"

"You know this recording will be admissible in court. In fact, I can arrest you, right here, right now. And you'd better believe I can and will use this against you."

A scuffle. Landry could see them. Waldrup had the gun and Carla pulled at his arm. The gun aiming wild. A dangerous situation. Waldrup grunted, his ugly little face turning beet red. Carla gave up on the gun and closed her hands around his neck. They danced across the elegant Mexican tile floor, the clumsiest dance in the history of the world, neither of them able to get the upper hand. With a gun waving around, Landry wasn't about to get in the middle of it.

Jolie caught his gaze and mouthed something—he thought she was saying it was time to intervene. That was the moment Carla went for the sheriff's gun, grasped it hard, and pulled the trigger. The loud gunshot stunned the air.

Waldrup staggered. His throat was blown out like an old tire, blood squirting and drenching his shirt. He stared at Carla with a look of surprise. Then his legs buckled and he fell sideways into a chair, knocking it over.

Landry stepped in first from one side and Jolie right behind, each covering their own side of the room.

Carla stared up at them in shock. She dropped the gun. "Self-defense!" she shouted. "He tried to kill me!"

Quick on the uptake, Landry thought.

"Carla!" Jace yelled from the darkness. "Carla! *Carla!* What happened? Did he shoot you? If you killed my sister, I can tell you right now, you're a *dead* man!"

"Get down!" Landry shouted as he hit the floor. A bullet shattered the edge of a Spanish armoire—bits of wood turned into projectiles.

Jace shot another volley into the room. By that time everyone was down on the floor, friend and foe alike.

Landry couldn't see him, but he'd try to pinpoint the kid's voice. "Jace—you want to talk about this?"

"This is all I'm gonna say."

Another fusillade of bullets.

"You want to kill Carla? She's still alive, Jace."

No sound at all from outside. Landry crawled to the doorway and saw—

Nothing.

The night seemed empty, except for the sounds of crickets, and a restless breeze that lifted the leaves of the cottonwood tree outside.

"Oh, *God!*"

Jace's voice, close by. It had come from less than twenty yards away. But all Landry saw was the dark green lawn, the tree, in the ambient light from the streetlamp down the hill next to the road. Jolie fired in the direction of Jace's voice. She'd fallen back and was hidden behind an arch in the colonnade. This covered Landry for the moment it took him to get outside behind another pillar.

More fire, although Landry couldn't see where it was coming from.

A bullet chipped the stone of the pillar, shrapnel hitting Landry a glancing blow on the cheek. He needed either better cover or to go full-bore at Jace.

He stared into the night. He could see the pool, and beside that, the tennis court. He could see the lawn, a dark hump of velvet slanting down to the road—

"Four o'clock!" Eric yelled.

Landry saw something running toward him—

Something.

Not a figure. It was more like a paper cutout of a man. Lighter than the grass but the same color. Enveloped in something flowing that moved with him and against him, like a dress.

Like cloth.

The figure hurtled toward them, firing what looked like a toy stick gun. Like those old-fashioned wooden toy guns. Dull, hard to see. He could see the lawn through it, could see the figure. A ghost.

Jace. Running toward them. Screaming like a Sioux warrior at Custer's Last Stand. Hurtling across the space like a phantom. Now you see it, now you don't—

But locked in on Landry.

Eric shot at the same time Landry did. Landry didn't know which of them blew Jace Denboer to kingdom come. The running creature fell down on the grass and disappeared, as if it had never been.

Landry squinted. He could see the puzzlement on Jolie's face, even in the half dark. He saw Eric shrug.

What just happened here?

Landry nodded to the other two, pointed to himself. He crouch-walked up the hill. Eric came from another vector. Jolie and Carla were now standing outside the door, out of the light, but he could see them in the ambient light of the colonnade's lamp.

SPECTRE BLACK

The kid lay on the ground, dead. Jace Denboer was covered from head to foot in what was a pretty good imitation of a burqa. Landry could see the folds of the cloth and he could see the crushed grass underneath. He could see where the bullets had seared through the material and into the body. He could see some of the blood, but not all. Landry knew there was a lot more here.

He could not see the outlines of the mass—center mass—of a human body. He couldn't see the chest. He squatted down beside the body and felt the small snaps where the material came together. He had to pull the garment apart by the snaps to truly see it: the bullet-torn torso, the shirt, the blood. They were all there, once he spread the front of the garment apart. The hood remained, cowling the kid's face, and Landry pushed that back as well. Then he could see the rest of Jace's face—the part that had been hidden by the hood.

Landry rubbed the material between his thumb and forefinger. It felt like any other cloth material he'd ever felt, but he knew the recorders and the projectors were sewn inside, held together by a net that was too small to be seen by the human eye.

Carla came to stand behind him. She rubbed her arms. Shaking. Tears seeping from her eyes, rolling down over her elegant cheekbones.

She said, "I knew he wouldn't live long."

Landry looked at her.

"Jace was the best lover I ever had." She held Landry's eyes. "And you're *nothing* like him."

Landry was silent, thinking about their strange encounter—more of a marathon than a sexual romp.

He wondered if there was something odd about her relationship with her father, Miko Denboer. Maybe he had molested her.

Or maybe it was someone else.

Or maybe it was nothing.

Carla was holding a tennis ball in her hand. Squeezing it along with the beat of her heart.

"Where'd you get the tennis ball?" he asked her.

"From your duffle."

"I'd be careful with that." His eyes met Jolie's. She knew about the tennis balls. A little magic of his own.

It seemed as if everything was standing still.

Landry looked around for Eric, but knew he wouldn't see him. Eric was hidden, keeping an eye on them, covering them with his sniper rifle.

Making sure.

He knew they would meet up later.

The police were on their way. Had to be.

The police department was way across town. He assumed there would be plenty of cars patrolling the area, though.

"What are you going to do now?" Landry asked Carla.

She shrugged. "I'm finished as an FBI agent."

He knew that was true.

"The funny thing is, I loved my job. You know?" She swiped at the tear near the corner of her eye. "It all went bad with Atwood. I hate men who prey on women."

Landry knew that something else lay behind that statement. Something besides an FBI agent who hated sex killers.

"God, I hate this place!" Carla said.

Her hand squeezed the tennis ball. Landry opened his mouth again to tell her not to do that, but realized it didn't matter. The only way to arm the ball was with the racket.

Jolie stared at the body, at the cloak. She seemed to be memorizing every line of it.

Pretty soon the police would drive up the winding road from the city below.

No sirens.

Yet.

Landry looked at Carla.

"I think I can help you out."

She looked at him, bewildered.

"Wait here."

Landry went back down to the colonnade and collected his duffle. Inside the duffle were the rest of the tennis balls and two rackets. He walked back up the short hill.

He handed them each a racket. Asked Carla, "Can you hit the house?"

"What is this? A test?"

"Can you hit the house?"

"Sure I can."

She hefted the ball in her hand. The neon yellow-green orb shimmered in the darkness. And then she whacked it, hard and true. Hit the Spanish tile roof of the covered walkway.

An explosion.

Ignition.

Fire. It started under the eaves and quickly spread, flowering up before running for fresh air.

Carla stared at Landry. For a moment, Landry could see the child she must have been.

Carla picked up another tennis ball. She held it, ready to hit, then looked at Jolie.

"Why don't you take a shot?"

She handed Jolie the ball.

Jolie tossed the ball up and whacked it hard against the glassed-in atrium. The atrium exploded, big and small shards of glass shattering, turned into sharp, jagged missiles.

They hit tennis balls until they were all gone, until flames consumed the whole Spanish monstrosity of a house.

It was *then* that Landry heard sirens. They were far away, but they were coming.

Carla's eyes were bright, avid, as she watched the Denboer palace burn.

"Now what?" Jolie said to Landry.

Landry looked at his watch. "Is there a place in town that serves breakfast at night?"

Jolie considered him. Finally, she gave him the smile he loved to see. No one could smile like Jolie.

"I'm sure we'll find something," she said.

ACKNOWLEDGMENTS

So many people have helped me with this book, or supported me as I wrote. Many thanks to my mother, Mary Falk, and my husband, Glenn McCreedy, for always being there for me.

Thanks to John Peters, whose knowledge and advice have informed my stories in so many ways, and to William Simon and Pam Stack, who are always there to help me turn possibility into an actual book.

I am especially grateful to Kevin Smith, my editor extraordinaire.

Thanks to Kjersti Egerdahl, who shepherded me through the editing process at Thomas & Mercer, and to the Thomas & Mercer team: Jacque Ben-Zekry, Marketing; Tiffany Pokorny, Author Relations; Sean Baker, Production; and Justine Fowler, Merchandising.

Special thanks to the fine people at Gelfman Schneider, especially my agent, Deborah Schneider.

ABOUT THE AUTHOR

Hailed by bestselling author T. Jefferson Parker as "a strong new voice in American crime fiction," J. Carson Black has written fifteen novels. Her thriller *The Shop* reached #1 on the Kindle Best Sellers list, and her crime thriller series featuring homicide detective Laura Cardinal became a *New York Times* and *USA Today* bestseller. Although Black earned a master's degree in operatic voice, she was inspired to write a horror novel after reading *The Shining*. She lives in Tucson, Arizona.

Photo © 2013 Galen Evans